# Vienna Waltz

### The Imperial Season
### Book One

## Mary Lancaster

Copyright © 2016 by Mary Lancaster
Print Edition

Published by Dragonblade Publishing, an imprint of Kathryn Le Veque Novels, Inc

All rights reserved. No part of this book may be used or reproduced in any manner whatsoever without written permission, except in the case of brief quotations embodied in critical articles or reviews.

# Table of Contents

Chapter One .................................................................... 1
Chapter Two................................................................... 12
Chapter Three................................................................ 22
Chapter Four.................................................................. 37
Chapter Five .................................................................. 48
Chapter Six..................................................................... 58
Chapter Seven................................................................ 70
Chapter Eight................................................................. 82
Chapter Nine ................................................................. 93
Chapter Ten.................................................................106
Chapter Eleven ............................................................119
Chapter Twelve ...........................................................131
Chapter Thirteen .........................................................141
Chapter Fourteen.........................................................148
Chapter Fifteen ............................................................159
Chapter Sixteen............................................................168
Chapter Seventeen.......................................................182
Chapter Eighteen .........................................................192
Chapter Nineteen ........................................................205
Chapter Twenty...........................................................217
Chapter Twenty-One...................................................232
Epilogue .......................................................................243
Author Bio ...................................................................246

# Chapter One

*T*HIS WAS THE man she needed.

He stole blatantly, yet with such speed and composure that Lizzie almost missed it. In fact, she wasted nearly four precious seconds before the realization hit her.

In mitigation of her uncharacteristic slowness, she had many distractions in Vienna's gorgeous Theatre an der Wien. Quite aside from the pretty ballet on the stage and the exquisite music that went with it, the theatre's sumptuous blue and silver furnishings were a feast for the eyes in their own right, as were the beautiful pastel gowns, glittering jewels and dazzling, gold-braided uniforms of many in the audience.

Lizzie had only arrived in Vienna with her siblings, aunt, uncle and cousins the day before. Despite exhaustion after the arduous journey, she was enchanted by everything from the historic and picturesque narrow streets of the inner city, to the sophisticated fashions of the European elite who still flooded into Vienna for the peace conference. She was quite happy to sit behind her family in their private box, so kindly donated for the evening by the British Ambassador, Sir Charles Stewart, and observe the wonders, leaving her cousin Minerva to display her charms at the front beside her mother and brother.

It crossed Lizzie's mind occasionally that she might actually be embarrassed to be seen in her old, ridiculously unfashionable dress. Not that she cared for clothes and primping and displays of jewelry—really, she didn't—but she had no wish to be ridiculed. Besides which, she had plans to make. So she sat back in her seat, letting the music surround her, and divided her attention between those plans, the stage dancers and the audience.

The theatre was packed and rather stuffy in the unseasonably warm October evening. Young men propped up pillars and doorways in the pit, many making eyes at the dancers on stage or the pretty young women seated close by. Some aimed higher, at the wealthier ladies in the tiers of boxes surrounding the stage. Lizzie thought Minerva drew a little attention of her own, which would gratify Aunt Lucy.

Of course, Lizzie's sister, Henrietta, even at her present tender age of fifteen, would have eclipsed Minerva and all other females present, too. But there was no point in brooding over ill fortune that none of them could do anything about now. If the old gentleman had only followed everyone else's advice about that wretched horse that had thrown and eventually killed him…but she refused to dwell on that. She and her siblings might have lost their father and their home, but Lizzie hadn't lost her wits and she was determined to win another home so that her sister—all of her siblings, in fact—could choose their paths from a position of at least minimal comfort.

More than once since they'd sat down, Lizzie's attention had been caught by the lady in the next box. A young matron, fashionably dressed in white with dramatic splashes of scarlet trim, she was one of the loveliest women Lizzie had ever seen. Not surprisingly, male companions surrounded her and she was being openly quizzed by several gentlemen in the pit as well as more discreetly by Cousin James. Lizzie wondered who she was; although when James mumbled an excuse and bolted from their box—presumably to fight his way into the beauty's instead—she rather thought she'd find out in more detail than she'd ever need.

It was as she waited expectantly for James' lanky figure to appear next to the unknown lady that the robbery occurred.

The music, at that moment, was particularly rousing, distracting Lizzie just as a very un-James-like man pushed unceremoniously through the throng in the beauty's box. She had an impression of someone large and dark and improperly dressed in no more than mud-stained shirt and breeches.

Then, before Lizzie, or anyone else by the look of things, had even registered his surely alarming presence, he went right up to the lady, grasped the delicate chain of the necklace around her pretty throat and tugged.

For the smallest instant, the lady gazed up at the thief, wide-eyed with shock. His lips moved, speaking only one syllable, but already he was turning away, incongruously casual. And the next moment, he'd vanished, leaving the lady gasping and clutching her suddenly bare neck.

Lizzie blinked. *Did I really see that?*

A few startled exclamations in German from the surrounding boxes convinced her she had.

And then the truth crashed into her. This was an opportunity that would never come again. And she was letting him get away.

Without so much as a glance at Aunt Lucy or Minerva, Lizzie sprang up and left the box. A flash of grubby white disappeared around the corner of the corridor. Lizzie flew after it. As she passed the victim's box, she heard a female voice say in French, "Oh, ignore it. I have another just like it. Besides, the police will catch him."

*How wonderful to be so blasé!* Lizzie thought as she raced past a few lounging men, one or two of whom may have tried to speak to her. Too focused on her quarry to pay them any attention whatsoever, Lizzie gained the staircase in time to see the thief running down the last few steps to the bottom. Bizarrely, he didn't even look like a fugitive, just a man in a hurry. In fact, he was whistling as he crossed the grand foyer, as if mightily pleased with himself. He even called something in a friendly voice to the doorman as he strode out.

However, by the time Lizzie reached the foot of the staircase, the hue and cry had gone up from the top. One of the victim's numerous male escorts was shouting the German equivalent of "Stop thief!"

Inevitably, a gaggle of staff began to close in on Lizzie.

*Oh, drat the fools, how will I catch him now?*

Fortunately, the same German voice fumed, "Not her, you idiots! The man with no coat! After him!"

At least Lizzie imagined that's what he said, for the approaching staff suddenly sprang in the opposite direction, like deer started by a shot. Lizzie was able to escape close on their heels, even to slip by them as they stopped outside the doors and asked each other questions about who they were looking for, what he'd stolen, and from whom.

Spying a shadow vanishing around the corner of the theatre building, Lizzie hurried after it. She knew she was running out of time. Everyone said Vienna was full of police and police spies, and she couldn't imagine any of them taking the blatant theft of a lady's necklace very lightly. And sure enough, voices and footsteps were converging from all directions. Lizzie clutched her flimsy shawl more tightly around her shoulders, walking as fast as she dared along a street full of abandoned carriages belonging to the theatre patrons. A few coachmen were gossiping and smoking together; others must have sloped off to the nearest tavern. She wondered if their own Viennese coachman, Wilhelm, was among them, but was too occupied to look.

She glimpsed the thief still some yards ahead of her, striding down the road, hands in pockets. She even heard the whistling blown back to her on the wind. But the footsteps behind were growing quicker and louder. One of the pursuers said in English, "He definitely went this way." So far their quarry seemed to be hidden from them by the distance, and the shadows, and, perhaps, by Lizzie herself.

The thief glanced over his shoulder. He must have at least heard if not seen his pursuers, for she thought he laughed, although the sound could have come from one of the nearby coachmen. However, he was clearly a thinking thief, for he didn't immediately bolt and draw attention to himself. Instead, he seemed to look about him as he walked. Then he paused, gazing at the crest on a waiting carriage. Lizzie hurried on. With a jolt of excitement, she realized the carriage was her aunt's.

The man walked on, but at least his brief halt had given her time to catch up.

"Wait," Lizzie hissed.

He turned and the glow from the nearby street lamp showed her black brows raised in surprise on a lean, handsome face. Although unexpectedly young, he gave off an air of recklessness and sheer danger that caught at Lizzie's quickened breath. His hair looked wild and unkempt and his rather hard eyes glittered in a way she recognized.

No one was perfect.

She grasped the handle of the carriage door and yanked it open. "Get in."

At that, a hint of confusion crossed his face, making him seem more boyish than dangerous. Which was some comfort, before a whole array of much more worrying expressions chased after it. She was fairly sure one of them was pure lechery and began to frown furiously to quash any such nonsense. Only then, his gaze shifted beyond her to the approaching police and their helpers. So far, the obstructive gaggles of coachmen and her own carriage door must have hidden him, for she could hear questions being fired at the servants farther back.

The thief drew in a breath that sounded suspiciously like laughter, strode the few paces toward her and leapt nimbly inside. Lizzie followed, closed the door behind her and sat on the other bench. It wasn't the most comfortable carriage in the world, but it had carried her across Europe already, so at least it gave her familiarity to hang on to.

"You had better hide under the seat," Lizzie advised.

"Are you coming, too?" he inquired out of the darkness in the opposite corner. He spoke in English, surprisingly, although with a hint of foreign intonation she couldn't place.

"Of course not," Lizzie said with dignity. "*I* didn't steal anything." She peered out of the carriage window. The pursuers had stopped some yards back, some gazing up the street, some in earnest conversation with the nearest coachmen. She thought one of them was Wilhelm and prayed he hadn't spotted her. Providing neither he nor anyone else had seen them enter the carriage, she thought they were safe.

The theatre staff among the group began to drift away, back to work, she supposed.

"I think they're giving up," Lizzie said in relief.

In the darkness, the thief seemed very still. "What makes you think I did?"

Frowning, Lizzie turned her head toward the shadowy figure in the corner. "Did what?"

"Steal something."

"I saw you," Lizzie said dryly. "Half the theatre saw you."

"Rather less, I should think," he argued. "But never mind. Given that you saw me, why are you hiding me?"

Lizzie took a deep breath. "Because I want you to steal something for me."

The figure opposite stirred. His boots scraped against the floor as if he were stretching his legs out. "What do you want me to steal?" His voice wasn't quite steady. He might have been laughing.

"A necklace," she said repressively.

"Ah. Because I've just proved I'm good at those?"

"No, no, it has to be a *particular* necklace."

"I see. And from whom am I to steal this particular necklace?"

"My aunt."

As if that finally startled him, he leaned forward into the light, peering at her more closely. She'd been right. There was no softness, no fear of anything in the dark, careless eyes searching her face.

He sat back into the darkness again. "You know, even thieves generally regard robbing their own families as beyond the pale."

Lizzie felt a flush rise to her cheeks. She hadn't expected to be lectured in morals by a thief. "It isn't robbing her if the necklace isn't hers to begin with," she said tartly.

"It isn't hers? Is it yours, then?"

"Well, no, not exactly," she confessed. "It belongs to my father's estate and should be passed on to Ivan the Terrible—" She broke off, biting her lips as the family nickname for her abhorrent cousin spilled out unbidden. The figure in the darkness didn't move or speak, although a hiss of breath escaped him. It might have been laughter, or impatience. "I beg your pardon," she hurried on. "I mean it should be passed on to my father's heir, some distant foreign cousin, along with the title and everything else."

"Everything else?"

"Our home and just about everything in it. All our lands and property. It's all entailed. So you see, the new baron won't miss one necklace. There's plenty more jewelry for his wife."

"Then this heir, your Ivan the Terrible, is married?"

"I don't know anything about him," Lizzie said loftily. "And don't want to."

"It's not his fault he inherited your old home," the thief pointed out.

"No, but he didn't need to kick us out of it the same day we buried my father, when he isn't even in the country. So far as anyone can ascertain, he doesn't even have any fixed plans to take up residence there."

From his pause, the thief was surprised by such callousness. "Did he do that?"

"Yes, he did. My two sisters, my brother and I have had to inflict ourselves on my aunt, just when they were preparing to leave the country. Which, in fact, has worked out quite well," she allowed.

"Brother?" the thief repeated. "But if you have a brother, shouldn't *he* inherit everything?"

"Unfortunately not, because my father never quite got around to marrying Michael's mother. He couldn't really," she added in the interests of fairness. "Being married to *my* mother at the time."

"I see the difficulty," the thief said gravely.

Lizzie peered into the shadows with suspicion. "Are you laughing at me?"

"Not in the slightest. I'm reviling the behavior of this unspeakable cousin who kicked you all out of your home."

"It is vile," Lizzie agreed cordially. "Because my brother and sisters are too young to live on their own, and even if I got a post as a governess, which I do quite intend in time, they couldn't really come with me. They'd have to live with my aunt."

"The aunt I'm to steal this necklace from?"

"Precisely."

"But you said the vile cousin has taken possession of everything already—how could he, by the way, if he wasn't in the country?"

"His solicitors sent in his own people."

"I see." The thief's voice was unexpectedly grim, as if he were now genuinely shocked at such unfeeling behavior. "So how came your aunt to have the necklace?"

"She'd already borrowed it for Minerva's coming out—Minerva is her daughter, my cousin. But, apparently, there is a great deal of competition among debutantes in London and my aunt was convinced that Minerva would have better luck finding a husband at the peace conference in Vienna, since all the world is here. And she feels the necklace adds consequence."

"To Minerva?"

"Indirectly. If her mother wears the necklace on special occasions, it makes Minerva's family appear to be of consequence."

"Isn't it?"

"They're well enough, but my uncle is employed at the Foreign Office. They're not the wealthiest people in the world, so they want Minerva and James to marry well."

"I see. So wouldn't it be better to leave the necklace with your aunt until after the Congress?"

"Well, no, because then we'll go back to England and the opportunity will be lost. I can't sell the necklace in England. It's too well known."

"So I'm to steal it and you will sell it?"

"Well, I expect you know better than I how and where to accomplish the selling."

"I presume you're going to pay me for my trouble?"

"Of course."

"How much?"

Lizzie closed her mouth. She'd expected to be given a price and whatever that was, had resolved to beat it down as far as she could. She had no idea of the going rate for thieves. Finally, she lifted her chin. "How much do you want?"

"Make me an offer."

"One percent of whatever you sell the necklace for," Lizzie said cunningly.

"Don't be ridiculous. The risk is all mine. Fifty percent."

Panic widened her eyes. "Oh no, that can't be the normal rate. If I give you fifty, I won't have enough!"

"For what?"

"To hire a cottage and live in it for two years and pay something toward Henrietta's first London season when she's seventeen. If I can't do that, there's no point in stealing the necklace at all."

The thief shrugged in the darkness. "Maybe you shouldn't."

She scowled in his direction. "Are you trying to talk yourself out of a job? You're a very odd thief."

"So are you."

She glared at him indignantly, though she was forced to concede the point. Perhaps the thief saw that, for he relented somewhat.

"Very well," he said. "I can see you're in need. I'll take ten percent."

"Ten," Lizzie said, her shoulders drooping. "I suppose that *might* do." Though unless he got an excellent price for the necklace, she thought she'd still be a few hundred pounds short of what she needed.

"You're not very good at this, are you?" the thief said. "You should offer me two."

Lizzie brightened. "Will you take two?"

"No, but I'll take five."

"Done," Lizzie said, impulsively offering her hand to shake on the deal. The thief's stretched out of the darkness and grasped hers. His fingers felt warm and rough. A faint scent of horses emanated from him, along with alcohol, which gave her pause. "How foxed are you?" she inquired.

His breath of laughter ruffled the back of her hand. "Drunk enough to make a bad deal for a pretty face," he said, suddenly dipping his head and kissing her fingers.

Her skin flushed under his lips and she snatched her hand back in outrage. "But not so drunk that you'll forget our agreement in the morning, I trust?"

He sighed. "No. Though I may regret it."

Approaching voices from the street jerked Lizzie out of her isolation. Wilhelm, her aunt's coachman, was returning.

"Oh dear, the performance must be just about over!" she exclaimed. She slid along the seat, reaching for the door on the road side of the carriage. "Can you escape now without being caught?"

"Easily," the thief said. He moved quickly, opening the door before she could reach it and jumping down. He didn't lower the step, but simply seized her round the waist and spun her out of the carriage. Her feet barely hit the ground before he propelled her across the road behind a passing carriage.

Lizzie, unexpectedly shocked by such careless treatment, could think of nothing to say except, "Don't you have a coat?"

His teeth gleamed in the light from the carriage. "Yes, of course. I just left home in too much of a hurry."

"To go thieving?" Lizzie asked, with more interest than condemnation. After all, she was making use of his services, but she'd never thought of it quite like a position one could be late for, like her uncle's at the Foreign Office.

"Exactly. Didn't want to miss my chance."

Lizzie suddenly had a lot more questions about the theft of the beautiful lady's necklace, but she had run out of time and all was not yet settled between them.

"Twenty-five Skodegasse," she said hastily. "There's a lane that runs behind the houses. I'll speak to you there tomorrow, when it's quiet. Noon."

As she hurried away from him, she couldn't prevent a quick glance over her shoulder to see where he went. But there was no sign of him. He'd vanished like the proverbial thief in the night.

"THAT GIRL," WILHELM the coachman said, pointing to the young English woman's ill-dressed back scuttling into the theatre against the flow of the rest of the audience, "met with someone in her own coach. A man. The police were chasing him."

He spoke to the shadowy figure he knew only as Agent Z, who lounged against his coach door, watching the world go by as only the Viennese could. Though Wilhelm doubted Agent Z was a true Viennese, he'd never ask. At once bland and chilling, the secret policeman was not someone Wilhelm wished to get on the wrong side of, hence his new double employment with the state police and Mr. Daniels. He'd been afraid to say no. Besides which, the double pay was good.

"And she is...?" Agent Z prompted.

"Niece of my master, Jeremy Daniels, one of the British diplomats, if you remember. He arrived yesterday. Don't know who *he* is, though."

"I'll find that out easily enough," Agent Z said, with a nod. "Good work. Keep your eyes open."

# Chapter Two

On her way to bed, Lizzie found herself snatched into her brother's chamber. Well, she thought of it as Michael's, though, in fact, he shared it with the currently absent Cousin James, much as Lizzie shared with Minerva as well as her two sisters. The house was much more cramped than they were used to. However, at this moment, her sisters were with Michael, waiting to ambush her.

"How was the theatre?"

"Did you see Herr von Beethoven?"

"Was the tsar there? Or Emperor Francis?"

"Did you see the Duchess of Sagan? She's meant to be the most beautiful woman in the world."

"Did Minerva attract many admirers?"

Bombarded with questions, she had to admit to seeing none of the famous personages and allow that Minerva had seemed to attract respectful interest.

"Sounds pretty tame," Georgiana, her youngest sister, said with clear disappointment.

"Not in the least," Lizzie assured her. "In fact, there was a robbery in the box right next to ours. A lady—one James admired excessively—had her necklace stolen quite blatantly, in full view of anyone who happened to be looking at her rather than the stage."

"What a coincidence!" Michael exclaimed. "Did you observe his methods?"

"Better than that," Lizzie said modestly. "I followed him out of the theatre and engaged his services."

"Oh goodness, Lizzie, how brave of you!" Henrietta breathed. "Was he terribly fearsome?"

"Not fearsome *exactly*," Lizzie said doubtfully. "Though I had the impression he cares for nothing and is afraid of nothing. In truth, he wasn't really anything like I imagined a thief would be. But he's agreed to steal the necklace for us and will come at noon tomorrow to receive his instructions."

Henrietta said, "You don't think we'll be ruining Minerva's chances by stealing the necklace?"

"Not in the slightest," Georgiana said stoutly. "Why should the fact that Aunt Lucy's wearing a particular necklace have any bearing at all on who does or does not offer for Minerva?"

Lizzie, who was of a similar opinion, merely nodded. She rather thought her aunt liked the added consequence of wearing such a fine piece of jewelry for its own sake.

"Where is the dog?" she asked, frowning with the sudden realization she hadn't had to fend the animal off since returning from the theatre.

As if on cue, the dog hurled itself through the bedroom door, lunging at Lizzie with insane delight. The children, who all understood that though old and unfashionable as it was, this was her best gown, all threw themselves at the dog to save the garment from the inevitable muddy paw prints.

"Well done!" Lizzie approved.

"Well done to you, too," Michael said. "Very clever of you to find us someone so quickly!"

IN THE MORNING, since Lizzie needed to be free at noon to meet her newly engaged thief, she made herself particularly useful arranging the house and organizing the servants to her aunt's liking. Aunt Lucy complained of the tiny size of their accommodation and the number of stairs, but in truth, they were lucky to have a whole house at all in the overcrowded inner city. Most diplomats of Jeremy's rank had to make do with an apartment or even a couple of rooms in someone's attic. No doubt, Aunt Lucy's rank and influence had pulled a few strings.

Fortunately, such activity excused Lizzie from accompanying Aunt Lucy and Minerva on their shopping expedition. New gowns were apparently required to prevent Minerva living up to the reputation the British had already managed to acquire in Vienna of being ill-dressed, and most especially needed for the masked ball at the Imperial Palace which would formally open the Peace Congress.

As she bustled about the house, her cousin, James, kept leaping out of his bedroom door to ask her opinion on coats and the style of his cravat, until his anxiety finally penetrated her own distracted thoughts.

"Are you going somewhere special, James?" she asked.

He flushed, making his appearance even younger than his years. "Madame Fischer invited me to her salon this afternoon."

"Well that was amiable of her! Um…who is Madame Fischer?"

"The lady in the box next to ours at the theatre!"

Lizzie, about to hurry on her way, held still, instead. "The lady whose necklace was stolen?"

"Yes, wasn't that shocking? But she is a great sport, didn't let it upset her evening at all. She wasn't even frightened."

"Well, I suppose she'd no reason to be frightened since the thief ran off with several stout men after him. Leaving you to guard her," Lizzie added hastily. "Have a pleasant afternoon."

Leaving him, she hurried downstairs to join the children in the garden, where they were setting up a picnic in the midday sunshine and squabbling over who should be fending the dog off the food.

"Tie his leash to the clothes pole," Lizzie advised. "That way he won't reach the food, but he can still sniff around a bit."

Michael duly dragged the dog a few feet away and tied his long leash around the pole. "We've been talking," he said over his shoulder. "And though you've been very clever finding a thief, we think I should go with you to meet him. Just to show him you're not alone."

Lizzie didn't have the heart to tell him that the presence of a twelve-year-old boy was unlikely to intimidate a hardened criminal like her blatant thief.

"Actually," Georgiana interrupted her brother's reasoning, "we decided we should all come, but Michael thinks it's the male presence which is important. Rot, if you ask me."

"No one *would* ask you," Michael retorted.

"Because I'm a girl?" Georgiana fired up.

"No," Michael said at once. "Because you're—"

"Enough," Lizzie interrupted. "I don't want to scare him off, so I'll go alone. Besides, I need you here to cover for me if anyone else comes into the garden – and to keep the dog quiet if he hears a stranger's voice."

"But we've never met a thief before," Georgiana objected, clearly disappointed.

"Well, that's one of the desired, if unwritten, accomplishments of a lady," Lizzie assured her. "Do not, under any circumstances, number thieves among your acquaintance."

The children giggled, although, sobering first, Henrietta pointed out in her soft voice that Lizzie had already ruined this accomplishment in herself.

"It doesn't matter if I'm going to be a governess instead of a lady," Lizzie claimed.

Georgiana crowed with laughter, but Michael said sternly that it would matter more. "What respectable family would employ a governess who associated with thieves?" he demanded, not unreasonably.

"Don't be silly. Of course I won't associate with him again once he's stolen the necklace and sold it."

"Indeed, why would you?" Henrietta said supportively.

"All very well," Michael said, throwing himself down on the rug beside his sisters. "But what's to prevent your thief from just taking off with the necklace and keeping all the money himself?"

"I thought of that," Lizzie admitted. "But in truth, I'd find it hard to sell it myself. I think the only solution has to be that I stick with him from the moment he steals the necklace until we have the money."

"Oh no," Henrietta exclaimed. "What if he murders you in a back alley?"

Lizzie thought about the thief jerking the necklace from Madame Fischer's elegant throat, then their rather odd conversation in the dark carriage. Although he hadn't harmed his victim, there had been suppressed violence in his casual gesture and, she thought, in his hard, turbulent eyes. Drunk as he'd undoubtedly been, his true nature was difficult to guess.

"I can't see him *murdering* me," she said judiciously. "But all the same, I shall take Papa's pistol with me."

The dog began to growl as she spoke, pulling against his leash toward the back of the garden, where a gate in the wall led to the alley.

"What is the time, Michael?" she asked, her stomach twisting with excitement.

"Almost noon. Do you suppose that's—"

The gate in the wall opened and a gardener in a big, floppy hat came in and immediately began raking fallen leaves into a neat pile. The dog stopped growling.

Lizzie rose to her feet. "Remember your parts," she urged her siblings and tripped down the lawn to the main path that led to the gate.

The gardener pulled his rake out of her way and tugged the brim of his hat. She spared a glance to thank him because she was still getting to know the servants here and the breath seemed to flee from her body.

The gardener tipped his hat back on his head and smiled.

Lizzie's heart jolted as the blood drained from her face. Although it was a rather charming smile, making his eyes gleam beguilingly, it only emphasized the recklessness she'd read in him last night.

"This wasn't our agreement!" she hissed.

"No, but it looks much less suspicious than skulking in the lane, don't you think?"

"No!" In fact, her main objection was to prevent him being near her siblings, though he did have a point about lurking.

"Are they your brother and sisters?" he inquired, casting a quick glance over the children.

"They're just orphans," she blurted, without much hope that he would believe her. "And their dog. Listen. I want you to take the necklace from my aunt in public, just as you did last night with Madame Fischer."

"Couldn't I just walk into the house and steal it now?"

"No! I can't have suspicion falling on us and, besides, there's no guarantee that the maids will see you do it."

His lips twitched. "I have to be seen doing it? You know, for that kind of risk my percentage should be higher."

"We have an agreement," Lizzie said sternly. "And yes, the robbery has to be seen, just in case Ivan the—the vile cousin accuses my aunt and uncle of hiding it from him."

The thief blinked. "You've thought of everything, haven't you? So where am I to steal it from?"

Lizzie drew in her breath, glanced around at the children and then back to the thief. "The Emperor's masked ball the night after tomorrow. Do you think you can get into the Hofburg?"

"Anyone who likes it will get in," the thief said wryly. "Austrian security concentrates on much less tangible threats than thievery."

"Good," said Lizzie. "Because I have to get in myself without an invitation."

"Why? If you're to be nowhere near the theft?"

"I need to point out my aunt and the necklace to you," Lizzie said. "But I shall be in disguise. Like everyone else, I'll have a mask and domino. Oh, do you have such things?"

"I can borrow them," the thief said blandly.

In the circumstances, it was hardly Lizzie's place to quibble. She merely nodded. "Very well. So, you must steal the necklace—without hurting my aunt," she added anxiously, "or the whole deal is off."

"I'll strive to control my violence."

Lizzie frowned at him. "You know, you sound very educated for a thief. Your English is excellent."

"So was my grandfather's. And I haven't always been a thief."

Intrigued in spite of herself, Lizzie opened her mouth to ask more but fortunately a burst of laughter from the children reminded her that she needed to get rid of him quickly.

"Once I've pointed her out to you, I'll leave and wait for you in a hired carriage. We'll go straight to your buyer and split the money as agreed."

The thief blinked. "Selling it may not be as simple as that," he warned.

Lizzie narrowed her eyes. "You had best make sure it is, because I shall be with you until the deal is done."

To her surprise, a half-smile sprang to his lips and hovered. "Is that supposed to be an incentive?"

She frowned with incomprehension then began to flush as an unlikely meaning filtered through. "Oh for goodness' sake, I don't have time for such nonsense and I'm certainly not foolish enough to fall for your flim-flam. Five percent as we agreed. And only on the terms I've just stated."

"You had really better do some gardening," Henrietta's soft voice said behind her. "James is at the upstairs window."

A swift glance upward showed her James, back in his original choice of coat, his hair exceedingly well brushed. Catching her eye, he grinned and posed, pointing to his cravat. Lizzie gave him a hasty thumbs-up sign.

"You *are* Lizzie's thief, aren't you?" Henrietta asked.

"Oh dear," Lizzie said faintly. "Henri—" She was about to tell her sister to go away while casting a quick, forbidding glare at the thief, who, like most people on first acquaintance, was staring at Henrietta's incomparable beauty.

But at that moment, Michael and Georgiana both yelled as the dog, having finally broken his rope, launched himself across the garden toward Lizzie and the gate, which he was more than capable of jumping.

Resigned to the indignity, Lizzie leapt into the dog's path and spread her arms wide to catch him. But it wasn't the first time Dog had played this game either. He swerved, bounding between her and the thief. Michael darted after him and Georgiana ran wide to begin the hemming in process. Dog skidded to a halt in the corner and turned. He knew this ploy, too, and understood he had to bolt fast before Georgiana got too close. So he did.

The thief took something from his pocket, saying something casual in a language Lizzie had never heard before. As everyone readjusted their angles of approach to close in on the animal, Dog skidded to a halt and turned to face the thief, wagging his tail. The thief held out a piece of biscuit and Dog trotted up to him, happily taking it from his right hand while his left closed around the dog's collar.

"Oh, well done!" Michael exclaimed. "Thanks!"

"Pleasure," said the thief, clearly amused as he surrendered the dog to Michael's charge.

"We were sure he'd go for the food," Georgiana said, waving one hand toward the picnic. "Instead, he bolts for freedom and is then distracted by a much tinier amount of food than he could have wolfed up there!"

"He's not very bright," Michael agreed, pulling the dog's ears. Dog licked his hand.

"He's been cooped up for too long in carriages and inns and now this house," Lizzie said guiltily. "We need to take him out somewhere and let him run. Somewhere we can actually catch him again before he exhausts us."

"Take him out to the Vienna woods," the thief advised. "With a large supply of bribes. He doesn't actually want to lose you, you know. He will come back."

"I know," Lizzie said. "But it's what he does *before* he comes back that worries us. After the Green Park incident—But never mind that," she interrupted herself hastily. "You were going, weren't you?"

"He could have some pie first," Michael pointed out.

Lizzie glared at him. She didn't want to say, "He's the gardener!"

Besides sounding far too lofty, it wasn't remotely true. On the other hand, he *was* a thief, as Henrietta at least had already worked out and hardly a desirable luncheon guest.

"James would find it odd," she said at last, aware of the thief's gaze on her uncomfortable face.

"James finds everything about us odd," Georgiana pointed out. "Even though he's known us all our lives."

"Well, imagine the difficulties strangers have," Lizzie said tartly. "Bring him some pie, Georgi, and let him leave about his work."

"I haven't swept up the leaves in here yet," the thief said provokingly.

Lizzie took a step nearer him. "You can't be seen with us," she hissed. "You'll ruin everything."

The thief leaned on his rake, a half-smile just dying on his lips. His unwavering eyes on hers didn't blink. For some reason, that close gaze flustered her, though she refused to admit it by stepping back.

"What do you mean?" Michael demanded behind her. He lowered his voice dramatically. "Oh lord, Lizzie, is this *him*? Your thief?"

The thief laughed while Lizzie turned on her brother, scowling furiously.

"Don't flap, Lizzie," Michael said. "No one can hear. And I always meant to meet him, you know. To be honest, I'm relieved. He's not so bad and he speaks well. So if he has to open his mouth at the ball, he won't give himself away."

The thief bowed ironically. Georgiana, arriving back with Henrietta, gave him a generous piece of pie. He accepted the delicacy with a murmur of thanks and then as an afterthought, a tug of his hat.

"What's your name?" Michael asked.

The thief considered him. "Johnnie. What's yours?"

"Michael. Do you—"

"Enough," Lizzie interrupted, pushing boy and dog in the direction of the abandoned food spread out at the upper end of the garden.

Although Lizzie shooed her siblings back toward the picnic, bidding Michael tie the dog properly this time, her brother had brought up a point that had niggled at her since she'd encountered the thief last night.

Turning back to find him making a decent pile of leaves by the gate, she said, "How come you speak as you do? And in English, because you aren't, are you?"

He seemed to hesitate. Then he said, "I was a soldier."

"Ah." *I haven't always been a thief*, he'd said. It made sense if he was one of the many returning soldiers released in peace time from whichever European army he'd been with. There was a glut of such men with little to return to except unemployment, poverty and trouble. It made her feel better about engaging him, for almost a second, until she realized Michael had overheard.

"Really?" he demanded eagerly. "I'm going to be a soldier, too, just as soon as Henri buys me a commission."

"Your sister?" the thief, Johnnie, inquired, apparently puzzled as to why Henrietta should have the honor—or, indeed, the means—of purchasing Michael's commission.

"Well, yes, that's what the necklace is for. Even I can see Henri's prettier than any other girl. When she's had her London season and caught her wealthy husband, she's promised to buy me a commission in any regiment of my choosing."

"It's one plan," Lizzie said, waving Michael away.

"And a very excellent one," the thief approved. "I prefer to steal in a good cause. Miss Lizzie—until the ball." With a last tip of his hat, he strolled out of the gate, closing it carefully behind him.

# Chapter Three

TWENTY MINUTES LATER, the thief who'd told Michael his name was Johnnie found he was still grinning off and on as he strode down the busy Graben. It was a wide, open space that crossed the city, through which the whole world seemed to be travelling today. Weaving amongst the wealthy and the indigent and all shades between, he dodged between a green, Imperial-crested carriage and a hired fiacre. Nowhere else in the world, he reflected, had you ever been likelier to rub shoulders with a king and a washerwoman at the same time.

"Vanya! Vanya, it *is* you! Come here!"

Dragged out of his entertaining reverie, he gazed around, searching for the woman's voice, which came from a smart carriage making its slow way down the middle of the road. A lady—surely Sonia, whom he hadn't seen for two years—hanging out of the window waving at him with one hand while she hung on to her very elegant bonnet with the other. "Vanya! Over here!"

Never one to pass over an old friend, let alone one who brought back such pleasant memories, he veered at once toward the carriage. He eased among the crowd until he could stride along beside her window and swept off his disreputable hat.

"Countess Gelitzina," he said and kissed her gloved fingers. "I should have known you would be here among the great and the beautiful."

"How very formal, Ivan Petrovitch! I must confess I *did* know you were here, though no one told me you'd taken to such eccentric dress. What in the world are you up to? Are you incognito? Dodging Prince Metternich's spies?"

"Of course. What do you think?"

"Er...what are you?"

"A jobbing gardener, of course, with additional skills of a somewhat more nefarious nature."

"Even you cannot be so short of cash as that! Is it a wager?"

"No, just something I agreed to while the worse for drink," he said cheerfully. "But I was right. It is vastly entertaining and one day I might even tell you all about it. Where are you staying?"

"Just over there." She pointed to a half-hidden building which faced onto the Graben. "When it's not my turn to attend the Tsarina in the Hofburg."

"But you will be at the Emperor's opening ball?"

"Along with the rest of Europe. Come to Princess Bagration's tonight and tell me all!"

"She doesn't invite me," he said, hand on heart in mock sadness.

"Oh, she does now," Sonia said with an arched smile. "Everyone wants the truth about the rumor that you snatched a necklace from the perfect bosom of some Viennese woman—in full view of the entire theatre. Oh, Vanya!" She clutched his shoulder through the window. "Is that why you're really in disguise? Are you in hiding from the law?"

Vanya gave a shout of laughter that attracted the attention of several passers-by. "You had best let me go," he said, amused, "or rumors about your bizarre new lover will eclipse those of my thievery."

Sonia frowned suddenly, though not, as it turned out, in anxiety for her reputation. "You do still *possess* other clothes, don't you? You haven't wagered them away with the rest of your fortune in a night of drunken debauchery?"

"Why would I do anything so foolish? Supposing I actually had access to a fortune."

"You wouldn't be the first in Vienna to do so since the Congress arrived! And you needn't look so innocent, either."

"I *am* innocent," he protested, although a high-risk plan was beginning to form in his brain. "At least for the moment." Her carriage began to veer to the right, while he wanted to go left, so he clapped his hat back on his head, kissed his fingers to the countess, and dodged across the road.

IN HIS RAMSHACKLE attic, Vanya did, indeed, find a card of invitation from Princess Bagration and another from Lady Castlereagh. Taken together with his standing invitation from the Duchess of Sagan, he'd have to be careful, he thought cynically, not to let such popularity go to his head.

"Wake me at six," he instructed Misha, his faithful batman, and threw himself face down on the creaky bed. Though still fully dressed, he was asleep in an instant.

Misha, used to his master, merely covered him up and set about brushing his uniform. As he polished the buttons by the window, be became aware that the man lounging against the building on the other side of the road had been there when his master came home.

"Bloody spies," he muttered under his breath.

PRINCESS BAGRATION, WIDOW of the late great General Bagration, who'd died so heroically at the Battle of Borodino, had taken up residence in the Schenkengasse in one wing of the luxurious Palm Palace. In the other wing lived her great social rival, the Duchess of Sagan, whom Vanya had visited on several occasions. This time, while exchanging pleasantries with acquaintances in the entrance hall, he took the other left hand staircase to the princess' salons.

No one would have been surprised. The tsar and all the most notable Russians attended Princess Bagration's soirees. It was largely Austrians, led by their allegedly smitten foreign minister, Prince Metternich, who frequented the duchess' salons.

The princess spotted him immediately and glided over to welcome him. By any standards she was beautiful, with shining blonde hair, a perfect white and rose complexion, and light blue eyes a man could happily drown in. She wore a diaphanous, almost transparent white gown that clung to her delectable frame and exposed a dangerous expanse of her alabaster bosom.

It always intrigued Vanya how she dressed like an expensive whore and yet never appeared less than a great lady. Perhaps it was the intelligence behind the provocative beauty on display. Whatever, Vanya could never do less than flirt with her. On one memorable occasion she'd allowed him rather more, which he remembered vividly, as she took his hand and playfully tapped his cheek with her fan.

"Vanya! How dare you take so long to visit me!"

"But I came the very moment you sent for me. I wouldn't otherwise have dared intrude."

"Frightened of His Majesty?" the princess teased.

"Everyone should be frightened of His Majesty, in my opinion." He looked about in mock terror. "Is he here?"

Princess Bagration laughed. "He has promised to look in later on. In the meantime, I can offer you two kings and a crown prince. Would you like an introduction? Or shall I point you toward old friends?"

"Can't I stay with you? I won't be any trouble."

"Vanya, you were *born* trouble! Which I understand is irresistible to many ladies less averse to risk than I. Sonia Andreievna, for one." As she spoke, Princess Bagration nodded across the room to where Countess Gelitzina held court surrounded by two heavily-braided officers, Prince Czartoryski, the tsar's Polish adviser, and a quietly dressed man whose eyes lit up when they glanced over and connected with Vanya's.

Vanya couldn't help the grin that split his face. Count Boris Kyrilovitch Lebedev was one of the few people in the world he welcomed with undiluted pleasure.

Boris broke away from Sonia's group of satellites with a faintly murmured excuse and strode towards Vanya with his hand held out.

"Vanya. I heard a rumor you were here."

Vanya embraced his old friend, thumping him on the back enthusiastically enough to attract considerable attention. "Well, I certainly didn't expect to find *you* in the midst of such frivolity."

"Frivolity? My dear Vanya, if the rest of the engagement is like the pre-battle skirmishes, the fates of nations will be decided in just such places as this."

"Now I understand," Vanya said wryly. "So how exactly are you contributing to this fate?"

Boris wrinkled his nose and lowered his voice. "I liaise with the British Embassy."

"Is that bad?"

"Only in places. I found them mind-bogglingly ignorant of European affairs and even geography, but to give them their due, they're learning."

Vanya took two glasses from the proffered tray in front of him and handed one to his friend. "Don't suppose you've come across a British diplomat called… Daniels? Geoffrey Daniels. Or was it Jeremy?"

"Yes, he's a good enough chap. Easier to deal with than Stewart, that's for sure. Plus he works harder. Why?"

"I think I might have come across his niece," Vanya said vaguely.

"I never heard of a niece, but there's certainly a daughter. I met her at Lady Castlereagh's this afternoon. Wouldn't have thought she was your type, Vanya. Let me rephrase. I'm *praying* she's not your type."

"Save your prayers, I've never met her. The girl I mean is definitely a niece."

"I think my prayers probably cover the entire British mission and all their extended families. At least until we have a peace agreement. What are you doing in Vienna, anyhow?"

"Theatricals," Vanya said disparagingly. "My Cossacks are barracked outside the city, ready to show off whenever they're required. I was ordered here *until* they're required. I'm supposed to be on leave."

"Which means you're ripe for mischief."

"Then isn't it as well I've got your sober face to keep me on the straight and narrow? They play cards here," he observed as they strolled through into the next room. "For money?"

"A *lot* of money if you have it."

"Well, I do. I just don't have it on me. Lend me a few roubles, Boris?"

"Not to play with."

"Just want to test my luck, see if I can win three thousand pounds."

"Three thousand!" Boris exclaimed. "What do you want that kind of money for?"

Vanya smiled. "To buy a lady a necklace."

The fun leaked out of Boris's eyes, leaving them just a little desolate. "To replace the one you took from that woman at the theatre?"

"Boris!" Vanya mocked. "I'm surprised at you repeating gossip. And no, it's nothing to do with her."

Boris sighed. "You can have what's in my pocket, providing you don't accuse anyone above the rank of count or colonel of cheating. And don't shoot anyone."

Vanya grinned and strolled towards the card tables.

IT WAS ONLY one plan and too risky to rely on, so he didn't really mind if he lost. He'd only borrowed a trifling amount from Boris, which he could easily repay just as soon as his mother forgave him and started sending him his money again. And sure enough, he lost the first two hands, won the third, and lost the fourth. After which, fickle fortune decided to smile on him and he was well into a winning streak, much to the disgust of his opponents, when a minor commotion in the main salon seized his erratic attention.

"The tsar," Sonia reported from the doorway. Having applauded his last few wins, she was bored with the game and ready to seek attention elsewhere.

Vanya sat where he was. Although quite ready to rekindle his old liaison with the countess, he reckoned he could win enough in another fifteen minutes, half an hour at the most—providing the cards stayed with him—and be free to pursue her wholeheartedly.

Somewhat to his surprise, his opponents didn't immediately rush to fawn upon the tsar, either. Vanya could only suppose that His Majesty's presence at such minor social gatherings had become too familiar.

And certainly, as he strolled into the card room twenty minutes later, the tsar's manner was informal to the point of casual. Tall, fair, handsome, and well-made, Alexander, Tsar of all the Russias, was an impressive man. Vanya, who was and had always been quite prepared to die for him, thought it a shame that he couldn't actually like him. To Vanya, he was a bad mixture of arrogance, brilliance, ineptitude, idealism, optimism, petulance, charm, and tyranny. People called Vanya volatile, but truly, the tsar was the embodiment of such a description.

Tonight, His Majesty was in affable humor, even pressing Vanya's shoulder to prevent him rising when he realized the tsar stood behind him. "No, no, Colonel," he said jovially. "My heroes shall not bow to me in private!"

Princess Bagration's salons were hardly private, but no one argued.

"Are you winning?" the tsar inquired.

"Moderately," Vanya said, to the accompaniment of snorts around the table.

The tsar was pleased to laugh and pass on. Which is when Vanya finally noticed the officers who flanked him. The one on the right was sneering at him openly when he should have been following the tsar.

"Blonsky," Vanya said in surprise, although he did vaguely recall hearing Blonsky's regiment had been assigned to guarding the tsar.

There was a time when he'd have cared, when at least hatred and anger would have risen at the sight of him. Now, the boy he'd been was so far removed as to not matter anymore. Even Katia had grown blurry in his memory. He'd shed too much blood in the last six years to be very eager to spill more. Even Blonsky's.

Blonsky curled his lip and looked right through him, a difficult combination to achieve, then turned and marched off after the tsar.

"Bad blood?" one of the players drawled.

"No," Vanya said. "It was never his blood that was the problem."

The player leaned closer, confiding, "Did you know he is pursuing Countess Gelitzina?"

Vanya, about to deal the cards, paused for a fraction of a second. "No. I didn't know that."

"He's dangerous in a duel," the young man said bluntly.

Vanya glanced at him and set down the cards.

But the player on his other side had overheard with some amusement. "So's Vanya. Who do you think gave Blonsky that sabre scar on his hand?"

"Play," Vanya said impatiently.

Ten minutes later, Vanya swept his winnings into his pocket and, ignoring pleas for revenge from his erstwhile opponents, went in search of Boris.

"He left on some business of the tsar's," Sonia said when he encountered her in the hallway beside the cloakroom, receiving her flimsy shawl from a wooden-faced servant.

Vanya propped his shoulder against the wall, waiting for the maid to leave. "What is Blonsky to you?" he asked, when the girl had effaced herself.

Sonia glanced up at him, a smile just curving her luscious lips. "Jealous, Vanya?"

"I don't care to step on another man's toes."

Sonia's eyes flashed. "It didn't bother you when my husband was alive."

She had a point, of course. He shifted uncomfortably. "Perhaps I've grown up."

"Good night, Vanya," Sonia said deliberately and turned her back, heading for the staircase.

Vanya straightened. "You could," he suggested, "drop me at Boris' lodgings."

Sonia stilled. After a moment, she looked back over her shoulder and regarded him. He'd always liked the way her smoky eyes seemed to smolder.

"I could," she agreed and walked on.

Vanya smiled and followed her.

IN THE QUIET of the morning after she'd given Johnnie, the thief, his instructions. Lizzie decided they should take the dog out for a long walk in the direction of the Vienna woods. Dog, thrilled to be outside of the confining walls of the house and garden, pulled on his leash so wildly that Lizzie was dragged all over the place. She only just managed to prevent him from throwing himself in front of a fast-bowling carriage.

By the time they reached the Graben, they'd developed a system whereby everyone else held on to the person who controlled the leash, ready to dig in their heels at Dog's next lunge. It was quite an amusing way to travel and it caused a good deal of hilarity among the children and the few passers-by they encountered. Fortunately, fashionable Vienna was still abed, since it never went to sleep before three o'clock in the morning and frequently later.

However, Lizzie soon discovered that even this ridiculous method was not foolproof. As Henrietta controlled the lead with Dog walking nicely beside her, he made yet another lunge at a maid carrying several parcels – presumably containing food. Lizzie and the others applied the anchor as usual and Henrietta remained in place. However, the leash unraveled, allowing Dog to run rings around the poor maid and tangle her in the lead. When the maid dropped some of her parcels in fright, Lizzie knew they were in trouble.

"Oh no," she said, releasing Henrietta and lunging after the dog. But Michael was ahead of her, throwing himself on top of the animal.

"So sorry," Lizzie said, untangling the frightened maid. "He won't hurt you but he's greed personified."

Georgiana and Henrietta were already picking up the maid's parcels. Dog, under Michael's restraining body, wagged his tail. The maid, looking more outraged than frightened, released a torrent of French, interrupted by a rather delightful peel of laughter from a lady Lizzie hadn't even noticed. She was about Lizzie's own age and exquisitely dressed in a blue morning dress and pelisse with matching chip hat. More than that, even holding her sides in mirth, she possessed an enviable, unconscious elegance.

"Thank you for rescuing my foolish girl," she said breathlessly, coming up to Lizzie and quieting the maid with a flick of one casual finger. "And for the entertainment. That's the funniest thing I've seen since I arrived in Vienna."

"You must thank Dog for that," Lizzie said dryly. "We are merely his slaves. Well done, Michael," she added. "You can release him now, but slowly." She shortened the leash to prevent the dog jumping on the elegant lady as soon as he'd bounced to his feet and shaken himself. The lady let him sniff her gloved fingers and stroked his big head. Dog fawned.

"He likes you." Georgiana observed with unflattering surprise.

"I like dogs."

"He's more of a disgrace than a dog," Lizzie sighed. "We never trained him properly. It didn't matter in the country, but in the city he's a menace."

"A beautiful menace," the lady insisted. Not many people would have called Dog beautiful, so Lizzie was disposed to like her.

"I don't think he ate any of your parcels," Lizzie said. "But if he's damaged anything, you must let us pay."

"Ah no, I believe this young man's quick actions saved the day. Or at least my breakfast."

Michael gave an embarrassed and slightly bedazzled grin.

Even more in accord with the lady, Lizzie said, "Well, if you find teeth marks in any of it, send word to me! I'm Lizzie Gaunt and staying with my aunt and uncle in the Skodegasse. Number twenty-five."

The lady held out her hand. "Dorothée de Talleyrand-Perigord, and I'm staying with my uncle in the Johnnesgasse. I believe they call it the Kaunitz Palace."

"You're French!" Michael exclaimed, fortunately detracting from Lizzie's astonishment with his own shock. Lizzie's was more to do with the recognition of the name Talleyrand.

"Oh, the blood in my veins comes from all over Europe," Dorothée said carelessly. "Besides, we're all at peace now, are we not? Is your uncle with the British Embassy? Mine is with the French."

Lizzie, allowing Dog the space to lift his leg at the nearby lamp-post, caught her new friend's eye with a wry twitch of her lip. "Madame, your uncle *is* the French Embassy."

Dorothée laughed. "He will rejoice to hear you say so."

By mutual if tacit agreement, they'd begun to walk together, the maid keeping a strategic distance behind, well away from the dog. Before they parted ten minutes later, Lizzie knew that her new friend was married, hadn't seen her husband for months, and didn't appear to mind, and that she had two children whom she'd left with her mother so she could come to Vienna to play hostess for her uncle. But more than that, they'd laughed together and Lizzie rather thought that if things had been different, they might have been close friends.

VANYA HADN'T YET made it to Boris' lodgings. Sonia had proved such a delightful distraction that he'd never got further than her apartment overlooking the Graben.

Vanya seldom slept in daylight, so he rose early, leaving her sprawled face down and contented in the bed. He flung on his clothes in careless fashion and sat down in the chair by the window to pull on his boots.

From here, he suspected, you could see the whole of Vienna pass by in a single day. Wherever you went, it was nearly always necessary to go via the Graben, this vast, open space stretching out before him. Even early as it was, several people were already abroad – scurrying tradesmen and merchants, a few servants and an elegant lady in blue…

He blinked, his restless heart suddenly soaring with unexpected excitement, for he'd just caught sight of a cavalcade of three young girls, a boy, and a large, hairy dog of indeterminate parentage. The youthful beauty of the family, Henrietta, was holding the dog's lead while everyone else held on to her.

Vanya stood up and grinned, leaning one arm across the wooden window frame to watch them process across the Graben amidst a great deal of hilarity. The sight tugged at him, reminding him of more innocent days, of childhood fun with his own siblings and cousins, before war and the awfulness of fear and violence had soured him.

Not that many people would have called him sour. But the sheer *joie de vivre* of the English family made him laugh and ache at the same time, especially when the dog assaulted the maid.

His shoulders shook silently as the scene unfolded before him. He couldn't tear himself away. The trouble was, he couldn't help liking the whole eccentric family; and, of course, the lady in blue whom they adopted into the adventure of their everyday life, was a stunning beauty by any standards. And yet for some reason, it was Lizzie his gaze clung to with ever-growing fascination. Something about her mix of innocence and boldness, fun and determination, surpassed even the unconscious loveliness of her face and figure, which had first attracted him, when she'd hustled him into her family's carriage outside the theatre.

Actually, he didn't even know if she *was* beautiful. Not like the tsarina or Sonia or the lady in blue who looked oddly familiar, but it didn't seem to matter anymore. Sheer vitality surpassed mere beauty. Or perhaps merely enhanced it, for he defied anyone to find a pair of finer dark eyes than Lizzie's. Somehow, they sparkled...

Sober, of course, he understood that she was off-limits to him for any number of reasons, but that hadn't stopped her popping into his mind at all sorts of inconvenient and inappropriate moments, not least of which had occurred last night while he was making unbridled love to Sonia.

Something very like shame churned in his stomach as he glanced toward the bed. It seemed...*wrong*, to be here with Sonia, watching *her.* As if he could somehow sully the English girl.

And yet, still he didn't turn away. He watched her laugh and hang on to the dog and all her dependent siblings while she made unlikely friends with the fashionable lady in blue. And he enjoyed it. He enjoyed *her*, even from a distance, with something that threatened to run far deeper than mere physical desire.

When the family eventually passed out of his sight, he sat down again and pulled on his other boot. Then, seizing his coat, he left his lover sound asleep in her tiny apartment and set off to walk to Boris' lodgings.

Boris was already awake and looking harassed as he sorted out a huge bundle of papers.

"You're up early," Vanya observed.

"Comes with the job," Boris said grimly. He spared him a quick, half-amused glance. "I suppose you haven't been to bed yet."

"I wouldn't say that," Vanya replied in the interests of strict truth. "Just came to give you this." He placed a bundle of roubles on the table.

"You won, then?"

"Surprisingly, yes. But I won't let it go to my head. I'm sure God was only smiling on that *particular* cause."

Boris raised one wry eyebrow. "Don't drag the Almighty into your vices." He set down his papers and fixed Vanya with his clear, direct gaze. "What are you up to, Vanya? What is this particular cause? Are you still talking about a necklace? Or does it have something to do with your feud with Blonsky? I heard he cut you last night."

Vanya shrugged. "The man's a boor. But you needn't worry. I'm not going to risk my life or anyone else's."

"But I've heard such odd things of you recently that you really do have me worried."

Vanya curled his lip. "Afraid I'm finally going to the devil?"

"Yes," Boris said frankly. He leaned both hands on the table. "Look, I know everyone thinks it's such an amusing start, but taking a woman's necklace, ripping it from her throat…*stealing*, Vanya!"

"Oh, for the love of—" Vanya cast his eyes to heaven. "It wasn't *her* wretched necklace, it was mine! *She* stole if from me!"

Boris frowned. "How did she do that? And what were you doing with a woman's necklace anyway?"

"It's my mother's. She forced it on me, said I should wear it under my uniform in battle. So I do. It may be my one act of filial obedience, but I've stuck to it and, if you must know, it's a bit of a secret talisman."

Boris's brow smoothed. "You imagine it keeps you safe."

Vanya shrugged impatiently. "Something has. So far. Besides, Louise Fischer is a nasty piece of work. I wouldn't have my mother's necklace on her cheating little throat."

"But you didn't mind her cheating little throat in your bed?"

"That's different. Or at least it was. I thought we both understood the nature of the game. Then she took the necklace from my trunk while I slept, crossing one of my very few lines."

"Why? Isn't she wealthy?"

"Getting wealthier by the day," Vanya said cynically. "She and her husband entertain the rich and gullible, drawing them in with Louise's beauty. She flirts with them while he fleeces them. They have high-stake card games in their apartment twice a week and nobody wins in the end."

"Even you?"

He shrugged. "I saw what they were up to. After losing, of course."

"So you took your revenge by bedding the woman and then humiliating her in public."

Vanya hated the hint of defiance he was sure must show in his eyes as he met his friend's gaze. Boris could always do this to him, show him how badly he was behaving and make him ashamed. In the end, he'd always been grateful, because Boris had always been right. At least until now.

"Something like that," Vanya said steadily.

Boris' eyes bored into his and then unexpectedly they smiled, and his shoulders relaxed. "No it isn't. You were drunk, weren't you?"

Vanya's smile was twisted. "Inevitably."

"And you never denied the accusations because if you'd told the truth you'd have revealed the Fischer woman publicly as your mistress. Or your whore. After everything, you were protecting her reputation."

"How saintly am I?" Vanya said flippantly, throwing himself into the nearest chair.

Boris hurled a cushion at him. "Not very. You just have an odd saving grace."

Vanya caught the cushion and put it behind his head so that he could lean back and pretend to close his eyes. "Well, one more scandal makes no difference to me. And who am I to quibble at the enterprising Fischers making a few kopeks from the wealthy fools who've invaded their city?"

Boris shook his head. "And I suppose you're going to be giving the rest of *that* money—" He flapped one hand towards the pile of roubles on the table. "…to charity?"

Vanya laughed. "Almost. You might say I'm righting a wrong with it. Or just enjoying the fun."

# Chapter Four

THE DAY OF the Emperor's ball dawned fair and sunny. Lizzie found herself much in demand, running errands and making last minute adjustments to the gowns of her aunt and cousin.

"I wish you were coming, too," Minerva said once, as their eyes met in the glass. "It would be so much more fun, then. On my own, I feel like a piece of meat left in the butcher's window too long."

Lizzie didn't really blame her. Like all debutantes, Minerva was being displayed for sale to the most eligible husband. But Lizzie only smiled and squeezed her cousin's hand. "Trust me, you look nothing like a piece of meat. And if you were such a thing, you'd be the one snapped up as soon as the shop opened for business."

Minerva laughed but caught at her hand. "Seriously, Lizzie, why don't you come?"

"I have nothing to wear," Lizzie said lightly. "And I didn't come to Vienna with you to go to balls, but to help if I could." Her conscience twinged a little at that.

Although she wasn't stealing, the act of taking the necklace was bound to frighten her aunt and cause considerable anxiety. Until now, she had been able to thrust such awareness aside with the resolve to comfort her aunt after it had happened. But suddenly, the whole great plan seemed just a little mean.

"Maybe I shouldn't do it," she said worriedly to her siblings when she found them all with the dog in the garden.

"Why ever not?" Georgiana demanded.

"It's bound to scare poor Aunt Lucy into a fit. Maybe Johnnie was right and he should just steal it from the house. Let Ivan the Terrible have what suspicions he likes, he'll never prove anything."

"Even when we suddenly have enough money to set up our own home?" Georgiana asked.

"Well, that's going to be an issue anyway," Lizzie said ruefully. "Not so much to the world, who might imagine Papa left us a little unentailed property. But to my aunt and uncle who must know there was no such thing."

"I thought you had a plan for that," Michael said.

"Well, I thought we could forge a letter from Ivan the Terrible appearing to make us an allowance out of the goodness of his heart, but you know that would only work if my uncle never actually speaks to him."

Georgiana and Michael both gazed at her with a mixture of anxiety and accusation. Henrietta, much more evenly tempered, looked from one to the other and then to Lizzie.

"I don't think you *can* call it off now," Michael said at last. "You won't see Johnnie until it's done."

"I will, since I have to point out my aunt...Why do I feel like Judas Iscariot? Anyhow, there may or may not be a chance to speak to him, but I definitely have to go."

"What's brought on such doubts?" Henrietta asked.

Lizzie sighed. "I don't know. The approach of the reality probably. And then I was talking to Minerva who wished I was going with her to the ball. I felt like a...a *cad*."

"Well, she has a point," Henrietta said. "Why *don't* you ever go to the balls and parties with them? You could make a splendid match here, Lizzie."

"*That's* the problem," Georgiana said, nodding wisely. "Lizzie would cast Minerva in the shade and catch all the best suitors."

Lizzie laughed with genuine, if touched amusement. "Hardly. I'm twenty-three years old and quite on the shelf. Even when I was seventeen, I was no beauty."

"Yes you were," Henrietta said loyally. "You still are, if only you could see it."

"Why didn't you have a London season like everyone else?" Michael asked.

Lizzie shrugged. "I don't know. The time passed. I never actually wanted one. Papa was ill off and on. It made more sense to everyone if I just stayed at Launceton. To be honest, I was grateful no one pushed me into it because you know I could never behave well for an entire evening, never mind several weeks. Our neighbors are used to my eccentricities, but London society would not be so forgiving."

Her gaze settled on Henrietta, whose dreams had always been of romance, husbands, babies, and decorating houses. "However, it would be a crime if *you* never had a London season, Henri. So one way or another, we need the necklace."

A knocking on the window drew her attention back to the house. Benson, Aunt Lucy's maid, was beckoning her inside. Lizzie waved and went dutifully back to help with the preparations.

※

WALKING TO THE Hofburg presented no difficulty to Lizzie. In fact, the proximity of the palace was the main reason she was so easily able to talk the children out of accompanying her with the dog.

"I would love to see all the emperors and empresses, kings and queens as they arrive," Henrietta said hopefully.

"But you wouldn't see the really important ones from the street anyhow," Lizzie assured her. "Most of them are staying in the Hofburg itself. It's only the lesser mortals who'll arrive by carriage. But I promise I'll tell you all about it and tomorrow night, providing I'm back, I promise we'll all go and gawp outside Prince Metternich's house to see all the royalty arriving for *his* ball."

Having fastened "the" necklace around her aunt's throat and positioned the elegant pearl clip in Minerva's beautifully dressed hair, Lizzie admired their appearances with quite genuine generosity. James seized her for a quick, private confab about his cravat, which she pronounced fine without a great deal of interest, before frowning suspiciously.

"Are you trying to impress someone in particular?" she asked.

James looked at once sheepish and awestruck. "*She* will be there. Louise."

"Then Madame Fischer is no longer the sole object of your admiration?" she asked, pleased for no reason that she could account for.

"Of course she is," James said haughtily, straightening to look down his nose at her. "Louise *is* Madame Fischer!"

Lizzie had to swallow a laugh. In fact, her main worry, despite Johnnie's assurances, was how she would persuade the palace doormen to let her in without a card. But as she tripped out into the street with the rest of the admiring household, to watch her aunt, uncle, and cousins step into their carriage, someone pressed an envelope into her hand.

Startled, she glanced around her. She had an impression of flashing white teeth and a small figure vanishing up the street. An urchin younger than Michael. Hastily, she crushed the envelope, hiding it as casually as she could in the folds of her gown while she waved the carriage off.

When she got back inside, alone in the parlor with the children, she tore it open – and found a card for the Emperor's ball.

There was no note with it, nothing to show where it had come from.

"Johnnie," Michael said with certainty. "I think you picked a very clever, thinking, planning kind of a thief."

Lizzie thought rather doubtfully about the hand snatching the necklace from the throat of Madame Fischer in full view of the theatre, about the blatant escape of the thief and his casual admission of drunkenness when she'd hidden him in her uncle's carriage. And yet, he hadn't ever been caught for the crime. So far as she knew.

"I think he's a very strange kind of a thief," she countered. "But since we don't know any others, how would we tell?" She took a deep breath and stood up with a decisive spring. "So, you remember your parts? I'll come and see you as soon as I return, but try and cover for me if that isn't tonight." They'd already agreed she should stay with Johnnie until the necklace was sold.

"You can't be alone with him all night," Henrietta said suddenly. "That would be *too* improper, even for us!"

"I doubt it's any less proper than engaging a thief in the first place," Lizzie said dryly. "In any case, who will know? But hopefully, it will not be anything like all night. In fact, if Johnnie has a buyer set up, I hope to be home before the others."

———

EVENTUALLY, WHILE THE children kept watch for passing servants, Lizzie crept out of the house in her mask and the voluminous black domino cloak that hid her small carpet bag in its folds. Henrietta had said, awed, that she looked mysterious and just a little dangerous, which pleased Lizzie excessively. From such a description, no one would ever recognize her.

The streets were thronged with carriages heading to the Hofburg, and with crowds of curious Viennese, many of whom also wore cloaks and masks as if hoping to sneak in to the festivities like Lizzie. She hurried on, mingling with the crowds until she stood in line for admittance.

As she neared the great doors with agonizing slowness, she realized what was causing a large part of the delay. As she suspected, many waiting to enter didn't have cards at all, but money was surreptitiously changing hands as the doormen sold on the cards they'd already collected. Lizzie feared the ball was going to be a horrible crush.

It was. But at least she was admitted without fuss or interest and no one seemed to notice that she had neither escort nor female companion, even when she quietly left her bag in the ladies' cloakroom. And then she was among thousands of people in a blaze of light and beauty. At first, she just wandered in a daze through the huge, white and gold panelled ballroom, where thousands of candles in magnificent chandeliers dazzled her, to one scarcely smaller, and then along an orange lined, covered pathway to another magnificent ballroom in the Spanish Riding School. Smooth, parquet floors seemed to glide under her outdoor shoes which she did her best to hide under the cloak. Galleries and seats full of glittering women and brilliantly braided men overwhelmed her. Most wore their cloaks casually open, revealing gorgeous attire and expensive jewels.

*How the devil*, Lizzie wondered in dismay, *am I to find my aunt, never mind Johnnie, in this throng?*

For some reason, she'd never imagined this sheer number of people. On the other hand, from overheard snippets of conversation, neither had anyone else. Someone claimed the ball had been oversubscribed to begin with; someone else was outraged by the number of guests who'd bribed the doormen to let them in.

And then the royal party arrived. Lizzie had only the tiniest glimpse when everyone bowed and she could finally see over their heads. A frail, white-haired man with a bony face led the procession, presumably the Emperor of Austria himself, his Empress on his arm. Towering behind them, was the tall, fair, angelically beautiful couple that could only be the Tsar and Tsarina of Russia.

A whole host of glittering dignitaries followed, too dazzling for Lizzie to separate. They made their stately way down the grand staircase, processing around the room to the raised platform draped in white silk and silver, where the two empresses took their seats at the front, the lesser queens, grand duchesses, and princesses behind.

It was luck in the end that directed her to her aunt. As she again wandered through the ballrooms, she became aware of a conversation nearby between an English voice and a German-sounding one.

"Perhaps *that* is Lady Castlereagh, with her niece," the German voice suggested.

"No, I can guarantee it isn't," the Englishman disputed. "Lady Castlereagh does not break the Sabbath by attending. If I'm not much mistaken, that's Mrs. Daniels and her daughter. Daniels is on Stewart's staff."

Lizzie immediately turned to see where they were looking and finally found the figures of Aunt Lucy and Minerva, masked but blessedly familiar, their amber and white domino cloaks open to reveal the finery of their attire. And the necklace around her aunt's throat. So all Lizzie had to do now was keep them in sight—while finding the thief, Johnnie...

The orchestra struck up while she weaved anxiously among the scented and bejeweled crowd, glancing alternately over to her aunt who appeared to be introducing young men to Minerva, and around the room in search of the ball's least respectable guest, if only to call off the theft. She had quite decided this was the best way to proceed. In fact, she couldn't imagine how she hadn't considered the effect of such a personal assault before.

Possibly because Madame Fischer had seemed to take it so much in her stride. But once she actually thought of it, it was Madame Fischer's reaction which had been odd. She suspected the woman had to be positively unfeeling rather than brave, in which case, it wasn't at all good that James should pursue her...

The emperor and the tsarina were advancing to the center of the floor to open the ball, followed by the tsar and the empress, and a stately Polonaise began, the couples in a long line parading around the ballroom. Minerva was dancing with a young man in green, much to Lizzie's relief and approval, while Aunt Lucy watched proudly from among a gaggle of other matrons. Her uncle, she finally discovered, was in conversation with several other serious looking men, masks dangling from their hands rather than on their faces. And James...where was James?

"Mysterious Mademoiselle Noire," a masculine voice said at her shoulder. "May I have the honor of dancing with you?"

"Oh no," Lizzie said fervently. This was another unforeseen event. She spared a glance at her suitor, a young man in a dark blue domino cloak hanging over one shoulder to reveal a military uniform with much gold braid, his fair hair short and tidy beneath the mask strings. Her instant, unqualified rejection made him blink, so she added hastily, "Perhaps later. I'm searching for my aunt."

"Let me help you find her."

"Then you'll miss the dance," Lizzie said, and with quick smile, slipped into the throngs away from him.

※

VANYA, MEANWHILE, WAS amusing himself by flirting outrageously with beautiful women, most of whom he didn't even recognize. One he knew to be the Duchess of Sagan, not least because Metternich was giving him the evil eye from across the room. Vanya contented himself with kissing her fingers and then, daringly, the inside of her wrist, which made her laugh and shoo him away as he'd known it would.

He'd postponed judgement on how to handle the necklace affair at least until after he set eyes on the aunt, which he managed by the simple expedient of asking people where she was. Perhaps they imagined he had his eye on the cousin, for a German diplomat pointed out a much younger woman waltzing in the arms of none other than Boris.

Casually, Vanya circled the dance floor, and eventually found the person he was most eager to discover: a female almost entirely enveloped in black, quite unconscious of the stir she was causing by being just about the only woman not revealing the elegance of her gown and figure. At least the cloak hood was down to reveal dark brown chestnut hair, fetchingly piled on her head and tied with a gold ribbon. He wondered who'd done that for her and decided it was most likely to be Henrietta, the acknowledged family beauty. Her mask was rigidly in place and her intense gaze was divided between her cousin and frequent sweeps of the room. Her gaze flickered over him once without interest. His lips twitched.

The waltz ended and Boris, always the perfect gentleman, conducted Miss Minerva to her protector who was, of course, a middle-aged lady wearing a very fine gold and diamond necklace on her plump bosom. Vanya smiled and derived further entertainment by strolling directly in front of the black dominoed lady, who was peering anxiously through the doorway.

"*Excusez moi, mademoiselle,*" he murmured politely.

Her gaze flickered over his uniform braid without even rising to his face. "*De rien, monsieur,*" she returned and passed on.

Vanya's shoulders began to shake as he hurried on, managing to reach Boris before he had left the Daniels women. Behind his mask, Boris' eyes lit up before he remembered to be suspicious.

"Allow me to present my friend," he said, scowling a warning at Vanya. "Colonel—"

"Vanya," he interrupted smoothly. "Since we're masquerading!"

"Colonel Vanya," the aunt said graciously. "My daughter."

"Enchanted," Vanya said smoothly, just as an Englishman butted in to claim his promised dance with Minerva. Boris could barely contain his grin. Vanya ignored him. "Perhaps I might solicit your daughter for a later dance," he suggested. "In the meantime, perhaps you, Madame, would do me the honor?"

The aunt blinked rapidly. "Me? My dear sir, I haven't danced in years!"

"But this is Vienna," Vanya said, taking her hand. "Everyone dances."

Since it was not the waltz but a staider country dance, Mrs. Daniels finally accepted with grace. After a few moments, as she turned in the figure, he let his gaze dwell on the back of her neck and then, very quickly, he reached up as if to grasp it and deftly loosened the clasp.

"Madame," he said at once. "The clasp of your necklace…"

Mrs. Daniels paused, her hand flying to the jewels at her bosom and giving them an experimental tug. The necklace came away in her hand. "Oh my," she exclaimed. "Oh dear!"

"Well, at least you have not lost it. Look, put it in your reticule until you get home. You can have it repaired tomorrow."

"Very true," she said. Vanya couldn't tell if she was more relieved not to have dropped and lost the necklace or disappointed not to be wearing it still. Good humoredly, he led her back into the dance.

When the dance was over, he returned her to her chair, made sure she had a glass of wine, and went off to find Sonia for the waltz.

~

MAJOR BLONSKY SCOWLED through his mask at the unedifying sight of Countess Gelitzina waltzing in the arms of the man he considered his greatest enemy, Napoleon Bonaparte and the entire French army notwithstanding. He appeared to be whispering outrageous blandishments in her receptive ear for her laughter was breathless and her cheeks flushed by more than the exertion of the dance.

"Major," murmured a quiet voice at his side. He didn't need to turn to recognize the voice as that of the man he knew only as Agent Z, but he glanced over anyway, if only to prove he was unafraid. The spy was in his element, masked and cloaked in silver-gray, hidden from the dance floor by the pillar he lounged against, and which Blonsky appeared to be sharing with him.

"I thought you were guarding His Majesty the Tsar," Agent Z observed.

"I am," Blonsky said shortly. "His Majesty is dancing. I don't see the countess as a huge threat to his life."

"I'm always glad to have my theories confirmed," the spy said politely, although Blonsky was sure the words contained a wealth of hidden sarcasm. "And what of the Russian officer I asked you about? The one who met secretly with the English woman."

"Colonel Ivan Petrovitch Savarin," Blonsky said with loathing. "It's my belief he's trying to sabotage relations between the Russians and the Austrians by promoting a secret treaty with the British."

The spy's eyes burned into his averted face. Blonsky smiled.

"You have evidence?" the spy inquired.

"Isn't that your job?" Blonsky said rudely.

"Not when I'm paying you. Why do you hate him?"

Blonsky felt no need to deny it. Unconsciously, he touched the scar on his hand, souvenir of their last unexpected and humiliating encounter. He'd never expected the boy he used to beat up regularly would have turned into such a good fighter. Graceless, perhaps, but efficient...damn it, even that wasn't true. Vanya had still possessed the swashbuckling panache that had so annoyed Blonsky as an adolescent. It had just been honed and focused by his years of soldiering.

"You fought a duel," Agent Z observed.

Blonsky could sneer—had sneered, and in public—at Vanya's half-wild Cossacks, but it was they who'd not only seen but fought in all the battles from Borodino to Leipzig. It had rankled when Vanya had instantly snapped back, insulting Blonsky's regiment as drawing room soldiers. It hadn't really been about regiments, of course; it had been about a peasant girl loved by the youthful Savarin and taken by the not much older Blonsky. But still, there had been too much truth in Vanya's insult and even Blonsky's promise to trounce the "barbarian" commander had been undeniably turned against him when the barbarian had trounced *him* in a humiliatingly short space of time.

"A stupid drunken brawl," Blonsky snapped. "We each imagined we were defending rather than disgracing our respective regiments." He pushed himself off the pillar. "You'll get your evidence," he snarled and walked away. It would have felt better if he hadn't suspected the spy had already melted into the crowd moving in the opposite direction.

# Chapter Five

L IZZIE, ON HER latest foray through the ballrooms and the riding school, had found no trace of Johnnie. She did see her cousin James mooning after Madame Fischer, in the company of some men she instinctively knew to be unsavory. She even began to approach, to extricate him and warn him to stop making a cake of himself over the Viennese beauty, before she remembered she shouldn't even be here.

Instead, she decided to leave the riding school and return to the main ballroom where she could keep her eyes on her aunt. Only where the devil was Johnnie?

*Perhaps he's been arrested over the other necklace or for something else entirely.*

On this unhappy thought, she swung abruptly away from the sight of James, leading Madame Fischer towards the dance floor, and cannoned into the hard body of a military stranger in a scarlet domino cloak.

"Oh goodness," she exclaimed, flustered by the force of their meeting. "I'm sorry!"

The officer, steadying her with a hand on either arm, said, "Don't be. I'm not. I've been trying to speak to you all night."

Something about his foreign voice sounded familiar, but though she peered up at him in the dazzling white light of the candles, the mask made him a mere stranger with black hair, steady, lazily smiling dark eyes and sculpted lips.

"Why?" she demanded, surprised by the unexpected tug of attraction. After all, she'd been gazing at masked military men for most of the evening and none of them had even momentarily distracted her from her mission.

The smile in his dark eyes intensified, spreading to his lips. "To ask you to dance, of course."

"I don't dance," she said hurriedly and added the excuse she'd been using all night. "I'm looking for my aunt." She began to slip away from the polite hands which hadn't quite released her, but although he let one hand fall away, his other slid down her cloak-covered arm to the fingers holding the domino closed around her.

"Why not?" he countered. "Why come to a ball not to dance?" When she opened her mouth to reply, he said it for her with quiet humor, "To look for your aunt. I know. Dance with me and I'll restore you to your aunt immediately."

It was, she knew, time to pull away into the crowd, forcefully if necessary, particularly since the orchestra had struck up a waltz. But as his fingers drew hers into his hand, his arm was already circling her waist.

There was nothing rough or coercive about it. She could still have got free quite easily and left him standing there looking just a little foolish. In fact, she tried to tell herself that was the reason she gave in, but in truth, something about his familiarity, about his voice and his person, all made her want to dance with him. He was a tall stranger in a mask, a foreign officer with his own life story far removed from her own, and he intrigued her.

And then the music, melodic, rhythmic and insistent, inspired her to recklessness. Or it might have been the novelty of the stranger's embrace. She'd only ever waltzed with Michael and her sisters; it was much too fast a dance for a country neighborhood.

"I've never waltzed in public before," she said bluntly. "I'll stand all over your feet."

"No you won't," he said with certainty, spinning her onto the dance floor.

She gasped, more with fun than fear. His head lowered slightly.

"The mysterious Mademoiselle Noire should not watch her feet as she waltzes."

"Gauche?" Lizzie suggested ruefully.

His eyes lit with laughter. "Sadly. And then you don't really want to draw attention to your outdoor shoes."

"Oh dear. You have found me out." She squared her shoulders and confessed, "I wasn't invited."

"You're in good company," he excused.

"You, too?"

"Sadly, I was bidden."

"Why sadly?"

"Your way is more adventurous," the stranger pointed out.

"Aren't you tired of adventuring?" she asked curiously.

He blinked. "Why should you think that?"

"Perhaps you have not been a soldier for very long," she guessed.

"Six years. Or is it seven?"

"Really? Then you must have fought Napoleon."

"All over Europe," he said flippantly. "And I see your reasoning. Maybe you're right and I should settle down."

"Oh no," she said with a quick frown. "Sometimes I wish I were a man and able to adventure about the world. Though I doubt I'd have made a very good soldier." She sighed. "Women are so hemmed in with respectability. Unless they wish to be ostracized."

"It isn't fair, is it?" he sympathized. "I've behaved badly all my life and no one has ever ostracized me."

"What did you do?" she asked, intrigued.

He laughed. "I can't tell you that."

She found herself returning his smile. "Because of my respectability?"

"And what's left of mine."

"But I'm the one intruding on the Emperor's ball. Here, *you* are the respectable one."

His breath of silent laughter seemed ridiculously familiar, but she couldn't catch the memory.

"I never thought of that," he said solemnly. "I shall tell all my friends. So tonight, the adventure is yours."

Reminded of the true purpose of the evening, she cast another rather guilty look around the riding school, searching for anyone who might possibly be Johnnie. Some plainly dressed man, hiding a hint of scruffiness beneath an all-enveloping domino. The trouble was, all the men she could see, including her dancing partner, wore their cloaks open, or even dangling off one shoulder like her current dancing partner.

"Who are you looking for?" he asked. "Perhaps I can help."

"I doubt it."

"Then it isn't really your aunt."

"Not *just* my aunt," she said cautiously.

"I sense an intrigue."

She let out a peel of laughter. "Don't be ridiculous. I don't *intrigue!*"

"Why ever not?" he asked outrageously. "It's one of the more fun and comfortable forms of adventuring. I suppose it comes down to respectability again."

"I suppose it does," she said with a twinge of regret. "Though to be honest, I've never yet encountered a man I wished to intrigue *with*."

"Mademoiselle, you cut me," he mourned, drawing her hand with his to his heart in mock injury.

She laughed. "No, I don't. We don't know each other at all."

"That is a large part of the fun in intrigue."

"I suppose you have a great deal of experience in that area," she allowed. Behind the mask, she was sure he was a handsome man. He was certainly charming in some indefinable way she couldn't help liking.

He said, "I suppose I do."

Catching an unexpected note of genuine regret in his voice, she peered up at him more closely.

He drew in a sudden breath. "Don't do that or I'll kiss you in the middle of the ballroom. Too blatant for intrigue."

"*And* for respectability," she scolded, although she felt a flush rise through her body to her cheeks as her wayward mind wondered how it would feel to be kissed by a masked stranger. *This* somewhat unconventional masked stranger who continued to gaze down at her, a faint, incomprehensible smile playing about his lips. She wanted, suddenly, to look away, but refused to give in to such cowardice.

Rather breathlessly, she said, "You should know I have no intention of either."

"Either what?"

She lifted her chin. "Kissing or intrigue."

His lips curved. "You could try one and if you liked it, move on to the other."

Laughter caught at her breath, perhaps in shock. "No, I couldn't. You're forgetting the respectability."

"But I thought you wanted an adventure?"

"Not like that," she said with dignity, although she may have ruined the effect by adding, "And certainly not with you. I suspect you're far too risky a proposition."

The smile died on his lips. "Why do you say that?"

"Because after tonight, after this waltz, we'll never see each other again." She was too used to speaking her thoughts as they occurred; she hadn't cleansed the unexpected regret from her voice.

And he caught it only too clearly. She saw the leap in his eyes and it caused an immediate commotion within her, like a flock of butterflies rising in her stomach. Even though she recognized it for what it was: a rake's triumph at the prospect of conquest. Worse, she couldn't make herself mind.

"Why should you think that?" he asked softly.

She shrugged, striving for carelessness. "Because even if we do, we won't know it. We won't recognize each other."

"Of course we will. There's an infallible way to ensure we do."

"What is that?" she asked unwisely.

"No two people kiss the same way."

For the first time, she missed a step. Heat surged through her so quickly she was glad of the mask to hide her flushed cheeks. She tried to introduce a haughty lift to her eyebrows, but already his arm was falling away from her back. The music had stopped and before her rather dazed eyes, he bowed over her hand, kissing the tips of her fingers in the continental fashion.

And then another voice intruded, speaking in jovial French. "Vanya! I might have known it would be you who finally persuaded the mysterious Mademoiselle Noire to dance!"

Startled, Lizzie's gaze flew to the man addressing her partner. She beheld, unmistakably, the Tsar of all the Russias, an unworn mask dangling from his wrist. Speechless, she sank into a deep curtsey. Any number of thoughts flitted through her brain, not least of them that despite her efforts at concealment, she'd been noticed enough to have a nickname coined by such an important personage. And yet, somehow more important was the fact that now she knew her stranger was called Vanya. It had a pleasing, exotic ring to it. It suited him. And like the tsar himself, the name had surely to be Russian.

Mr. Vanya straightened and inclined his head smartly to his monarch. "Sire."

"Won't you introduce me?" It wasn't really a request. The tsar had commanded.

"To the best of my ability in the circumstances," Mr. Vanya said smoothly. "Sire, allow me to present Mademoiselle Noire. Mademoiselle, His Majesty, the Emperor of Russia."

"Enchanted," the tsar said, smiling as she curtseyed once more. He even took her hand to raise her. "Perhaps I might hope for this dance."

He was, she supposed, dazzling, and she knew this was the most flattering invitation she would ever receive. And yet, all she could think of was how to get out of it. The evening was confused enough and she still hadn't found Johnnie.

"Perhaps a later dance, Your Majesty," suggested an aide in a green domino—surely the one who'd been dancing earlier with Minerva? Another aide, an officer from his fine moustache and fabulously braided uniform, stood on the tsar's other side, his gaze locked in some kind of silent communication with Vanya. The civilian aide said, "Your Majesty is promised to the Queen of Bavaria for this one."

The tsar frowned, as if he was quite prepared to slight the queen for Lizzie's sake.

Mr. Vanya said, "Then I am saved. *I* promised to return Mademoiselle to her aunt, under pain of death."

It smoothed the Imperial brow. The tsar even laughed, as Vanya drew her aside, her hand through his arm.

Behind them, the tsar said, "Who the devil is her aunt anyway?"

"I've no idea," his aide replied and laughter bubbled up in Lizzie's throat.

"Oh goodness, I almost had a tale to tell my grandchildren! That I danced with the Tsar of Russia!"

"Now you have a rarer one," Vanya said. "You *refused* to dance with the Tsar of Russia."

"No, I didn't. You and his aide refused to let me. He is excessively handsome, isn't he?"

"So I'm told." Vanya swerved in the other direction. "If we hurry, we'll catch him before he reaches the Queen—"

With a squeak of protest, she tugged him back toward the exit from the riding school. "Don't dare!"

"As you wish," he said gravely.

She eyed him with mingled amusement and disapproval. "Mr. Vanya," she began.

His black eyebrows lifted and her breath caught, carrying her on a quite different thread that led her back to reality.

She said abruptly. "He called me Mademoiselle Noire. So did you. Have I been noticed?"

"Oh yes."

"But why? People rarely notice me anywhere and this time I've gone out of my way to appear insignificant!"

"I doubt the first is remotely true and in this place, where everyone is trying to be noticed by everyone who matters, trying to be insignificant is significant in itself."

"Wrong strategy," she said ruefully, as they entered the covered walkway between the buildings. The cool air and the sweet scent of the orange trees were soothing. As, curiously, was the dark sky beyond.

And then, coming towards them, she saw the unmistakable figures of Aunt Lucy and Minerva, escorted now by Uncle Jeremy. Lizzie gave a quick, instinctive tug to free herself and hide, but Vanya's hand closed over hers in warning, or perhaps comfort. He was right. Rushing away would only draw more of the kind of attention she wished—*needed*—to avoid. She only hoped Vanya hadn't picked up who she wished to flee from.

Carefully, she kept her gaze on the end of the walk, on the ballroom ahead, as if searching for someone there, as her family advanced toward her. Her heart beat hard in her breast.

As they passed, Aunt Lucy said pleasantly, "Colonel Vanya."

*Oh no, he knows them!*

"Madame. Mademoiselle," Vanya murmured with a polite inclination of his head and then they were passed. From the corner of her eye, she realized none of them had actually looked at her. Relief was intense and lasted the rest of the way into the ballroom. "There," Vanya said. "People generally only see what they expect to."

She glanced at him with more than a hint of self-mockery. "Was I so obviously hiding?"

"Only to me. Brazening it out is usually best. Although here in the main ballroom, there are other options, such as pillars. And alcoves," he added, drawing back the curtain on one. It was empty and before she'd properly registered the fact, she found herself inside it. "Gather your breath," Vanya advised.

"Thank you," she said. "You're being very kind to me."

"No, I'm not. I have an ulterior motive."

"For what?" she asked.

"Helping you gather your breath."

Lizzie said, "You know she's my aunt, don't you?"

"I won't tell anyone."

"Why not?"

"Do you know the story of Cinderella?" he inquired.

Baffled by the change of subject, she blinked. "Pardon?"

A smile flickered across his lips. "Everyone loves Cinderella. I'm just making conversation until you recover your breath."

"How poor a specimen do you take me for? I'm quite recovered from so minor a disaster."

"Of course you are," he said, placing one finger under her chin and turning up her face, presumably to check for signs of the vapors.

She began to laugh, to reassure him that she never, ever had hysterics, only for some reason the words stuck in her throat, and it seemed she had no breath after all. Vanya's masked face dipped lower and his dark eyes, the texture of his lips seemed to enthral her. Certainly, she couldn't seem to speak or draw back.

At the last moment, she threw up one hand to ward him off, but it was too late. His lips closed on hers and, in shock, her defensive fingers curled instead on the braid of his uniform.

It wasn't a long or aggressive embrace. Perhaps it was his gentleness that confused her, because when he raised his head, she neither slapped him nor ran. Incurably honest, she admitted to herself that it had been a nice kiss and that she rather wanted another. Torn, she swallowed convulsively and his head lowered once more.

This one was longer, sweeter, exploring her mouth, and when it ended, she touched his mask, the skin of his cheek, just because she wanted to, and lifted her face to be kissed again. A delicious sort of heaviness spread from her tingling lips through her whole body. Excitement, delight…and danger.

"That's enough," she whispered against his lips.

"No," he said, releasing her. She thought his voice wasn't quite steady, but that may have been the pounding of her heart distorting her hearing. "But it will do for now." His lips curved. "You see? Now we'll always know each other. When we meet again."

A choke of laughter broke from her. "We won't, you know. Goodbye, Colonel."

As she reached up to pull back the curtain, forcing herself to think of Johnnie and the necklace, she suddenly froze.

"She wasn't wearing it," she blurted. "Oh God!"

She hadn't stopped Johnnie in time. He hadn't needed her to point out his victim. And now, she'd no idea where either the thief or the necklace was. She fled.

# Chapter Six

LAUGHTER SHOOK VANYA'S body as Lizzie rushed away from him. But though he'd enjoyed himself so much, he didn't actually want her to suffer. After a discreet moment, he strolled out into the ballroom and turned his steps back toward the riding school. Since Boris was on the "nanny" shift with the tsar, he was easy enough to locate.

"Swap dominoes with me," he said without introduction.

"What? Why? Who are you hiding from?" Boris demanded, though he obligingly took off his cloak. "Countess Gelitzina and Madame Fischer were both glaring daggers at you on the dance floor."

"What the devil for?" Vanya asked, throwing his cloak to Boris and swinging his friend's around his shoulder before striding off without waiting for an answer.

On his way out of the riding school, he stopped a passing waiter. From his pocket, he took a pre-scribbled note and a handful of coins and discreetly passed them across the tray. "For Mademoiselle Noire, the mysterious young lady in black," he said. "You know who I mean?"

"Yes, sir, I do."

"Hurry, then."

As he found his way outside into the grounds, he threw his mask away and unfastened his regimental coat. Shrugging it off, he left it under a bush for either himself or Misha to find later. Then, with Boris' domino covering his shirt sleeves, he moved around toward the front of the palace to wait for Lizzie. Ruefully, he acknowledged that he'd just endangered his own plan. By dancing with her, by forcing her to notice him, especially in such a way, he'd left himself open to recognition.

It probably wouldn't matter, of course. The disreputable Colonel Vanya could sell the necklace as easily as Johnnie could and it had been rather fun flirting with her on a more equal social footing. In truth, he rather wanted to remain Colonel Vanya to her, so that he could openly protect her, and perhaps put his arm around her in the hired carriage and kiss her a little more. Her kisses were sweet: a little shy, a little curious, with a latent passion he would be a complete cad to awaken fully. She was off limits and still he'd crossed the boundary. Or at least pushed it back a little.

Johnnie would undoubtedly be best at this point, but he didn't hold out a great deal of hope that he'd fool her just by wearing a different colored cloak. Even though she hadn't recognized Johnnie in the masked and military Vanya, he was now, surely, rather more firmly established at the forefront of her mind.

People were still milling about in the grounds—more illegal entrants to the ball, he presumed—as well as around the main entrance trying to bribe the doorman. It was easy to blend into the shadows. It reminded him of the rather deadlier games of hide and seek in the winter of 1812, when he'd led ambushes and sudden night attacks on the retreating French army.

He drove the memories away, thinking himself into the slightly furtive role of Johnnie the thief. And yet, his whole mind seemed to be full of *her*, vivid and fun and totally unaware of her charm.

She hurried out of the palace, drawing the hood of her cloak up over her head. She'd acquired a small carpet bag from somewhere; it hung from the edges of her cloak.

He stepped out of the shadows, ridiculously tense as he waited for recognition to hit her.

But she barely glanced at him as she hurried on. "Oh Johnnie, why didn't you wait for me to point her out? I'd decided I didn't want you to do it that way, but to rob the house, instead."

"It's done now." As Vanya, he'd unconsciously let the Russian intonations more into his speech with her and, in fact, mostly they'd spoken in French, the generally accepted common language of the Congress. "I couldn't come anywhere near you. Everyone was looking at you."

"Oh dear," she said worriedly. "I'd hoped that was nonsense… None of this has gone according to plan, has it?"

"Well, there's the necklace," he said, jangling the coins in his pocket as they walked across the square.

It didn't seem to comfort her, although she did glance up at him through the gloom with her eyes so big with worry that it was all he could do not to kiss her there and then. "What did you do? Did you scare her? Why was there no hue and cry after you? She didn't *look* frightened…"

"Stop worrying," he said, leading her to a waiting fiacre for hire. "It was all quite civilized."

Lizzie stopped in her tracks, eyes widening. "She doesn't know it's gone," she said in wonder. "You flim-flammed her!"

He grinned. "Unladylike."

"But she *will* know it's stolen?" Lizzie said anxiously. "Once she notices, I mean. She won't just think it's lost and blame herself?"

"She won't think it's lost," he assured her, handing her into the fiacre before he turned and spoke quietly to the driver.

"Where are we going?" Lizzie demanded as soon as he joined her and the horses began to pull. "Do you have a buyer ready?"

"At an inn just outside the city."

Lizzie frowned. "Really? I imagined some mean back street with thieves in every corner."

"You sound disappointed."

In the pale light shining in from the coach lamps, she regarded him with some suspicion. Her fingers tightened convulsively on the bag in her lap. "You wouldn't…let me down, would you, Johnnie?"

Vanya sat back and stuck his hands in his pockets, meeting her gaze through the shadows. "What do you think?"

She shivered slightly, hiding her moment of fear in a glare. He had to admire her courage. There weren't many young ladies of her upbringing who could put themselves in such a situation, let alone deal with it as she was.

She took a deep breath. "If you take advantage of me, I'll kill you."

Vanya blinked. "*Kill* me? How are you going to do that?"

"Pray you never find out," she said loftily. "Stick to our agreement."

"I always meant to. If you insist on mean back streets, we'll go there and hope for a decent-ish price, but my buyer will be at the inn and he'll give us twice what any back-street fence would."

Lizzie searched his face and he held his breath, glad of the poor light but still waiting to be recognized.

"You trusted me when I was drunk," he observed, when she didn't speak. "I'm a better man sober."

Her eyes fell. "I'm sorry. I suppose I just don't feel very good about this whole plan now we're actually doing it. I feel dishonest and…dirty."

"Don't," he said, leaning forward and touching her tense hands. "Who are you hurting? Not Ivan the Terrible and not your aunt. The necklace can make no real difference to your cousin's chances of a good marriage. And I'm sure your father would have been happy to know you and your siblings will be comfortable."

"Maybe," she said doubtfully. "He wasn't a terribly responsible parent."

"He looked after Michael," Vanya pointed out. "That is definitely in his favor."

"Yes, but in truth, although he didn't *object* to having Michael with us, it was my mother who insisted on it when Michael's mother died shortly after his birth. There was a bit of a scandal, I believe, but it didn't touch us much in the country."

"Is your mother still alive?"

Lizzie shook her head. "No, she died some years ago." Although she spoke matter-of-factly, a shadow of grief crossed her face. She squared her shoulders. "I think, after this, you should give up thieving."

"But I've only just begun to enjoy it," Vanya protested.

She gave a little choke of laughter, swiftly swallowed. "You won't enjoy it when you're caught," she said severely. "Why don't you use the money from this to begin some other trade? Do you have a family?"

"I have a mother and several sisters."

"Maybe you should go home."

"I will. Eventually. I've a few things I need to do first."

"Not more thievery?" she asked with an anxiety that seemed genuine.

He shrugged. "Just a little duty, a little sorting out and a little kicking."

"Kicking? You're not going to hurt someone, are you?"

"No one you know," he soothed.

"Well, I suppose that's all right," she said doubtfully. "If they deserve it."

"Oh, they do."

She leaned forward. "Tell me, Johnnie, did you know Madame Fischer before you stole her necklace?"

Several evasions sprang to Vanya's mind. He really didn't want to get into a discussion about how, precisely, he knew Madame Fischer. In the end, he simply said, "Yes."

"What is she like? Is she a good person?"

"On the whole I would say…why do you ask?"

"Just because my cousin seems most smitten with her. And I'm not convinced she would be good for him."

"She wouldn't," Vanya said bluntly.

"Because she's married?"

"No, that's the one thing in her favor. She can't marry anyone else."

Lizzie's eyes widened. "You don't think she'd commit bigamy with

James, do you?"

"No, I don't. You told me his family isn't wealthy."

"Ah." Lizzie sat back, deep in thought.

"Does he go to her house?" Vanya asked reluctantly.

Lizzie nodded. "Is that bad?"

"It would be better if he didn't."

"Maybe I'll go with him next time," Lizzie said with a sigh.

"Good God, no," Vanya said with enough fervor to attract her astonished stare. "I'll sort it out for you," he promised recklessly.

She regarded him, her head leaning slightly to one side. "I don't think you're cut out to be a thief, either," she observed. "You're much too good."

"No one's ever called me that before," he said with perfect truth.

"What do they call you?"

"Wastrel. Rakehell. Irresponsible. Reckless. Foolish."

"Are they desirable traits in a soldier? Because I don't think Michael has any of those."

"No, they're not. I wasn't a bad soldier, though. It was always civilian life I messed up."

"Where did you fight?" she asked.

"Oh, all over the place." He nodded out of the window. "Look, we're making good time while the city is quiet. We should be there soon."

If she noticed his rather blatant change of subject, perhaps she merely put it down to the understandable reticence of a thief, for she didn't press him. She merely looked out of the window, allowing him to examine her profile without distraction.

Hers was a much subtler beauty than her sister's, he thought. And very different again from Sonia's or Louise's or any of the other women who'd passed through his erratic life. They were like a different species from her.

It wasn't even that he was in danger of placing Lizzie Gaunt on a pedestal—where she would be most uncomfortable. She just...stood out from the crowd. He wondered what she'd say or do if Johnnie the thief kissed her as Colonel Vanya had done. Would she finally connect the two?

Really, he had to stop caring. He had only to get tonight over with and take her home with her money. After that, Johnnie could disappear. And sooner or later, she'd find out who Vanya was. Perhaps he'd be gone by then. To Russia or even England. Perhaps she'd remember him kindly in the end. Or with spitting fury for his pretense.

The fiacre was slowing, turning onto a quieter road. They were nearly there. Vanya thought he'd chosen pretty well. The inn was far enough off the beaten track and well-hidden enough to be a possible den of thieves. In fact, it was, so far as he could gather, a respectable house where Lizzie was unlikely to come to any harm.

"You wait here," Vanya said, as the fiacre pulled into the yard. "Stop the driver from abandoning us and heading back to Vienna without us."

"Just don't pay him," Lizzie advised with unexpected worldliness. She prepared to rise. "I'm coming with you."

"That's not a good idea," Vanya said. "Unless you want to get a lower price once my buyer sees the aristocracy's involved. Or worse, connects you to the crime."

Lizzie paused, her hand already on the door.

"I won't run away with it," Vanya assured her. "This is the only way out, so you may watch just as well from the comfort of the carriage."

With obvious reluctance, Lizzie sat back down. "You won't be long, will you?"

"A quarter of an hour, no more." He winked at her. "Hold on to your hat. It's nearly finished."

He jumped down from the fiacre, gave the driver instructions to wait for him and to have a care for his passenger still inside, and strolled across the courtyard to the house. He crossed with the ostler who approached to see what the horses' needs were.

Vanya entered the inn and turned into the taproom. Misha rose silently from the table nearest the door. Vanya nodded to him and jerked his head toward the door. Still wordless, Misha went out to keep watch on Lizzie as they'd agreed in this eventuality. There was another plan for Misha to play the buyer, should Lizzie have insisted on accompanying him inside.

Vanya stretched out his legs, smiled at the buxom girl approaching him, and ordered a beer.

※

LIZZIE WAS ONLY too aware that she was out of her depth. Worse, her mind had developed a wayward habit of slipping away from the present to dwell on the unsettling encounter with the masked Colonel Vanya at the ball. An odd way to receive her first kiss. Well, her first serious kiss. She didn't count the rather embarrassing lunge of Maurice, the vicar's son, when they were both eighteen. She'd boxed Maurice's ears and that had been the end of the matter. But for some reason, she'd had no inclination to slap Colonel Vanya or, indeed, to stop him at all.

The Russian officer had been fun, cloaked in an air at once dashing and self-deprecating, experienced and devil-may-care. And although he'd taken liberties, there had never been any doubt that she could dismiss him whenever she chose. When she finally had, he'd stopped. Her heart smote her at the memory of his eyes at that moment. She touched her lips, wondering...

Outside, the inn door creaked open again and a man mooched out. Not Johnnie, but a smaller, fair man with exotic whiskers and a leather jerkin. He leaned against the wall of the house and lit a pipe. Getting some air, perhaps, because he'd drunk too much ale? Or...Lizzie's heart beat at the thought....a lookout making sure no police interfered with the transaction Johnnie was making on her behalf.

Another vehicle bowled quietly into the courtyard, an undistinguished trap driven by a nondescript man in a peaked cap. He got down, gave the reins to the ostler and walked toward the inn. Without any obvious interest, he spared a glance at Lizzie's waiting fiacre, then went inside, ignoring the smoking man who watched him.

Lizzie was aware she had too great a tendency to trust. And now that she thought of it, she knew no more about Johnnie than she did about the stranger who'd just entered the inn after him—the buyer?—or the man who propped up the inn wall near the door.

Would Johnnie just take the money and run? He owed her nothing.

At any rate, it simply wasn't in her nature to sit here and do nothing. With sudden decision, she opened the fiacre door, clutching her carpet bag, and jumped down.

"All good, Miss?" the driver asked.

"Oh yes. Just getting some air," she said. "I won't be long."

Just long enough to walk around the building and make sure Johnnie wasn't lying about there being other exits. She hurried out of the lit courtyard around the side of the house. Some of the light followed her, more shone out from the inn windows, so it wasn't pitch dark. On the other hand, she couldn't see very much as she blundered around the building.

Behind her, something cracked and shuffled, and the hairs on the back of her neck stood up. Was someone following her? If so, she couldn't go back for fear of running into them. Trying not to panic, she hurried on her way as fast as she dared, hugging the wall of the house.

She did, at least, discover one other door, apparently leading out from the kitchen. A pig was asleep in a small pen with a pile of her babies. The mother opened one eye and snorted. Lizzie hurried on, looking around her. If Johnnie did come out that door, there was nowhere obvious for him to go except over the back wall into fields, and she couldn't really imagine there was much point in him doing that. So it seemed her suspicions were unjustified. Only…

Behind her, she heard nothing. She wondered if her sense of another presence there was pure imagination. When she finally fought her way through a large rose bush back into the front yard, the fiacre was still waiting. The new arrival's pony and trap had been taken into the stable, and the smoking man had vanished—back inside? Or behind her, following her…

Another crack, a swish and a breath of annoyance from the rose bush at the side of the house, told her what she needed to know. Someone *had* followed her. With sudden decision, she swerved away from the fiacre and inside the inn. She was undoubtedly safer among people.

---

THE MAN KNOWN as Agent Z was, in fact, a police officer, who had risen through the ranks to be one of Baron Hager's most trusted lieutenants. He'd done so by a mixture of intelligence and diligence and an instinctive perception that led him to the heart of most cases. Since the Congress had come to Vienna, this perception had been vital in cutting through the mountain of information dumped on him by his many spies, new and old, to those few snippets of information that actually mattered to his country and his Emperor.

Major Blonsky's accusation against Colonel Savarin was one of those few which interested him enough to merit further investigation by himself. He was only too aware that getting such a thing wrong could cause havoc, not to mention embarrassment. But if it were true, then Austria needed a countermeasure.

Agent Z doubted that it was true. Blonsky's personal hatred of Savarin was obvious and the choice of an indiscreet, womanizing Cossack commander as the tsar's go-between to the British didn't make much sense either. On the other hand, many of the tsar's choices baffled Agent Z and no one had ever questioned Savarin's loyalty or bravery. Discreet inquiries had revealed that he was something of a hero in Russia, considered an intelligent commander by both his superiors and his men, which was rare enough to make him worthy of further investigation.

So, although Z suspected Blonsky's accusation came from a desire to say *something* to earn his fee and get Z off his back, while at the same time paying off old scores, the connection between Savarin and Jeremy Daniels' niece did give it a certain vague credence.

The niece was certainly up to something. She'd been observed leaving her home alone and had been followed to the Hofburg where Z had himself seen her with Colonel Savarin. He'd watched them vanish together into an alcove, which may have been an amorous assignation, as perhaps was this.

Z had witnessed the couple meet again outside the Hofburg and hurry into the fiacre, which he'd followed in his own waiting vehicle, throwing off his domino and mask and donning a peaked cap and a tatty overcoat, instead.

The inn was an odd place for a lovers' tryst...and he'd seen at once that the girl waited alone in the fiacre. As if they were returning to Vienna tonight. On the other hand, Z clocked the colonel's servant leaning against the wall outside, smoking, as if keeping watch. So what the devil was Savarin doing in the inn?

Drinking beer. He sat alone and looked perfectly comfortable, his elegant legs stretched out in front of him, ankles crossed. Z did what he did best, melted into the crowd, insignificant and unnoticed, while he observed his prey.

He learned nothing, until the girl came in. Savarin glanced up without interest, as did everyone else, then leapt to his feet with almost comical speed. The surrounding noise of talk and laughter died down as the other denizens of the taproom blinked at the sight of a clearly noble young woman, however ill-dressed, in their midst.

The girl halted inside the door, her eyes searching the room. They skimmed over Z, glimmered with rather worrying recognition—Z wasn't used to being recognized by anyone—and moved on to Savarin with some relief.

Savarin was already starting toward her.

"What is it?" he demanded in English, taking her arm and spinning her around to face the door once more.

"Someone was following me," she hissed.

"Following you where?"

"Around the building in the dark."

"I thought we'd agreed you should stay put in the fiacre." The colonel sounded harassed and more than a little frustrated.

"It was hardly a solemn and binding oath," the girl retorted.

"Well, never mind, we can go now."

"Really? Is it done?"

"Of course it is. I was just finishing my beer."

That definitely interested Z. *What* was done? And when? Z couldn't have been more than a couple of minutes behind Savarin and the Russian hadn't said or done *anything* in that time. Z could almost have imagined he'd been escaping for five minutes from a nagging wife, only the man's posture was all wrong: hovering, protective rather than truly annoyed to be discovered. And yet, Z was fairly sure Savarin had just lied to her.

His nose told him *something* was going on here. And he needed to know if it was important or just some amorous intrigue that hurt no one but the participants.

"Where is it?" the girl whispered.

Savarin patted his pocket once and Z knew he had to see whatever was there.

"Put it in my bag," the girl instructed.

"Yes, but not here." Savarin sounded more amused than harassed. "Have you no concept of discretion?"

"I suppose I lack your training," she said with a faint curl of her lip.

"And common sense," the colonel retorted, all but bundling her out of the door. Z was already moving quietly and quickly enough to catch the door before it shut completely. Thus he was able to slip out, slouching to blend with the place he'd left, and unseen by his quarries.

The colonel's servant still leaned against the wall. In the shadows, without looking, the servant passed something to Savarin who pocketed it unobtrusively. Whatever it was, it weighed down the colonel's pockets.

This interesting transaction, of course, had the added advantage of distracting the servant from Z's presence. Z, more determined than ever to get to the bottom of this intrigue, flitted through the shadows and behind the fiacre, unnoticed by anyone in the courtyard.

# Chapter Seven

"I'M SURE THAT'S the man who followed me," Lizzie hissed as they hurried across the courtyard to the fiacre.

"Him? You don't need to worry," Johnnie said hastily.

"Then he's an ally?" Lizzie asked with some relief.

"You could say that," Johnnie replied, glancing up at the snoozing fiacre driver. He opened the door himself and handed Lizzie in with an unconscious grace and civility she was sure must be rare in a thief.

However, her speculations got quickly lost when he climbed in after her, saying, "Open your bag."

Lizzie obliged, carefully shifting the pistol she'd brought to one side, protecting it under her hand as Johnnie took handfuls of banknotes and silver coins from his pockets and dropped them into the bag. She felt her eyes widen.

"How much did you get?"

"More than you hoped," Johnnie said. "Have a look. I'll just have a quick word with—um…my ally there, and then wake the driver so we can be off."

As Johnnie jumped down, she gazed in wonder at the money piled in her bag. It was in Austrian gulden, so she'd have to take it to a bank and calculate its worth in pounds, but it seemed an awful lot. Her heart warmed with gratitude to the thief as well as with relief that she finally had something, some security for Michael and the girls that would surely last until Henrietta could come out and catch a wealthy paragon of a husband to make her happy and provide for Georgiana and Michael as she would never be able to.

The carriage door opened again, very quietly.

"Johnnie, this is—" She broke off as a total stranger stood there, reaching in to the fiacre quite blatantly to seize the bag on her lap.

With a gasp of shock, she slapped his hand, before her brain engaged and she remembered she had a more powerful weapon. In the instant his slapped fingers paused, she snatched the bag out of his reach and jerked out her other hand with the pistol.

"Get away from me," she commanded.

The man wore a peaked cap and was, she could swear, the man who'd arrived in the pony and trap shortly after herself and Johnnie. He paused with one foot on the step. He'd clearly meant to climb in with her until he found himself gazing at the not quite steady barrel of her pistol.

"The bag," he said peremptorily. "Show me."

"It's nothing to do with you. Go away or I'll shoot you."

"If you shoot me, Miss Gaunt, you'll be in more trouble than you could ever envision. Give me the bag."

Something in the grim authority of his voice made her want to comply. However, she had no intention of giving up her siblings' future to anyone, let alone to a total stranger. Even one who knew her name. She lifted her chin and opened her mouth to give a haughty reply.

She never made it. Quite suddenly, the intruder was seized by the shoulder and spun around to receive a crashing blow to the jaw.

Johnnie stood there, fist clenched, his mouth a straight hard line of fury, his eyes positively murderous, reminding Lizzie that there had always been a hint of danger and suppressed violence about him. Well, the violence was no longer suppressed.

The blow should surely have broken the stranger's jaw or perhaps laid him out cold. Instead, he was already rolling as he fell to the ground, as if preparing to spring back to his feet. Johnnie went after him and the stranger hooked one foot around his ankle, jerking him to the ground.

Lizzie let out a squeak of distress. Abandoning the bag inside the coach, she jumped down. "Stop!" she commanded, then resorted to pleading. "Oh, please, stop!"

The two men paid her no attention. They rolled together, aiming and parrying blows so that only a few ever connected.

"You fight dirty," Johnnie observed, panting as he leapt to his feet, giving himself space. He held a wicked-looking dagger in his hand, presumably one he'd wrenched from his opponent's grip. "Now, get out of my way."

"So do you," the stranger replied. His hand delved into his coat pocket and suddenly he held a small pistol pointing straight at Johnnie's heart. "Now, get out of mine."

Johnnie raised his dagger arm. The stranger cocked his pistol, his finger curled around the trigger. And Lizzie couldn't take anymore. She rushed between them, yelling "Enough!" Much as she did when Michael and Georgiana were squabbling. Her fingers curled with more fury now than fear, because they were behaving so childishly.

Her arm jerked and a huge bang rent the air. The stranger stared at her in ludicrous astonishment, and then crumpled to the ground.

"Oh God," she whispered. She'd forgotten she was holding the cocked gun. She wasn't normally when she stopped a fight...

Her fingers opened in revulsion, letting her father's pistol fall to the ground. "Oh no. Oh God, what have I done?"

She dropped to her knees before the fallen man. Johnnie crouched by his other side.

"Bring a light," he commanded the fiacre driver. But by the coach lanterns, Lizzie could already see the ominous dark stain on the man's coat.

"Is he dead?" she whispered. "Have I killed him?"

The thief shook his head. "Not yet," he said. He jerked his head around to the inn building where several men had spilled out, presumably attracted by the gunshot.

One of them, the smoking man, was already running toward them. Johnnie gestured with his arm, a peremptory gesture that suggested he was used to giving orders that were promptly obeyed. Perhaps he'd been a sergeant in his army... And right now, why did that matter? She'd shot a man who lay dying at her feet.

Johnnie yanked off his necktie with one hand, opening the injured man's coat with the other. The smoking man spoke to Johnnie in a strange language. It might have been Russian. Johnnie answered in similar vein, pressing his hastily folded cravat over the red wound.

"What can I do?" Lizzie demanded.

"Hold this over the wound when we lift him," Johnnie said. "Press hard." He looked up at the man who'd just arrived and, in German, ordered a room for the injured man and the summoning of a doctor. The landlord bristled, hands on hips, releasing a torrent of protesting words that Lizzie couldn't follow, and which cut off quite abruptly when Johnnie looked at him again.

In silence, the landlord ran back the way he'd come. Lizzie could hear him issuing commands as Johnnie and the smoking man lifted her victim between them. They were surprisingly gentle although efficient. Blood oozed over Lizzie's hand as she pressed the pad of the cravat to the wound and trotted along beside them.

"Press harder," Johnnie said. "You want to stop any more blood coming out of him."

"Won't I hurt him more?" she asked anxiously.

"He won't mind if he lives. Besides, he's out cold. Best if he stays that way until we fish the ball out of him..."

A woman met them at the door of the house and led them up to a clean, tidy room on the first floor. While between them, Johnnie and his ally wrestled the injured man out of his coat and cut away his shirt, the woman and Johnnie babbled in German. Among the few words Lizzie picked out were "police" and "brother" and "doctor". The woman went unhappily away, though she came back a few moments later with tweezers, for which Johnnie politely thanked her.

The smoking man with the fine whiskers, took the tweezers and held them in the nearest candle flame.

"Lift the pad," Johnnie instructed, "And let's see what we've got.

Miss Lizzie, you won't like this next bit. Why don't you go and see if you can extract some clean bandages from the landlady? I asked her to bring them up but you'd better chase her up here."

Eager to do her part, Lizzie nodded and hurried to the door.

"Oh, I told her we were eloping," Johnnie said casually. "That this man is your brother who tried to make you go home with him."

Lizzie's mouth fell open. "Why?"

"Because I suspect the truth is rather more dangerous. Fetch the bandages and I'll tell you."

To avoid the landlady's questions—asked with a mixture of avid curiosity, sympathy and disapproval—Lizzie pretended to understand less German than she actually did and returned almost gratefully to her victim's room.

A bowl of gory red water stood on the wash stand which had been dragged over beside the bed. The tweezers and a small red ball had been dropped into it.

Lizzie felt queasy as she set her armful of bandages on the bed. "You got the ball out then," she managed. The smoking man seemed to be sewing up her victim like a dress seam. She swallowed. "Will he live?"

Johnnie touched her shoulder. "He has a chance. It's a pity there's no doctor nearby, but Misha and I are quite used to dealing with such wounds. Our man is strong and fit, so his chances are better than most."

With almost unconscious efficiency, Lizzie had begun to make a dressing for the wound. When Misha's needlework was done, she placed it over the wound, running the bandages around his chest to hold everything in place, while Johnnie and Misha lifted the patient for her. That done, they settled him on the pillows and covered him with the crisp sheet and blankets.

"He's very white," Lizzie said doubtfully, sinking onto the bed beside her victim. She frowned. "Doesn't the landlady think it odd that my brother is Austrian, while I speak so little German?"

"Clearly, he's a half-brother," Johnnie said.

"Clearly," Lizzie agreed with a catch in her voice. She cleared her throat with determination. "So why did you make up this ridiculous story?"

"He has no identity papers with him," Johnnie said, perching on the foot of the bed. "None at all. He arrived here shortly after we did and tried to take your bag when he saw the opportunity. He didn't expect you to fight back. His coat is vile, I'll grant you, but I suspect we'll find a finer one in his possession. His shirt is of good quality, as were his breeches before we muddied them in our scrap."

Lizzie dragged her gaze away from her victim, twisting around to look at Johnnie, instead. "Who is he?"

"I don't know. But I suspect he's an officer of Metternich's secret police."

Lizzie's jaw dropped. She swallowed. "You mean I shot a policeman? Of rank?"

"Well, he's not Baron Hager. He gets his hands dirty. But he's not a ten-a-penny spy, either."

"You can't *know* this," Lizzie protested. "It's just as likely to be true as the story you made up about our elopement!"

"No," Johnnie said with apparent regret. "Misha's seen someone watching our rooms. And your house is almost certainly watched, from inside or out, because of your uncle's position."

"Oh no!" Lizzie stared at him. "Then he—this man whom I shot—knows all about the necklace and what we did?"

"I doubt he's interested. State secrets are what interest him."

"Well I have none of those and I very much doubt you do, either!"

"I think it's our connection, from different camps, if you like, that probably drew his attention. I suspect we were seen in your carriage outside the theatre."

"What do they think?" Lizzie demanded. "That I read all my uncle's papers and pass the information to you?"

"Maybe."

"Then who do you give it to?"

"Whoever pays me, I suppose."

She frowned. "Where are you from, Johnnie? Which army were you in?"

For an instant she couldn't understand, he hesitated, then he answered quite steadily, "The Russian army."

She'd already suspected it. She seemed to have developed an unhealthy attraction to Russians of all ranks. Perhaps it made up for her un-Christian hatred of Ivan the Terrible.

"The thing is," Johnnie said, "The Austrians have spies everywhere. The word is, no one of any importance in Vienna can sneeze at dinner without Metternich knowing about it by supper. So you need to be careful about your secrets."

"I think I've rather blasted that one," she said, turning back to the wounded man. "He'll be missed, won't he?"

"Eventually. Yes."

"Who should I tell?"

"No one. Not yet. If and when he awakens, we can tell him we really were eloping. Shooting him by accident changed your mind. If he believes us, he won't be interested in more."

"And if he doesn't?"

"He was trying to steal from you. The British will never let you be charged with such a crime in such circumstances."

"But there would be a terrible scandal. Aunt Lucy would never forgive me."

"Which is why it would all be hushed up. It's very unlikely to get that far."

"And if he dies?" Lizzie whispered.

Johnnie shrugged. "Then we stick with the elopement story to anyone who's interested. It will be all right. You didn't mean to shoot him. Anyone could see that."

"To be honest, I was never that accurate," she said tremulously. "I can't hit a barn at fifty paces."

"You've never had the right gun," Johnnie said. "I'll teach you with mine and you'll be able to hit a silver penny in no time."

Lizzie gave a wavery laugh. "I doubt it."

Johnnie grinned. "We'll see. Now, you'd better get back to Vienna with your bag."

Lizzie blinked. "I can't leave him like this. What if he has a fever?"

Johnnie exchanged glances with Misha. "We can be here most of the night."

"It was I who shot him," Lizzie said grimly. "The least I can do is nurse him."

"And what of your sisters and brother? Your aunt will miss you."

"The children will cover for me," Lizzie said. "At least until noon tomorrow. We weren't sure when I'd be back, you see, how long it would take us to—"

"Do you know how to deal with a fever?" Johnnie interrupted.

"Of course I do," Lizzie said disparagingly. She wasn't the Baroness of Launceton's daughter for nothing.

"Then I'll pay off the fiacre," Johnnie said. "And give the driver enough to bribe him to silence. Here, we'll split the night into three watches. Misha and I will take the first two, then wake you. Hopefully, by the time we have to go, we'll have more idea how things stand with our friend here."

Lizzie stood up. "You must have been a very good sergeant," she observed.

Misha, in the act of drinking, spluttered.

Johnnie frowned at him. "If only I could rise so high," he said quellingly, getting to his feet. "I'll find the landlady and procure you a chamber."

---

IT WAS A good plan, though, in fact, it didn't work out quite like that. Since Lizzie wasn't tired, she hung around in the patient's bedroom. Eventually, Misha brought in another more comfortable chair for her, while he curled up on the floor and went to sleep, reminding Lizzie of Dog.

Johnnie sprawled in the hard chair a couple of feet away from her, leaning his elbow on the bed itself, and frequently resting his head on his hand while he watched their patient or spoke to Lizzie.

When the injured man finally opened his eyes, Lizzie said, "Oh no!" And then, when she read the dazed expression of pain and confusion in them, she leapt up in relief. "Oh, thank God!"

He jerked, thrashing his head from side to side on the pillow until Lizzie smoothed his brow with her fingers. "Hush, sir, we're looking after you. I'm so sorry I shot you, but you must lie still now and we'll bring a doctor in the morning. Can you drink this?"

While Johnnie lifted him, Lizzie held the cup of water to his lips. It was laced with a few drops of laudanum, courtesy of the landlady who said it had been left by a previous noble guest. Their patient obviously recognized the smell because he drew back instinctively.

"For the pain," Lizzie said gently. "It's only a couple of drops to make you more comfortable."

The confused eyes scanned hers and then Johnnie's.

Johnnie said, "You're still at the inn. I took the ball out of your shoulder, but you lost a lot of blood. You should rest. Is there anyone you want us to inform of this?"

The man's eyes didn't waver. He shook his head.

A smile flickered over Johnnie's face. "Stubborn, aren't you? She didn't mean to shoot you, you know. It was an accident. We shouldn't have waved weapons in her presence. It upsets her."

A frown tugged at the man's brow. Lizzie held the cup to his lips again and he drank. At last, Johnnie laid him back on the pillows. The man's eyes began to close.

"Sleep," Johnnie advised him. "It's the best healer."

Lizzie set the nearly empty cup back down on the table and sank slowly into her chair. "At least he woke up," she said in an effort to encourage optimism.

Johnnie sprawled once more across the vacant part of the bed, watching her. "Why did you say, '*Oh no*'?"

"My father," she said in a small voice. "He opened his eyes at the moment of death. I thought our man had died, too."

"How did your father die?"

And she found herself telling him about her father's fall from his horse in the late summer rain and how his initial recovery had quickly relapsed into fever, pneumonia and, finally, death.

"We'd barely buried him when Ivan the Terrible's people arrived to expel us," she finished.

Johnnie frowned. "How did they know so quickly?

"Oh, my father had spent some time looking for him, probably to extract some kind of promise from him concerning us. He'd traced him to Russia a few months before the accident, but Ivan never wrote back to him. After the accident, he wrote again, so I suppose by the time he actually died, the wheels were in motion, as it were, to replace him. My aunt took us in, although she was already packing to come to Vienna."

She shook off the memories, refocusing her gaze on Johnnie. "I don't think you're a very normal thief," she observed, not for the first time. "Thank you for helping us so discreetly."

For the first time in their acquaintance, she thought he actually flushed, although it may have been a trick of the candle light. "You're paying me," he reminded her gruffly.

"Yes, and talking of which, I haven't had time to count the money. How much is it?"

"About the equivalent of three thousand pounds."

"*Three*?" Lizzie sat up. "Oh, how wonderful. That's more than I dared to hope. Well done, Johnnie!"

He shifted. "Well, look after it. What are you going to do with it? Do you have someone who would bank it for you?"

"No one who wouldn't ask awkward questions," she said ruefully. "I think I'll have to hide it until we get home... Although I suppose we could live here. I rather like Vienna."

"Well, there's no hurry to decide. It doesn't look as if the Congress is going to *open* very soon, never mind end before Christmas as everyone used to prophesy."

Lizzie was silent, mulling over a few ideas and calculations.

She drew in her breath. "I don't think you should thieve anymore.

Wouldn't you like to do some honest trade, instead? Maybe marry and have children?"

"One day," he said vaguely. "Only I'm not very good at anything except soldiering. And there's not much call for that now we've finally beaten Bonaparte."

"But with a little money behind you, you could train to do something else," Lizzie insisted. "Think about it. I'll pay you twice what we agreed if you promise to use it to set yourself up with an honest living."

Head in his hand, he gazed up at her unwaveringly. "You really mean it, don't you?"

"Of course I do."

"It's very kind, but… I think you might find Henrietta's coming out will cost you rather more than you imagine."

"She has a very wealthy godmother I mean to approach to sponsor her," Lizzie said ingenuously.

A quick but intense smile flashed across his face, catching at an elusive memory. She didn't try very hard to place it. It had been such a strange, full evening…

"And then you will become a governess?"

"That's what I intend."

"You would make a wonderfully fun governess," he said. "My sisters would love you. My mother, on the other hand, would probably dismiss you in a day."

"Oh, I mean to be a lot staider by then," she said casually. "In any case, what do you know about governesses?"

"You'd be surprised. I've met a few."

"I hope you didn't steal from them," Lizzie said anxiously. "They don't have very much, you know."

"No, I can honestly say I've never stolen from a governess," Johnnie said. "But I can't quite see why you're so adamant about becoming one."

"Well, like you and soldiering, I'm not really fit for anything else. I was brought up to be a lady, not a very useful member of society, but

I've looked after my brother and sisters for as long as I can remember, so I think I have the necessary experience. How many sisters do you have?"

"Three. One married while I was away fighting."

"To a good man?" she asked, catching the shadow that crossed his face.

"I don't know. I don't think I ever met him."

"You should go home," she said gently.

Again the smile flickered across his face. "Maybe I will."

Lizzie was aware they were passing the time with idle chatter, distracting themselves from the problem—and in her case the guilt—of the injured and possibly dying man in the bed. But at the same time, there was comfort in the companionship, interest in her ally's life and view of the world. He seemed to know a lot about the political situation in Europe, from an angle she found particularly fascinating. He didn't like that Napoleon had been exiled merely as far as Elba, off the Italian coast, and blamed his own tsar for not being harsher.

"Oh, I met your tsar tonight," she crowed. "He even asked me to dance."

"I know. I saw."

Her words, however, had brought Colonel Vanya galloping back into her mind, and since she couldn't bear to think of him now, in this appalling and yet bizarrely comfortable scene, she hastily changed the subject. Johnnie, surprisingly, cooperated.

As they talked, their patient slept. Although he groaned occasionally and plucked helplessly at his bandages as though trying to prevent the pain beneath, he didn't wake. Gradually, Lizzie's own eyelids grew heavier and, in one of their companionable silences, she laid her head back on the chair wing and fell asleep.

# Chapter Eight

SHE SMILED, BECAUSE someone was tickling her cheek. Or caressing it, perhaps. It must be her mother, though it didn't feel like her mother's hand smoothing hair from her face. She opened her eyes and her lips fell open in shock.

Most definitely *not* her mother, who had been dead for nearly ten years. Johnnie the thief, his finger over her lips, while his own made a shushing motion, bent over her.

"What?" she whispered.

"We need to go," Johnnie said quietly. "Our friend's still asleep." He beckoned her further away from the bed, although their patient hadn't woken during all their conversations last night. Perhaps he was afraid the man was only pretending sleep now and wished not to be overheard.

She followed him toward the door, where Misha waited. "I've spoken to the landlord," Johnnie murmured. "I've given him money to care for our friend and he'll hire a conveyance to send you back to Vienna as soon as you're ready to go. I won't be able to return here until late tonight, but I think he's on the mend. And I'll send a doctor over. He should get here around noon, all being well. You don't need to worry."

"Oh dear, I'd better give you money for all that," she said worriedly, looking around for the carpet bag.

"It's taken care of," Johnnie said comfortably. "Go to your room and sleep for a couple of hours."

"Actually, I'm not tired." Instead, her stomach was rumbling. "Have you had breakfast?"

"No, but—"

"Let me fetch you something to eat on the way. Are you going far?"

"Well...a long way round to Vienna," Johnnie said evasively.

"I can smell new bread," Lizzie said, opening the door. "I'll fetch you some of that while you gather your things."

Lizzie tripped downstairs, where the delicious bread scent still managed to rise above the stale beer and smoke smells of the airing taproom. Following her nose to the kitchen, she obtained from a flustered maid two warm loaves, two pats of fresh butter, a knife, and a plate.

"Sorry we can't serve you better, right now," the landlord's wife said, almost apologetically as they met in the kitchen doorway. "Got a grand lady in the private parlor who's *most* demanding."

Lizzie accepted the implicit put-down meekly. She herself might be the daughter of a baron, but she certainly had no position in the world now. No one would describe her as a grand lady.

As she crossed the main hall toward the stairs, a woman's voice hailed her from the half-open door of a room on the right, presumably the private parlor. "Girl! Fraulein!" it called in unmistakably English accents.

Lizzie barely hesitated. Despite her need of discretion, curiosity was greater. She pushed open the door and went in.

"I can't drink coffee in the morning!" complained the room's only occupant. "I insist on tea!"

The lady was stout and of middle years, wearing a lace cap over largely brown hair that looked to Lizzie as if it didn't quite dare to go fully gray as it wished. Her gown was a dazzling shade of purple.

"How can I help you, madam?" Lizzie inquired civilly. "Shall I send the landlady or the maid to you? Or perhaps your own servant?"

The lady's head jerked up from contemplating the evil coffee in the cup before her. Lizzie found herself raked from head to toe by an exceedingly sharp pair of blue-gray eyes.

"You're not the maid," she observed.

"No, but I can fetch her for you."

"So you said. Are you the girl who's eloping?"

"Oh dear," Lizzie said. "I suppose I am, only I won't. And the landlady promised not to tell people about what happened."

The English lady gave a bark of laughter. "No hope of that. Why don't you join me?"

"Oh, I couldn't impose."

"Trust me, I would welcome the company. I've been cooped up in a carriage with no one but my maid for days and all the decent coaching inns are full."

"Well," Lizzie said. "I would be honored." She came farther into the room and set one loaf on the table with the butter. "Only I have to give this to my friends who are about to depart."

As she spoke, she heard their unmistakable steps clattering downstairs.

"Excuse me one moment," she said to the lady and scurried out to meet Johnnie and Misha in the hall. They stopped short, looking surprised as she ran up to them, proffering the bread and a packet of fresh butter.

"You can eat it on the way," she encouraged. "I'm sorry, I never thought to wrap it."

"No need," Johnnie said, taking it from her. "Misha will keep it in his bag. Thank you."

She gave him a slightly uncertain smile.

He drew in a breath. "Go back to Vienna and don't worry."

"Well, I will, because I don't wish to start a hue and cry. But I'll come back tomorrow to see to our friend."

"There's no need," Johnnie said.

"I think there is. I thank you for your help, but he is my responsibility."

Misha muttered something which caused Johnnie to frown impatiently though he didn't so much as glance at his friend. His eyes didn't leave Lizzie's face.

Then he said abruptly, "Goodbye, Miss Lizzie." And walked on without a backward glance.

Lizzie swallowed. It felt a very final farewell and, just for a moment, she felt quite forlorn. She walked back into the parlor to find the grand lady had stood up and walked across to the window. Lizzie joined her in time to see the ostler leading out two very skittish horses across the courtyard. Johnnie and Misha strode toward them. In one speedy motion that she barely saw, each threw himself onto a horse and galloped off out of the gate, leaving the ostler standing open-mouthed, his arms still held in the same position.

"Goodness," Lizzie said, blinking. "I've never even seen cavalrymen mount quite like that."

"Cossacks," the lady pronounced. "I saw them in London when they came with the tsar and the grand duchess. Finest horsemen in the world. Bred to it from birth, practically." She turned to face Lizzie. "But you'll know that. Are you not eloping with one of them?"

"No," Lizzie said firmly. "We've decided against it."

"Probably for the best," the lady said. "Society frowns on such ramshackle behavior. Pity really. Ruins a lot of fun, but there it is. Sit down and let's be comfortable. I'm Eleanor Fawcett."

"Elizabeth Gaunt. But please call me Lizzie. Everyone does."

"Gaunt?" the lady said. "One of Launceton's daughters?"

"Yes," Lizzie said warily. She had the feeling her honesty was now ruining what was left of her reputation and probably contaminating Minerva, but somehow, she couldn't bring herself to lie to the clear-eyed lady.

"Bad business," Mrs. Fawcett said, shaking her head and pushing her reviled cup of coffee towards Lizzie, who accepted it gratefully. "I'm sorry you and your sisters were left in such a situation. Entails are the devil's work. The secret is to marry before you're destitute."

"I'm afraid my father rather took us by surprise," Lizzie said wryly.

Mrs. Fawcett gave another of her barks of laughter. "He did that a lot one way or another. You should know I was madly in love with the man for almost a whole year."

"Good grief."

"I know, but he was a handsome devil in those days." She picked up the knife and began cutting the bread with unexpected skill. "Not sure he'd approve of you eloping with a Cossack officer."

Not even an officer, Lizzie thought ruefully. But then, they'd never really been eloping. It was merely a less heinous crime than theft. And murder. Aloud she said, "Well, at least he'd approve of my deciding against it. Are you travelling to Vienna, ma'am?"

"That was my intention, since it seems to be where the most interesting people are. England's deadly dull these days and since Bonaparte is now in chains—at least metaphorical chains—one can actually travel abroad again. I am taking advantage. What do you think of Vienna? Will I be amused?"

"Well, there are lots of parties," Lizzie said. "Balls and masquerades and soirees are planned for every night. Troop reviews and other entertainments during the day and, if you care for such things, there are emperors, queens, and princes coming out of the woodwork. Even though the Congress itself is not yet open. You missed the emperor's opening ball last night."

"I shall console myself with having met you. Are you with Lucy Daniels?"

"Yes...um." Lizzie, who was buttering a slice of bread, laid down her knife. "Aunt Lucy doesn't know I'm here. I hope," she added fervently.

Mrs. Fawcett blinked. "You mean you didn't leave a farewell note?"

"No," Lizzie said, shifting in her seat.

Mrs. Fawcett lifted her slice of bread. "Excellent. The trouble with notes is, one's folly is in writing and therefore undeniable. As it is, you may travel back with me and we'll make up some story to satisfy Lucy and the world."

"I'm hoping we won't need to," Lizzie said gratefully. "The children were going to cover for me until noon at least. Because of last night's ball, no one should be up before then."

"Children!" Mrs. Fawcett exclaimed. "What children?"

"My brother and sisters. They're also with my aunt."

For the first time, Lizzie saw Mrs. Fawcett's face grow wintry with disapproval. "You were going to leave them alone to run away with a Cossack?"

"Well, not exactly," Lizzie said desperately. "It was very wrong of me, I know, but it was all part of a plan to help *all* of us. Only…it wasn't a very good plan, so I won't explain it to you."

"You're quite resourceful, aren't you?" Mrs. Fawcett said thoughtfully. "Is your Cossack a decent sort of a man?"

*No, he's a thief.* The impossibility of saying any such thing closed up her throat. "He's always behaved to me with kindness," she said truthfully.

"And decency?" Mrs. Fawcett insisted, so significantly that even Lizzie finally understood her point.

She blushed. "Perfect decency."

"Well, that's something. To be honest, I was quite confused as to which one you shot. The eloper or the brother."

"Oh dear." She had no reason to trust Mrs. Fawcett with the truth. Despite the fact that she seemed to have been acquainted with Papa and Aunt Lucy, and appeared disposed to kindness, Lizzie knew she could not rely on a stranger's silence. And yet if Lizzie said nothing, God knew what stories the woman might spread in Vienna. "I didn't shoot my brother. He was a perfect stranger. I thought he was a thief, only he might have been an Austrian policeman who, for some reason, imagined I was carrying papers dangerous to his government."

Mrs. Fawcett's eyes widened. "Were you?" she asked so breathlessly that Lizzie realized she'd found an unlikely fellow spirit.

"Sadly no, but he tried to take my bag and Johnnie objected and hit him and then there was a fight and I tried to make them stop, only my pistol went off and the thief or the policeman or whoever he is, was shot."

Mrs. Fawcett ate her bread and butter in silence. At last she said,

"Of course you would have to take a pistol on an elopement... Where is he now? The man you shot."

"In one of the rooms upstairs. We watched him all night to make sure he didn't die, though to be honest, I haven't much—any!—experience with gunshot wounds and I'm not quite sure how I would have kept him from dying if he'd shown any signs of it."

"No, but it's in your favor that you tried," Mrs. Fawcett assured her. "So, what are your plans now? Once you've assured his continued existence, how will you prevent him charging you with attempted murder? Or espionage?"

Lizzie lifted her chin. "I'll tell him the truth," she said, although because she couldn't help it, she added, "Sort of... After all, if I'd truly meant him ill, why would I be helping him now?"

"That is a very good question. Why *are* you helping him now?"

Lizzie blinked. "I couldn't let him die."

"And your Cossack was of the same mind?"

"Of course. It was Johnnie who dug the ball out of him." She shuddered. "He must be in a lot of pain whenever he is awake. I don't suppose you could lend me some laudanum for him? The landlady only had a few drops and those will be gone as soon as he wakes."

"I'll see what I can do," Mrs. Fawcett said almost mechanically. Her gaze was fixed on Lizzie's face with clear fascination. Uncomfortable under such scrutiny, Lizzie jumped to her feet.

"Talking of which," she said brightly. "I had better get back and see how he does. Thank you for the coffee, ma'am, and your company."

"You are most welcome to both," Mrs. Fawcett assured her. "Come and see me when you mean to leave. We can travel to Vienna together."

"That would be more comfortable," Lizzie said gratefully. "If you're sure?"

"I insist."

With a quick smile, Lizzie left her inquisitive new friend and hurried back upstairs to the patient's room. As she climbed the stairs, she caught sight of three inn servants carrying trays of food into the private parlor and couldn't help smiling.

The patient appeared to be still asleep, although more restless than during the night, as if he were trying seriously to wake up. Lizzie patted his good arm with a few soothing murmurs, then, taking the carpet bag with her, she went on to her own room to wash her face and comb her hair. It would, she thought, be some time before Mrs. Fawcett was ready to leave, if she intended to eat even half of the food put before her.

So, carrying the bag once more, she returned to the patient's room, and for the first time, counted out the money Johnnie had got for the necklace. A quick calculation in her head proved he was correct, too, about the value. For a moment, she wondered if her new wealth was enough to employ him and reluctantly abandoned the idea. Besides, he didn't seem cut out for domestic service and she rather thought he could do more with his life, if he just left off thieving.

Thoughtfully, she shoveled the money back into the bag. As she covered it with her mask and domino cloak, something made her glance toward the bed. Her victim's eyes were open, glittering at her from the pillow.

"You're awake," she said, relieved. Part of her had been afraid he would never wake up at all. Dropping the bag on the floor, she went to the bedside table and filled the cup there with fresh water from the covered jug.

"Don't," he said hoarsely as she reached for the almost empty laudanum bottle. "Just water."

"Well, this time," Lizzie agreed doubtfully. "But you must be in an awful lot of pain."

Although she placed her arm under his shoulder to help him into position, she was pleased he did most of the work himself—surely a good sign of recovery. He drank the water greedily, then lay back on the pillows watching her.

The confusion of last night was not so apparent in his eyes now. On the other hand, they seemed to glitter in a way that tugged at her memory. On impulse, she brushed her hand across his forehead. His skin felt hot and tight.

"Oh dear, I think you've developed a fever," she said worriedly. Hastily, she went to the washing bowl and soaked the cloth before returning to bathe his head, hands, and wrists. For good measure, she pulled back a couple of the blankets covering him. "Sir, tell me where to reach your family," she pleaded. "They must be worried sick about you."

He shook his head stubbornly.

"Won't you even tell me your name?"

"You shot me," he said deliberately.

"Yes, I did," Lizzie confessed, "and I'm so very sorry! I didn't mean to. I was only threatening you with it because I thought you were a thief, but then when you were fighting with Johnnie, I got angry and clenched my fists...stupid thing to do when you're holding a pistol. But we can talk about that when you're well again. You must lie still now. I'll order some gruel for you to keep your strength up."

---

HER PATIENT ONLY ate a few spoonfuls of the gruel before shoving it away. Lizzie gave him some more water and this time he didn't seem to notice when she put the last of the laudanum in it. In fact, he was muttering to himself in German and his skin felt even hotter than before. Taking her courage in both hands, Lizzie changed the dressing on his wound, which no longer looked so neat. Instead, it was red and puffy and weeping slightly. She washed it and applied a clean dressing, then drew the sheet back over him.

For a few moments she stood anxiously over him, plucking at her lower lip with indecision. But she couldn't leave him in this state. She'd done this to him.

Hastily, she marched to the door. Encountering the flustered maid in the corridor, she asked for directions to Mrs. Fawcett's chamber.

She found the English woman with her maid, supervising two large footmen as they hefted a trunk onto their shoulders.

"Ah, Elizabeth," Mrs. Fawcett said, as if Lizzie were a pleasant familiarity in her life. She addressed the servants. "Miss Gaunt will be travelling with us—*as usual,*" she added significantly.

The maid and the footmen didn't even blink, merely nodded as if their mistress hadn't just commanded them to lie if required.

"But that's what I came to tell you, ma'am," Lizzie said hastily. "I'm afraid I can't travel today, and I wanted to ask you instead if you would be so good as to carry letters to my sister...and to my aunt, I suppose."

"You must tell me all about it," Mrs. Fawcett said comfortably. "Cartwright, make sure they stow the trunk safely. Take the dressing case and I'll be down directly."

"I can't keep this from my aunt any longer," Lizzie said ruefully when the servants had closed the door behind them. "I hate to cause her this trouble, too, but I truly can't leave here at least until the doctor has been. My patient has developed a fever and the wound looks so ugly I—"

"When do you expect the doctor?" Mrs Fawcett interrupted.

"Hopefully around noon, Johnnie said."

Mrs. Fawcett drew in a breath. "You had better let me see this patient."

"Truly, ma'am—"

"I've nursed two brothers, a husband, and four sons, three of them from battle wounds," Mrs. Fawcett said sternly. "All of them lived. Show me your patient."

Lizzie closed her mouth and meekly led the redoubtable Mrs. Fawcett along the corridor to her patient, who was now lying on the floor beside the bed.

"Oh no!" Lizzie ran to him. "He must have tried to follow me...and now he's gone back to sleep." She straightened. "I'll call the landlord to help get him back in bed."

"No need," Mrs. Fawcett said from the window. "I'll just call back my men."

Within five minutes, the burly footmen had lifted the injured man back between the sheets. Mrs. Fawcett peeped at the wound and sent the servants away to bring all her luggage back inside.

"I have a few medicines and remedies that might help," she said comfortably. "Take heart, Elizabeth, all is not yet lost. Now, let me think what is best… Yes, you must go to Vienna in my coach, while I stay here and watch our patient and speak to the doctor."

"That hardly seems fair."

"Well, I like to be useful and I think we should preserve your reputation if we can. Besides, your sisters—" She broke off. "You mentioned a brother as well. Why do you have a brother with you?"

"He's always been with us. His mother died, you see."

"And yours took him in." A smile flickered across her face. "She could always deal with your father. I'm glad to see you are so like her."

"Oh, but I'm not," Lizzie said earnestly. "It's my dearest wish to learn to be, but I keep having accidents and, well, it's difficult to be good and still look after people sometimes."

"Which is why we need to help each other now."

Lizzie smiled. "It's you who's giving all the help."

"Nonsense. You are supplying my entertainment. I shall write to your aunt, explain that I have been indisposed here and that, for your mother's sake, I would very much like your company tomorrow. I'll send the coach for you."

Lizzie regarded the older woman with considerable respect. Although she didn't like to leave Mrs. Fawcett with her mess, she did owe it to her siblings—and to her aunt and uncle—to return to Vienna and make sure all was well. Besides, Mrs. Fawcett clearly had more experience than she with wounds of this nature.

"You're very, very good, ma'am," she said fervently.

"I'm very, very good at organizing people as I want them," Mrs. Fawcett corrected. "Call Cartwright, will you? Tell her I want my pens and paper."

Within a quarter of an hour, Lizzie was comfortably ensconced in Mrs. Fawcett's well-appointed travelling coach, being waved off by the lady herself, the maid, and the landlady of the inn.

At the last moment, Lizzie stuck her head out of the window. "Oh, Mrs. Fawcett! When I return, do you think I could bring my dog?"

# Chapter Nine

MRS. FAWCETT'S COACHMAN dropped her at the door of the Daniels' house in the Skodegasse. She thanked him and he tipped his hat.

"See you tomorrow then, miss," he said cheerfully and urged his horses on.

Lizzie let herself in with her own key and while she removed her cloak, listened carefully. The house seemed ominously quiet. Of course, it still lacked an hour until noon, so it was unlikely the ball-goers would be abroad—with the exception of her uncle who, presumably, had to attend to diplomatic business. But it wasn't like her siblings, or Dog, to be so subdued.

She ran upstairs to the room she shared with her sisters and Minerva, entering with some trepidation. Both beds were occupied, the smaller by Minerva, and the larger by an ungainly heap which was clearly her sisters' representation of herself asleep.

Minerva didn't stir as Lizzie crossed the chamber on tiptoe. Crouching down, she drew the small trunk from under bed, replaced the carpet bag inside it, and pushed it gently back under. That done, she quickly smoothed and made up the bed, and quietly left the room. In the hallway, she encountered her aunt's maid.

"Good morning, Benson," she said brightly, searching the maid's face for signs of disapproval or any other unusual reaction to her presence. "Where are the children?"

"I saw them go out to the garden, Miss. With the dog."

"Then that explains the quiet in the house. Is my aunt awake yet?"

"Just about, Miss."

At least all seemed well with Benson and so, presumably, with her aunt. But before she could relax, she had to see the children.

They were, indeed, discovered in the garden. As soon as she opened the garden door, Dog launched himself at her. Undeterred by the pole to which he was tethered, he continued to run at her in short, pointless burst that always pulled him up short and should have hurt him.

Putting him out of his misery, Lizzie went to him at once, let him jump on her and lick her while she held on to him for self-preservation and the children ran at her with cries of relief and joy.

"Oh goodness, calm down," Lizzie begged. "You'll give the whole game away."

"We were just discussing where to tell Aunt Lucy you'd gone," Georgiana said. "I reckon we could have got you another couple of hours."

"Though I for one am very glad not to have to," Henrietta said.

"What happened?" Michael demanded. "Did you get it? Because they all seemed very cheerful when they came home."

"Really? Well, that is good, I suppose…although we may well have the panic tonight, instead. What is happening tonight?"

"Prince Metternich's ball," Michael answered, and when his sisters gazed at him in astonishment at his being aware of any such thing, he added, "What? Apparently, it has a military theme."

"Ah," Lizzie said, understanding. "Well, let's sit down here around Dog's pole so he can lie on top of me while we speak. I've had quite an adventure and it isn't all good—although at least we have the money."

She told them nearly everything, including speaking to the tsar, although omitting her dance and subsequent passage with Colonel Vanya. She told them of her difficulty finding Johnnie in the crush and his unilateral decision to steal the necklace by some flim-flam that meant Aunt Lucy didn't realize it had been stolen. When she got to the part at the inn and the stranger demanding her bag, they all gazed at her wide-eyed with shock. Michael and Georgiana both cheered Johnnie for hitting him and even when she described how she came to shoot the poor man, Michael declared stoutly that he'd deserved it.

Henrietta, in her kindhearted way, was touched by everyone's care of the wounded man, although Georgiana showed a disquieting interest in the gory details. For once, she appeared to agree with Michael that Lizzie had done the right thing in shooting him.

When she came to her encounter with Mrs. Fawcett, they all scratched their heads, wondering if she was a true friend or an interfering busybody.

"She seems to have known both Mama and Papa," Lizzie told them. "And while she's definitely most curious by nature, she does seem benevolently disposed toward us. She didn't need to stay there to look after my victim or send me back in her carriage. To be frank, if it hadn't been for her, our game would have been up. As to my reputation, my uncle's fury and Minerva's chances of a good marriage... I shudder to think. And she's written to Aunt Lucy to ask if I might visit her at the inn tomorrow, so I'll have an excuse to return to the patient."

"Can we come?" Georgiana asked as a knock sounded on one of the house windows. Lizzie looked up to see Benson summoning her from her aunt's room.

"I don't see why not," Lizzie said, standing up. "It's a big carriage and I already have permission to transport Dog in it. You're not *much* more destructive."

The children's laughter following her back inside the house gave her the strength to face her aunt calmly. She had no doubt that her aunt had finally discovered the theft of the beloved necklace. But when Lizzie, heart thumping with guilt and not a little shame, opened the door, she found her aunt waving a sheet of paper around.

"Did I know Eleanor Fawcett was your godmother?" Aunt Lucy asked.

"Only unofficially," Lizzie said. "*You* are my godmother."

"Yes, but it's also true Eleanor and your mother were very close for a time…until Jane married your father, of course. Well, it's very good of her to take an interest in you now. She's on her way to Vienna, but was taken ill at an inn not far from the city. She's asking that you visit her."

Lizzie said weakly, "How kind."

"I think you should go. It's a very good connection. She's an eccentric creature, of course, but she has a lot of influence in the fashionable world. She knows everyone. Everyone. Be kind to her and when she sets up her establishment in Vienna, we might all expect an invitation."

Her aunt had more to say on that subject and on the subject of last night's ball before moving on to her expectations of tonight's festivity at Metternich's summer palace, but it all floated over Lizzie's head. She was more concerned with how and why neither Aunt Lucy nor Benson had noticed that the necklace was missing.

She didn't discover that until the evening, when, as she was just finishing adjusting the hem of Minerva's enchanting pale yellow ball gown, Aunt Lucy bustled into the bed chamber to see if her daughter was near ready to go. Resplendent in deep turquoise, her aunt looked every inch the elegant matron of birth, wealth, and influence. Lizzie couldn't take her eyes off her aunt's bosom, on which lay the glittering diamond necklace Johnnie had stolen last night.

---

IT MUST BE *paste*, she thought as she and the children turned out dutifully to wave the carriage off to its second ball in two nights. *My aunt must have had it made up so she'd have something to keep when she hands the original over to Ivan the Terrible. She's got muddled and assumed the fake is the real one…*

Or was it? What if Johnnie had sold the fake one and the buyer found out? She'd have to give the money back. Though surely any receiver of stolen goods, any decent jewelry fence, would be able to spot a fake…

"Come on then," Michael said. With their aunt and uncle's permission, they were going to follow in a hired fiacre to watch the guests arrive at the ball. Reluctantly, Lizzie had vetoed taking the dog who could have caused untold carnage from one moment of inattention.

When they arrived, there were already crowds of people outside Metternich's palace and spilling onto the grounds themselves. In their usual manner, the children quickly latched on to a friendly Viennese, who good-naturedly pointed out the most important arrivals, including the enormously fat King of Württemberg and his handsome son, the crown prince, the long, lean King of Denmark, and the white-haired Emperor of Austria with his Empress who looked like everyone's favorite aunt and uncle apart from the fortune in jewels sprayed around the empress' person.

"Where is the Tsar of Russia?" Henrietta asked eagerly. "Is he not here yet?"

"This will be him," said their unofficial guide. "Escorted by his Cossacks!"

Michael jumped up and down with excitement, trying to see over people's heads. Their kind guide pushed Michael in front of him and made a space, too, for the girls. The good-natured Viennese moved happily out of the way to let the children see.

And the Cossacks were playing to the crowd. Although the tsar's carriage was travelling relatively sedately in their midst, the horsemen were galloping ahead and doubling back in constant, circular motion. They looked rough and wild, with fine moustaches and some very eastern faces, their horsemanship unparalleled in terms of skill, discipline, and precision. Michael was enchanted.

The tsar and the stunningly beautiful tsarina rode in an open carriage and were cheered as enthusiastically as the performing Cossacks. On either side of them rode brilliantly uniformed aides on horseback and, a little in front and farther to one side, rode another officer, resplendent in a green and gold uniform that she'd seen before.

Her heart gave a funny little flutter, because it looked very much like Colonel Vanya's. She looked up at his face as his part of the cavalcade approached, but she could see nothing to recognize – a hint of black hair beneath his tall hat, which covered a good part of his face, too. She saw only hollow cheeks and rather fine bone structure—the bits, mainly, that on Vanya had been hidden by his mask. She must have been wishing some kind of familiarity on him, for this man could have been anyone.

He appeared, however, to be the Cossacks' officer. One word from him reined them into proper order as they prepared to enter the front gates. With superb control, the Cossacks wheeled into sedate formation, separating to the front and rear of the tsar's carriage.

"Magnificent!" Michael exclaimed. "Lizzie, I know I said an infantry regiment would suit me very well, but I *need* to be a cavalryman!"

Lizzie laughed, knowing exactly how he felt. Unexpectedly, the Cossacks' officer, then waiting at the gate for the carriage to pass through, glanced over his shoulder and directly at her.

Something moved inside her, as if her heart were trying to come out of her throat. The officer smiled, dazzlingly, and inclined his head, then turned back to follow the carriage.

Colonel Vanya, she thought with ridiculous, laughable excitement. Surely Colonel Vanya…

Or, more likely, a complete stranger who'd caught sight of Henrietta. When her sister came out, she was going to need a dragon of a duenna.

---

ALTHOUGH VANYA HAD overheard the English boy's enthusiastic wish to be a cavalryman, expressed in a vaguely familiar, still breaking voice, it hadn't been enough to attract his attention, not until *she* laughed and answered him.

Just the sound of her voice made him smile and, yet, deluged him with quite uncharacteristic indecision. She'd spent all night in his company without connecting him to her masked admirer at the Emperor's ball. To see him now, unmasked, wouldn't she recognize "Johnnie" right away?

What did it matter? It was only a matter of time until he was completely found out and he couldn't quite understand his reluctance to end the charade. She'd been kind to the thief. But he didn't want her kindness. He wanted…whatever it was she'd shown the masked colonel, only more, deeper…

Forcibly, he cut off his mind's ramblings. In a nut shell, he wanted just a little longer of her time, of her company as an equal. And when it all came tumbling down, as it must when she learned the whole truth, well…Vanya wasn't used to dealing with the future. And right now, he'd settle for a glimpse of her. And so, deliberately, he turned.

Even if he hadn't been looking for her, she would have been easy to spy. With their beguiling mixture of vitality, fun, and beauty, it was no wonder the Viennese seemed to have made the English family into pets, an attraction to rival the crowned heads they'd come along to watch. And there *she* was, in her darned gown and her unfashionable bonnet and pelisse; and she seemed to be watching not his incorrigible show-offs, or even the tsar, but *him*.

His smile was totally spontaneous, not just because she was *there*, and more beautiful than all the bejeweled and fashionable women he'd find tonight, but because of the sudden widening of her eyes, a leap of surprise and excitement, wonder and confusion. Oh yes, he'd made an impression. It was all he could do not to wheel his horse around and gallop, straight for her, sweep her off her feet and away from the world.

It was the soldier in him who turned first to his duties and then to the realization that he was being unkind to both Lizzie and himself. There would be no more intoxicating flirtation with her. It was time even for Johnnie to extricate himself from her life.

Going through the motions as required, he ordered the men picked out to follow Metternich's servant through the grounds to a make-believe village. There, dressed as peasants, they were to perform dancing for the edification of the royal guests. He then directed the others to join the soldiers inside the house to show off their drill with their Austrian and Prussian allies.

But while he presented his most respectful and sociable manner to the distinguished world, he could feel the bitter recklessness rising up, clawing to get out. It was inevitable that it should; worse, he wanted it, too, because this was the kind of pain he couldn't deal with, the kind he couldn't solve, like losing his father, like losing Katia, like misjudging and losing more men than he should. Like being bored.

As soon as the soldiers were dismissed, to the appreciative applause of the sovereigns, he handed command to his lieutenant and swiped two glasses of champagne from the passing servant, who may have imagined he was carrying one to a lady. He drank them down, one after the other, mainly because he couldn't lay his hands on vodka, which worked much more quickly.

"That bad?" drawled a voice at his side.

Vanya brought his furious gaze back into focus on Blonsky. He laughed. "How perfect. Have you come to pick a fight with me?"

"Whenever you like," Blonsky said at once.

Vanya regarded him, considering. It seemed he could remember Katia's laughing face after all. And right or wrong, he still blamed Blonsky for her death. He flexed his fingers.

"Do you both want to be exiled?" Boris hissed, emerging at Blonsky's shoulder. "Because that's what'll happen if the tsar so much as gets wind of another duel."

"Vanya doesn't care for the tsar's approval anymore," Blonsky sneered. "His English ship has come in."

That gave Vanya momentary pause. "Where did you hear that?"

"A letter from home. I look forward to greeting your lady mother when she reaches Vienna. I only hope she brings your delectable sister."

If Blonsky imagined the bombshell of his mother's approach would save him, he was vastly mistaken. All the old pain over Katia swept over Vanya, rushing against the new pain he didn't yet understand but which definitely surrounded Lizzie Gaunt.

Boris scowled. "Mind your manners, Blonsky."

Blonsky was already turning away, smirking because he imagined there was nothing Vanya could do. Wrong.

Vanya hooked his foot around Blonsky's ankle and jerked. He was already moving on as Blonsky clattered to the floor. "So slippery," he said savagely.

Boris, of course, did his best to limit the damage, helping Blonsky rise as if he really had slipped on the polished floor. That irritated Vanya, too. He wanted a fight and, on the whole, he would far rather it were with Blonsky than with anyone else. He'd wanted to kill him for a long time. Failing that, he'd have to go to some low tavern and brawl like his Cossacks at their worst.

Or he could drink. He found another couple of glasses in the ballroom, drank one immediately and carried the other with him in search of distraction.

Unfortunately, the first people to attract his attention were Mrs. Daniels in her diamond necklace—he wondered what Lizzie had made of that—and her daughter, who was silently twisting her fingers together in clear discomfort if not actual distress. Some people thrived on huge social gatherings. To others, the quieter, shyer spirits, it was pure torture. And for a young, marriageable lady of Minerva's class, there was no choice.

He didn't want to feel sorry for the girl. He wanted to feel sorry for himself and wallow in a night—probably several nights, merging with the days between—of self-pity and overindulgence. And yet, the thought crept into his head that if Lizzie were only with her, she'd bear it better and Lizzie could enjoy some fun for a change. Worse, he knew what Lizzie would expect him to do for her wallflower cousin.

But he wouldn't. It wouldn't be a distraction at all.

He even walked right past them before, with an inward curse, he swerved back and bowed to the surprised matron. "Mrs. Daniels, good evening. We met last night at the Emperor's ball."

Gratified, Mrs. Daniels murmured a greeting, but before she could push her daughter forward—he could almost feel the girl tensing with the threatened humiliation—he'd spoken the words soliciting Minerva's hand for the waltz. He even expressed surprise that she wasn't already spoken for. As she took his hand mechanically, she seemed stunned.

Vanya was well aware he wasn't considered much of a catch by the parents of marriageable daughters. On the other hand, without any effort on his part, he had the kind of reckless cachet that induced foolish young men—and not just Russians—to admire him. To many such, if Vanya danced with a girl, she must be worth the effort.

As he'd fully expected, Minerva danced with grace but no joy. He could see only one way to get them both out of this: the direct approach.

"You hate this, don't you?" he observed, without heat or malice.

"Oh no, quite delightful," she protested, flushing.

"Whopper," he observed, borrowing from her young cousins' vocabulary, which at least won a surprised laugh.

"Not entirely, sir," she promised. "I just get a little…lost in such crowds of people."

"I'm not surprised," Vanya sympathized.

"Do you find that, too?" she asked, almost hopefully.

"Not lost exactly. I just ignore whatever doesn't amuse me and there is always *something* amusing somewhere. For example, did you see anyone purloining teaspoons at last night's ball?"

Minerva blinked. "Purloining…are you joking me?" she asked uncertainly.

"No, it's quite true. I have it on the best authority that half of the Emperor's silver teaspoons vanished overnight. So be vigilant next time you drink tea with your friends. See who serves it with Imperial teaspoons."

She gave another slightly shocked little laugh and he smiled encouragingly. By the time the dance had ended, she was almost relaxed. And by the time he returned her to her mother, several young men—not all entirely reputable—were waiting to be introduced.

At least it would pass the time for her. Vanya stayed for a moment to exchange banter and a few friendly insults, and then made good his escape.

Boris came up behind him as he downed another glass of champagne and reached for another. "Drinking in pairs tonight?" Boris inquired sardonically.

Vanya raised the next glass to him and drank about half of it.

"You're looking for trouble, aren't you?" Boris said worriedly.

"Well, I'm looking for something," Vanya acknowledged. "Another war, maybe, if only I could stomach it. Maybe a fight would do. Is Blonsky still pawing the ground?"

"Nothing so obvious. He doesn't believe you'll fight him again."

"He didn't believe I'd fight him the last time, either."

"Yes, he did. He just thought he could humiliate you as he did when we were children."

"I can't think why that upset me so much as a boy," Vanya said with odd detachment.

"Because he was supposed to be your friend. Because he enjoyed it. And because you were four years younger and easy meat for a bully. For what it's worth, it never made him the leader of all those boys."

"Oh, I discovered that quite early on. I knew we'd always be enemies because of it, too. I just stopped caring. Boris, what is this about my mother? Is she really coming to Vienna?"

"Apparently so. How come I know more than you?"

"I told you, she's not speaking to me and I never bother to write back to anyone else."

"So I've noticed. Why isn't she speaking to you?"

"I forget. Anyway, *I'm* not speaking to her now she's interfered in my English ship."

Boris blinked. "What the devil is that supposed to mean?"

"I might tell you one day," Vanya said, reaching for yet another glass of champagne. "Now, where's the card table with the most ruinously high stakes?"

Boris threw up his hands and left him, muttering that there was no doing anything with him in this mood. With a provoking laugh, Vanya took his champagne out of the ballroom and into the card rooms.

But even here, the distractions all seemed to speak of Lizzie. A very young man playing very deep caught his attention, mainly because he sat at the same table as Fischer. He wondered how that weasel had obtained an invitation from the fastidious Metternich and suspected Louise, who was probably here somewhere, too, if he could be bothered looking.

A quick question to a fellow officer elicited the losing boy's name as Daniels and the information that his father was on Castlereagh's staff.

Judging by the empty glass and the sick frown on the boy's face, it was already too late to save him. But there was a quick way to stop it from getting any worse. Irritated, because yet again he was going out of his way for a girl he couldn't have in any sense of the word, he strolled over to young Fischer's table and watched. The boy was still losing.

After a few moments, Vanya placed his hand on Fischer's shoulder and leaned. Startled, Fischer jerked around.

Vanya smiled into his shocked face. "Don't get up," he said and bent his head. "The Daniels boy has nothing, you know. So good to see you wasting your time," he murmured in the man's reptilian ear and walked away. He thought of searching out the Cossacks waiting to escort the tsar back to the Hofburg. Misha would have vodka or something just as bad.

But as he passed through the ballroom with focused intent, he finally found his distraction and the night's salvation. She looked beautiful in her low cut white dress trimmed with delicate orange. Her lovely, plump bosom hinted most temptingly at what lay hidden. Vanya already knew, of course, but he felt he should make sure.

"Sonia," he said, smiling and taking her hand, although she was in mid-conversation with several other people.

She broke off to greet him coolly, but he could see the conflict in her eyes. Although she wished to be distant, for some reason, she was actually flattered by his attention. He made the most of it, smiling into her eyes as he drew her toward the dance floor.

"My waltz, I think."

Protesting would have caused a scene. Perhaps that was why she came without demur. But in his arms, her stiffness relaxed and, with massive relief, he knew he would at least be able to lose the night in blind lust.

# Chapter Ten

Eleanor Fawcett dozed in the chair beside her patient's bed. She hadn't meant to and the commotion in the yard woke her after only a moment. Horses' hooves galloped on the cobbles; a peremptory shout for attention went up.

A quick glance at the injured man assured Eleanor that he still breathed, if not very comfortably, and so she stood and went to the window. A soldier threw himself off a very fine black stallion she'd seen before. Although she'd seen the rider before, too, his clothes were different. This time, he wore a very fetching military uniform.

"Well, well," Eleanor murmured. "The Cossack again. Or are you?"

A sleepy ostler emerged to care for the horse, which the soldier abandoned to his care with apparent reluctance before striding into the inn. Eleanor returned to her patient, bathing his hot face and neck and arms again. He shivered, thrashing his head in protest while his tight skin burned up. She heard the Cossack clattering on the stairs, charging along the corridor and then he barged into the room, kicking the door shut behind him.

He was halfway across the floor before he noticed Eleanor and pulled up short, staring.

As Eleanor had suspected, he was drunk. His face was clearly flushed from more than arduous riding and his eyes held a dangerous glitter that began to die under her calm scrutiny. She could see him wondering wildly if he'd just intruded on some stranger's room by accident, perhaps even if his man had died.

He looked every inch what he undoubtedly was: a handsome, young reprobate.

He dragged a hand through his tousled hair, roughly rubbed his eyes and his face before glancing at the bed, and then back to Eleanor. "Is he dead?"

Since he spoke in French, she answered in the same language. "No, not yet, but his fever is high."

To her surprise, the wild young man actually bowed to her with something approaching grace. "Forgive me, Madame, but I've no idea who you are."

"Then I have the advantage of you. You are, if I'm not mistaken, Johnnie."

He blinked, but didn't otherwise look remotely put out. In fact, he bowed again with a little more flourish. "At your service, Madame."

"I doubt that. You have an odd name for a Cossack."

"But then I'm not a Cossack."

She glanced pointedly at his uniform.

"I may command Cossacks," he allowed, "but I'm not one. I'm not really anything. While you, I have to guess, are a friend of Lizzie's."

"I was certainly a friend of her parents. Elizabeth is something in the way of a goddaughter to me."

"She never mentioned you," Johnnie observed.

"Well, she didn't know of my existence until this morning," Eleanor admitted. "Why are you here?"

He nodded carelessly towards the bed. "To check on him. Why are *you* here?"

"The same. It was the only way I could persuade Elizabeth to leave him and go home."

Johnnie walked toward the bed. Even drunk, his movements were such that Eleanor could see exactly why Elizabeth had been prepared to elope with him. If Eleanor had been twenty years younger, she probably would, too.

"He looks terrible," Johnnie said abruptly. Again, he dragged his hand through his wild hair. "I can't let him die."

"It strikes me it would be more convenient for you—and Elizabeth—if he did die. No one else saw who shot him."

Johnnie shook his head violently. "She'd never forgive herself."

Eleanor regarded him with more interest. Perhaps he wasn't just an average rake after all. Perhaps there was more.

She said, "You expect to nurse him in that state?"

"I've cared for men in worse."

"Did they live?"

His eyes dropped. "Sometimes. Did the surgeon come?"

"He did. He said the colonel had sent him." And now that she was speaking to this officer, she began to have a suspicion who the colonel was. Up until now, she'd imagined Johnnie had begged the favor from his commanding officer.

"And about *him*?" Johnnie asked, with a hint of impatience.

"That there wasn't much else he could do. He left something for the fever and laudanum for the pain. Otherwise, he needs cooling and water and, presumably, God will decide whether or not to spare him."

"Do you believe in God, Madame?"

"Not completely," she said, with a reprehensible urge to shock the arrogant young man before her. And it certainly drew his surprised gaze back to her.

Unexpectedly, he laughed. "I like you, Madame, whoever you are."

"Eleanor Fawcett," said, offering her hand. "Entirely gratified, of course."

"Of course," he said gravely, shaking hands with her, before suddenly tearing off his cloak and coat and sword belt, and rolling up his sleeves. "Now let's see about getting that fever down."

<hr />

IN THE MORNING, while the children were dressing and squabbling, Lizzie went to see if her aunt was awake, ostensibly to ask about the night's festivities and any messages for Mrs. Fawcett, but more importantly to see what she could discover about the necklace.

She found her aunt, sitting up in bed drinking hot chocolate and rather blearily reading her morning correspondence.

"How was the ball?" Lizzie asked, sitting on the edge of her bed.

"Exhausting. I think we'll all be glad of a quiet evening!"

"Did Minerva enjoy it?"

Aunt Lucy sighed. "She doesn't *try*, Lizzie!"

"Well, it is a little uncomfortable being hung out on display like a piece of meat."

"Lizzie!" Aunt Lucy scowled, throwing down her letter. "Where do you get such notions?"

"From Minerva, actually. I think she would prefer a quieter life."

"She won't once she's an old spinster with no one to keep her," Aunt Lucy retorted.

"Maybe she and I can join our poor resources and live quietly in a cottage in genteel poverty."

Aunt Lucy eyed her a little uncertainly.

"Sorry, I don't mean to tease you," Lizzie said contritely. She didn't really bear a grudge; it was natural that Aunt Lucy should care more for her own daughter's future. "And it's hardly your fault my father made no arrangements for us. On the contrary, we're very grateful you took us in."

"Took you in?" Aunt Lucy repeated disparagingly. "You are my nieces, my profligate brother's children, and, of course, you must live with us as long as is necessary. In fact, despite the noise of the children, Lizzie, I have to say you make a household run more smoothly. You're a very *useful* girl. But listen, couldn't you speak to Minerva? Advise her to…to *sparkle* a little?"

"She sparkles in her own way," Lizzie assured her. She hesitated, but now wasn't really the time to bring up her cousin's affection for Mr. Corner. "I think she's more comfortable at smaller events than at huge, formal balls. Especially here, where they are so crowded you can't move. According to Minerva," she added hastily. "Oh, and I meant to speak to you about the necklace, the diamonds you borrowed from the estate."

Aunt Lucy cast her a wary glance. "Oh?"

"I wondered," Lizzie said, not entirely disingenuously, "if you had ever thought of having a copy made? You know, a paste replica?"

Aunt Lucy stared at her. "Why would I do that?"

"Well, then you could wear one whenever you liked and give the other back to Ivan the Terrible."

"Don't use that ridiculous name, Lizzie, it will slip out at the wrong time. If you can't stomach calling him Lord Launceton or Cousin Ivan, call him by the name he uses in Russia—if you can remember it. I'm not sure I can."

"Sorry. Don't you think it's a good idea about the necklace?" Lizzie pursued.

Aunt Lucy shifted uncomfortably. "Don't be silly."

But the flutter of uncertainty in her face made Lizzie catch her hand. "Aunt, is there anything I can help you with?"

"Of course not!" Aunt Lucy gave a trill of a laugh and pulled her hand free with a distant pat. "I can't think what you mean."

"Well, the clasp was broken, but you still wore it last night."

Lucy's shoulders sank in incomprehensible relief. "Oh, that. It doesn't seem to be broken after all. Perhaps Benson just hadn't fastened it properly the night of the Emperor's ball, for when we looked at it yesterday evening, we could see nothing wrong with it."

"And you still have it."

"Of course I still have it. Why wouldn't I?"

"No reason," Lizzie said, getting up none the wiser. An unworthy suspicion was forming in her head. She stood up. "Do you have any messages for Mrs. Fawcett?"

Her aunt picked up the next letter from her tray and reached for her chocolate. "Just my regards and best wishes for her quick recovery. I look forward to seeing her in Vienna."

"I'm going to take the children and the dog with me," Lizzie said. "So, at least, they shouldn't worry you!"

"Excellent idea." She threw the letter down on the bed. "This is addressed to you, Lizzie."

Surprised, Lizzie came back to the bed and picked it up. It was in a bold hand she'd never seen before. In spite of all her common sense, her heart began to beat faster, because the letter could come from *him*. He could have discovered who she was...

Resisting the urge to tear it open to find out, she forced herself to break the seal without obvious urgency, scanning quickly to the signature. And, of course, it wasn't from Colonel Vanya.

"It's from Dorothée," she said in surprise.

"Who's Dorothée."

"A young French lady we met in the Graben the other day."

"French?" Aunt Lucy sniffed. "What does she want?"

"She's invited me to her house tomorrow afternoon."

Aunt Lucy set down her chocolate. "I don't think I want you visiting *French* people."

"Why not? The war is over. And she did seem very nice. She didn't object at all when Dog jumped on her and her poor maid. I would like to see her again, if you don't need me."

"Is she respectable?" Aunt Lucy asked bluntly.

Lizzie laughed. "She seemed so. She is here with her uncle. She is a married lady, I believe. She says she will send her carriage for me, so I won't need an escort."

"Oh good, because I planned to take Minerva to Lady Castlereagh's that afternoon."

"She'll like that," Lizzie said honestly, since Mr. Corner was likely to be there. "So I may visit Dorothée?"

"Yes, yes, but go now. Someone is ringing below and it's probably the carriage for you. Don't keep Mrs. Fawcett waiting and be on your best behavior...actually, Lizzie, now I think of it, perhaps you *shouldn't* take the children and certainly not the dog!"

"She said I might," Lizzie said, hurrying to the door, from where she blew her aunt a kiss. "Goodbye! Enjoy the peace of your day."

"Lizzie, your dress!" Aunt Lucy wailed after her.

"My dress?" She looked down, twisting around to inspect the back as well as the front. "What's wrong with it?"

"Everything. You must wear something of Minerva's. Why didn't I think of this before?"

"Because you have enough calls on your time and money," Lizzie soothed. "I'm respectable if hardly fashionable and Mrs. Fawcett quite understands how things were left."

She herded the children downstairs, paused only long enough to snatch up her reticule with Johnnie's share of the necklace money, which she'd forgotten to leave him in the hurry of his departure. She then followed her siblings and the dog outside and into the familiar carriage.

Dresses, after all, had never been terribly high on her list of priorities, and even if she'd had the means or the time to adapt something of Minerva's, she really saw no point in dressing in the height of fashion to visit a country inn and an old friend of her parents, to say nothing of the man she'd shot and, possibly, the thief who'd stolen Aunt Lucy's necklace. Or at least *one* of Aunt Lucy's necklaces.

"Do you suppose," she said to her siblings as the coach rattled over Vienna's cobbles, "that Aunt Lucy had a paste copy of the necklace made and now can't tell which is the real one? I think she imagines the stolen one is the fake and that's why she's so undisturbed by the theft."

"Maybe it *was* the fake," Michael suggested.

"I think Johnnie's buyer would know diamonds well enough to spot the difference."

"Probably," Michael agreed. "But it doesn't matter now, does it? We have the money and, even better, we haven't made Aunt Lucy cut up rough about losing it."

"Yes, but if the necklace she still has is the fake, what if Ivan the Terrible notices?" Georgiana wondered. "He does seem to be the kind of money-grubbing man who *would* notice such a thing and complain, even if he has everything else and certainly doesn't need another diamond necklace!"

"That's what bothers me," Lizzie admitted. "I hope Johnnie is at the inn so we can ask him how knowledgeable his buyer is likely to be.

And listen, this is still our secret. You mustn't say anything about the necklace in front of Mrs. Fawcett."

"As if we would," Michael scoffed.

It was another lovely, sunny day, although so far into the year. As the coach bowled out of the city and through the countryside, Lizzie opened the carriage window. Dog stuck his shaggy head out and sniffed the air with pleasure.

"Ah," Lizzie remembered in time. "One other thing. The inn servants and Mrs. Fawcett think I was eloping with Johnnie, so don't be shocked!"

Henrietta gave a peel of laughter. "With Johnnie?"

"Well, how else were we to explain why I was there with him? And the man I shot is our eldest brother, come to take me home. I have now decided not to elope with Johnnie."

Michael grinned. "All for the best."

"I think so. Only the brother that I shot had best be another half-brother since Mrs. Fawcett is involved."

"You do tell excellent whoppers, Lizzie," Michael observed with open admiration.

"I do, don't I?" she said ruefully. "Never mind, when this mess is cleared up, we'll *all* tell the truth *all* the time."

"Except how we came by the money for our cottage," Georgiana said reasonably.

"Apart from that," Lizzie agreed.

By the time they reached the inn, Dog was wheefling with excitement.

The coach rumbled sedately into the familiar courtyard and drew to a halt. Before either the coachman or the inn servants got near, Michael threw open the carriage door and the children and Dog spilled out with joy.

Lizzie emerged with marginally more decorum, laughing and holding onto her bonnet as Dog paused to jump at her before bounding around the yard and sniffing at the stable door.

Mrs. Fawcett emerged from the inn's front entrance, smiling. Lizzie went to her at once, hand held out. "Good morning, ma'am. I'm afraid we've come to cut up your peace. They're all a little exuberant!"

"You brought them all!" Mrs Fawcett sounded more amused than disapproving, fortunately.

Lizzie called the children to order and they trooped over at once to make their bows and curtseys to Mrs. Fawcett. At least, they remembered their manners, although Dog, barking at the stable door, had clearly forgotten his.

Lizzie called to him sternly, which he ignored. "Go and fetch him, Michael. I don't want him scaring the horses."

Michael ran over cheerfully, just as the stable door opened and Johnnie emerged, as casual as ever in shirt sleeves. Dog hurled himself at him as if he were an old friend.

"Morning, Johnnie," Michael said cheerfully, and the girls immediately ran over to greet him, too.

Johnnie paused to ruffle the dog's head, greeting the children with easy familiarity as he strode among them toward her.

"He seems at home with them," Mrs. Fawcett observed.

Lizzie flushed. "They're very open and friendly."

"I have to say I like him better than I thought I would."

"Then you've met him?"

"Oh yes. We nursed our friend together last night."

"How is our friend?" Lizzie asked.

"Not good. He's just about holding his own, but the fever is still raging."

"Oh dear! Well, I'm here to take my turn, so you and Johnnie can both get some sleep."

"Not a chance," said Mrs, Fawcett. "I want to get to know these remarkable children."

"Good morning, Johnnie," Lizzie broke off her conversation to greet the thief. Under Mrs. Fawcett's perceptive eye, she felt somewhat uncomfortable. She'd no idea how she was meant to behave toward a supposed lover she'd just jilted. "You'd better show me our patient," she blurted, before she realized how it would sound to Mrs.

Fawcett, who now must imagine she wanted to be alone with him.

Which, of course, she did, though not for any of the reasons Mrs. Fawcett might imagine.

"Watch the dog!" she called hastily to the children. "Don't let him run off too far."

"Or chase the chickens," Mrs. Fawcett added.

"Oh no, he's very good like that," Henrietta assured her. "He never worries chickens or sheep. I think he finds them boring because they won't play with him."

The rest was cut off as Lizzie preceded Johnnie inside.

"I didn't think you'd still be here," she said, low.

"I don't have to be anywhere else." He still sounded as stiff as she'd felt greeting him in the yard.

She tried for lightness as she began to climb the stairs. "But, of course, I forgot your fee."

"Which is, of course, why I came back."

There was no mistaking the bitterness in his voice.

Stricken, she stopped and swung around to face him on the stairs. "I didn't mean that. You've done far more to help me than even an old friend might have done."

Although he halted, too, her suddenness meant he stood too close, on the step below, eye-to-eye with her. But there was no time or, indeed, need to be embarrassed.

He said curiously, "Why should you care what I understand or misunderstand?"

"I don't know," she admitted. "I suppose I was brought up to care about other people's feelings."

His rather hard eyes scanned hers and slowly softened, which had an odd effect on her stomach. It reminded her of a different feeling, a different situation she wouldn't get into now.

"A courtesy not always returned," he guessed.

"Often enough," she said lightly. "You're not angry with me?"

Something that wasn't quite laughter surged out with his breath. He spread his arm, gesturing her to proceed. "How can I be angry with you? If we could only keep our friend up there alive, it would be the best diversion ever."

Lizzie walked on. "Mrs. Fawcett said his fever was worse."

"Worse than yesterday when you left. No worse than last night."

Lizzie didn't need to touch his forehead; she could see his fever in his face.

"We gave him a cold bath last night, which helped," Johnnie said.

Lizzie nodded, biting her lip in pity for her victim. Then, distracted, she cast an amused glance at Johnnie. "You and Mrs. Fawcett did?"

"Well, I and Mrs. Fawcett's footmen. Mrs. Fawcett supervised from a modest distance.

Lizzie's lips twisted. It wasn't quite a smile. "You're right. It would be fun if we weren't afraid he would die."

She found the familiar cloth and dipped it in the fresh bowl of water before she bathed his face and neck. As she worked, she felt Johnnie's gaze following her movements, but he didn't come any farther into the room or sit down.

He stirred. "Did you want to speak to me about something else?"

"Well, apart from the money—which is in my reticule, by the way, just take it—and to offer any help I can from my family's connections—"

He smiled, leaning his shoulder on the closed door. "You are a one woman reformist movement, aren't you?"

"Are you making fun of me?"

"Only in an admiring kind of way. I've only ever taken care of myself."

Lizzie moved on to her restless patient's hands and arms. "And our friend here and me. And if you were a soldier, I expect you took care of each other."

"That doesn't count."

She paused to glance at him in surprise. "Why not?"

He blinked, straightening, then walked farther into the room with a shrug. "I don't know. In war, there are just things one *needs* to do. You have no such need."

She grimaced. "And yet, I'm no saint, am I? Oh, that reminds me. How knowledgeable is your buyer?"

"I beg your pardon?"

"The man who bought the necklace from you. Would he know diamonds from paste?"

Johnnie halted on the other side of the bed, frowning. "I would hope so. Why?"

"Because my aunt still has a necklace that looks exactly like the one you stole. The only solution is that she had a replica made, probably to fool Ivan the Terrible. If it's the fake she still has, then Ivan will be mad as fire. But she must think she's *lost* the fake, so she's not much put out by its loss." She frowned at Johnnie's lack of reaction. "Johnnie, if she *has* lost the fake, then whoever bought the necklace for that huge amount of money is going to be furious with us when *he* finds out!"

Dropping the cloth back in the bowl, she looked over at Johnnie, expecting some kind of panic. But he looked perfectly calm as his eyes searched her face.

"It doesn't matter. We have the money and I assure you we're perfectly safe."

"Won't he be able to find you again?"

"No," said Johnnie flatly. "He's gone back to…Bohemia."

"Oh." She searched in vain for any signs of anxiety in his face. He looked tired, she thought, irrelevantly, noting the dark rings under his eyes, the rather tight lines around his mouth.

He said, "Don't worry. That part is over."

"It just seems wrong to cheat someone. Even a receiver of stolen goods!"

"Well, it can be a dangerous practice," Johnnie allowed. "But they leave themselves open to it. I assure you he'd have cheated us if he could. In fact, he probably did. Perhaps the necklace was worth ten thousand."

"Hardly." Lizzie sank into the chair by the bed, again watching her patient. "Has he been delirious?" she asked suddenly.

"I think he has bad dreams from the fever, but he's a close-lipped fellow, even in this state. He mutters occasionally, but nothing comprehensible."

"Then we still have nothing to tell us who he is?"

"I'm pretty sure Baron Hager could tell us that. He's the Austrian police minister."

"Maybe I should try to see him."

Johnnie opened his mouth to speak, then closed it again and swallowed. "Best not, just yet. We'll just get him in trouble for this mess. Once he's well, he can sort it out himself."

Lizzie nodded, agreeing that she'd done the man enough harm. Irrelevantly, it struck her that Johnnie was a very handsome young man. Those cheek bones, those lips… "It must be a Russian look," she blurted aloud.

Johnnie blinked. "What must?"

She blushed furiously. "I beg your pardon! I was thinking aloud. You just remind me a little of another Russian I met recently."

Johnnie grinned. "Not the tsar?"

She laughed with relief. "No, not the tsar."

"Well, I hope he is worthy of your notice, whoever he is."

Lizzie sighed. "It doesn't matter," she said, having coming to terms with reality rather than the sweet, if silly, fairy tale fantasy that had crept up on her. "He won't remember me."

Johnnie blinked. "I would doubt that. You're not easy to forget, Miss Lizzie."

She waved that away. "Not when we've stolen a necklace, shot a man, and nursed him together," she said humorously. "I assure you I don't have many such alliances."

# Chapter Eleven

MEANWHILE, ELEANOR FAWCETT was spending a very instructive half hour with the beguiling Gaunt children and their ridiculous dog. In the quiet inn courtyard, they sat at the wooden table beside her or ran about as the notion took them, chattering away to her without any self-consciousness at all. Even the staggeringly beautiful Henrietta, who was doomed to slay hearts across Europe, seemed to accept her gift without pride or even much interest. Even when the passing inn trade occasionally stopped to stare at her.

Despite their normal openness, they were a little evasive about Johnnie and how Lizzie had met him. Eleanor suspected they'd been sworn to silence on that score. But they spoke happily of life at Launceton Hall and their sudden departure due to the unfeeling and vulgar haste of the new baron, whom they referred to as Ivan the Terrible. The harassed but kind-hearted Lucy Daniels had clearly taken them in and swept them all off to Vienna with her own family.

However, reading between the lines of their funny stories and innocent remarks, Eleanor picked up that Lizzie had been the organizing force on the journey. It sounded as if she'd earned her keep well before they'd even arrived in Vienna, where they all lived in a cramped little house and cheered Cousin Minerva off to balls.

"Doesn't Lizzie go to the balls, too?" Eleanor asked innocently.

"Well, no, there isn't the money to buy her suitable gowns," Henrietta said, sadly. "The ones she used to wear at Launceton are too old and tired."

Georgiana snorted. "They're afraid Lizzie will cast Minerva in the shade and spoil her chances of a brilliant match. What?" she added aggressively as Henrietta and Michael both nudged her. "It's true!"

"But not for strangers' ears," Eleanor agreed. "Don't worry, I'm not really a stranger and I'm discreet to a fault. Don't you like Cousin Minerva?"

"She's all right," Michael said carelessly. "A bit dull and mopey. Lizzie thinks she wants to marry my uncle's secretary, Mr. Corner, and is unhappy being forced to all these parties."

"Well, in our position, one can't always do what one wants," said Eleanor, who, in fact, had always done exactly what she wanted. Except for marrying Launceton, of course, though with age and experience she could see that he would have been a terrible husband and they'd have made each other miserable. Michael was the living proof of that.

Eleanor straightened her shoulders. "Well, when I finally get to Vienna, you must all come to my parties. You'll make me the rage of the Congress."

They all laughed uproariously at that until Dog jumped on them to see what the fuss was about. But Eleanor wasn't really joking. She'd had an idea, which she continued to mull as Johnnie came back out of the inn, leaving Lizzie to tend to the patient.

He was vilely hung over, of course, but it seemed to Eleanor that he emerged somewhat brighter than he'd entered a quarter of an hour or so ago. Lizzie seemed to have that effect on people. She was clearly wasted combing hair and adjusting hems at this Congress.

While Johnnie took the children and the dog off for a walk, Eleanor dozed in the midday sun, remembering the past and dreaming of the future. She woke, smiling, to the laughter of children and the delicious smell of luncheon. The food here was tolerable now she'd made it clear to the landlord exactly what she expected of him.

Eleanor went up to check on the patient, pronounced him comfortable enough to be left for half an hour, and herded Lizzie downstairs for luncheon which, to please the children and cater to

Dog's partiality for human company, was served at the outside table.

Dog hurled himself at Lizzie as if he hadn't seen her for a week. "Goodness, what a filthy, muddy creature you are," she observed without rancor.

"We took him down to the river," Michael explained. "He tried to dry himself in the mud afterwards."

"I wonder if we could hose him down somehow before we take him home?" Lizzie mused.

"Wait until he's dry, then brush him like a horse," Johnnie recommended, holding a rickety chair for Eleanor at one end of the table.

Eleanor sat with a murmur of thanks and watched as he performed a similar service for Lizzie at the other end. He and the children sat on the benches while the food was brought out and placed on the table.

"We'll serve ourselves," Eleanor assured the staff, waiting until they'd gone before she leaned forward and whispered, "Go!" to the children.

They laughed with delight and fell on the food with gusto. And yet, they weren't little animals. They had manners and they knew not to be greedy, even thinking to pass certain plates to those who couldn't reach them. Eleanor was pleased.

Georgiana said, "Lizzie, can we go and see the man you shot?"

Eleanor choked.

"He's not very well," Lizzie said, not the least discomfited. "Maybe later."

"Is Papa's pistol still here?" Georgiana inquired with an innocence that made Michael grin.

Lizzie frowned at her. "No, it's back in Vienna, and you are *not* to shoot the poor man again."

"He might be sorry," Henrietta offered.

"He'd better be," Georgiana said darkly.

"Even if he isn't," Michael said, "you can't shoot a man when he's down."

Georgiana seemed ready to dispute this, until Lizzie said firmly, "Michael's right."

Georgiana shrugged and reached for more bread.

Eleanor opened her mouth to ask a few salient questions of her own about the shooting, but at the last moment, her attention was caught by Johnnie's steady gaze on Lizzie. Although no one, least of all Lizzie herself, noticed, the moment crashed over Eleanor with the force of a very large wave.

*So that's the lie of the land...*

Whoever and whatever Johnnie was, and whatever the truth of the elopement nonsense—and the more she saw of Lizzie, the less she was inclined to believe any of that—and its subsequent calling off. Johnnie appeared to be falling very hard.

---

AGENT Z'S WORLD had consisted of scary and impossible dreams for so long, that when he opened his eyes to find the beautiful girl who'd shot him, leaning over him and caressing his forehead, he compressed his lips to stop the words getting out and waiting for something worse to happen.

The English girl, Miss Gaunt, smiled. Her eyes seemed to be wet.

"Thank God," she said, straightening. Still smiling, she bathed the sweat from his forehead with cool water, then passed her arm under his shoulder to help him sip some liquid from a cup.

A very calm and unlikely dream. His shoulder ached and he was weak as a kitten.

"I'm so glad to see you better, sir," she said seriously. "And *extremely* sorry for shooting you. The gun went off by accident, for you must know I'm a truly dreadful shot and couldn't have hit you if I'd tried."

She bit her lip, as though to stop herself from babbling.

He tried to speak and croaked, instead. He coughed and tried again, remembering to speak in English. "Where am I?"

"At the Emperor Inn."

He found it difficult to think, but at least he could... "How long have I been here?"

"Two nights."

*Damn.* He made an effort to throw off the sheets and discovered he was naked beneath, apart from his drawers. He clutched the sheets upward again, but in any case, she was already pressing him back onto the pillows.

"Your fever was high," she said. "You need to rest."

"Where are my clothes?" he asked hoarsely.

She pointed to the wardrobe on the far wall. "They've been laundered and mended as best we could, though I'm afraid Johnnie was quite brutal with your shirt. He gave you one of his."

"He's here, too?"

"Oh yes. In fact, I must tell them. Don't get up, not yet..."

She ran across the room and threw open the door. "Johnnie! Mrs. Fawcett!" she called. "Our man is awake! The fever is broken!"

In the distance, he heard a clattering, as though chairs were being pushed back, and then the pounding and rushing of feet on the stairs. It all seemed too bizarre to wrestle with and he was so very tired. In fact, he thought he might be delirious again, for a lady in purple swept into the room like a ship in full sail, preceding the Russian officer who'd fought with him. Over the bag.

As the man leaned over him with an oddly proprietary interest, Z blurted, "The bag. Where is the bag?"

"Long gone," the officer said. "Don't worry about it."

He was weak and ill, or he'd never have asked so directly. "What was in it?"

"I can't tell you that," the Russian said. "But it was nothing that could ever harm your country or mine. It had nothing to do with you. That's why she didn't give you it."

He didn't understand any of this. He'd rarely felt so vulnerable in his life, but since no one was hurting him, it seemed safe enough to close his eyes and sleep.

"He'll be starving when he wakes," the older English lady said comfortably before the world faded.

With all the excitement of the patient shaking off his fever, it was growing dark before Lizzie noticed the time and sprang into action to round up the children and the dog and all their works.

"Wait, wait," Mrs. Fawcett interrupted. "Why don't you just stay here? They still have room. Probably."

"My aunt expects us," Lizzie insisted, although she'd grown so comfortable here she didn't really want to move.

Mrs. Fawcett waved that aside. "George and William will carry a note promising to return you in the morning."

"Won't they mind such a journey?" Lizzie asked doubtfully.

Mrs. Fawcett raised one cynical eyebrow. "Not if I let them stay in Vienna for the night. They may check on the apartments I rented while they're there."

"Oh, let's stay, Lizzie," Michael cajoled. "Dog loves it here."

"Besides," Mrs. Fawcett added, "I would be surprised if it weren't quite pleasant for your aunt and uncle to have less people and animals in the house for a night."

The landlord, duly summoned to the private parlor, said he had one more room that Lizzie and the girls might occupy and that he could put up a truckle bed for Michael with Johnnie, whom he referred to as "the captain".

"In that case," Mrs. Fawcett said, with no obvious idea of the havoc she was causing in the kitchen, "supper for six."

"Oh, and do you have something for the dog?" Lizzie asked. "He'll be starving."

"I doubt that," the landlord growled. "He's already had a string of sausages. But I'll see what I can do."

"Thank you," Lizzie said warmly and he retreated, mollified. "What?" she asked, catching Johnnie's gaze. A little smile played around his lips.

He shrugged. "Nothing. You just twist them all around your little finger without even trying."

"I don't know what you mean," Lizzie said loftily. "I'm going to check on our patient. Wouldn't it be nice to have a name for him?"

Since the patient was sleeping peacefully and comfortably, Lizzie didn't stay long but went with the girls to inspect their chamber, which was, in fact, the same one she'd been given the last time she'd stayed here. Like their bed in the Vienna house, this one was huge enough to accommodate all three of them comfortably. The girls pronounced it enchanting and giggled when Cartwright, Mrs. Fawcett's maid, brought them some night things lent by her mistress.

Lizzie shooed them away as Mrs. Fawcett herself sailed in.

"Will you be comfortable enough? You or one of the girls could always share with me."

"Oh no, thank you, we'll be perfectly comfortable here. The bed is huge and we've got used to sharing. Besides, we couldn't put you out any further than we already have." Lizzie thought for a moment, frowning. "Though I suppose I ought not to let Michael share with Johnnie."

"Why ever not? You all seem on remarkably good terms."

Lizzie flushed. She'd grown so comfortable; she'd forgotten that Mrs. Fawcett didn't know Johnnie's criminal background. She persisted in imagining him an officer, an illusion fostered by the staff of the inn calling him "captain", though Lizzie suspected that was their default title for any military person.

"Just thinking aloud."

"There's nothing depraved about him you haven't told me?" Mrs. Fawcett asked, fixing her with a stern eye.

"Of course not," Lizzie said lightly.

Then the idea hit her like a thunderbolt. Mrs. Fawcett, with her wealth and eccentricity and very different expectations of her servants, would make the perfect employer for Johnnie. She would keep him out of trouble and quite on the straight and narrow. And if there was a confused happiness that in this way she would continue to see him occasionally, well, he'd become a surprisingly good friend through all of this. Plus, the children liked him…

"I need to talk to Johnnie," she said breathlessly. "Excuse me…"

Discovering Johnnie in the courtyard, lounging at the wooden table in the gloom, Dog lying over his feet, she said, "Shall we take him for a walk?"

Johnnie sprang to his feet and then stood very still. In the darkness, she couldn't see where he was looking. In fact, she wasn't even sure he'd heard her, so long did he take to answer. Then his breath came out in a rush. "If you wish."

<hr />

IF ANYONE HAD told Vanya a week ago, that life could hold no greater happiness than walking in the dark beside a girl he didn't even touch, he'd have laughed in their faces.

But she made the night seem somehow magical. There was new beauty in the dark blue velvet of the sky, the moon and stars like jewels whose only purpose was to enhance Lizzie. The same magic welcomed the pain of his restraint and his knowledge that this was the one girl he could never have, the knowledge that it would all come tumbling down and bury him. But he wouldn't let her be hurt. He'd keep his distance and just bask in her presence. It felt inexplicably like joy.

They didn't speak much as they walked with Dog on the leash between them, sniffling at whatever attracted his erratic attention, although they did discuss the relief of their patient's recovery and speculate over his identity.

"Do you think he'll have us arrested?" Lizzie asked once.

"I don't know. I think it's unlikely, given your position."

"Perhaps you should disappear, though. Become someone else."

Vanya laughed, because he couldn't really cope with yet another identity. "Johnnie can disappear," he assured her. "Whenever he needs to."

"Good, because I've had a wonderful idea. I'll speak to Mrs. Fawcett this evening if only you agree to it."

"Agree to what?" he asked, turning to gaze at her in the moonlight. He wanted to touch her pale, delicate skin.

"Working for her. I can't imagine it would be like working for anyone else. She could send you all over the world, come up with tasks I couldn't even imagine. You would be a great asset to her, being so resourceful."

"I would?"

"Assuredly. What do you think?"

Johnnie wanted to laugh again. He wanted to take her in his arms and kiss her for being so wonderful. But he'd no idea what to say without hurting her feelings.

"I wouldn't make a good footman. Besides, she already has two who are clearly used to carrying out extra duties."

"I don't know… You like the outdoors, don't you? And you're so good with horses. Perhaps you could be trained to manage one of her estates? Do you think you'd be good at such work?"

Vanya swallowed. "I have a little experience in the area," he allowed humbly. "Mostly when I was younger. Before I joined the army. Of course, in Russia, we have serfs rather than free tenants, but I imagine most of the principles are the same."

"Then you'll let me speak to her?" Lizzie asked eagerly.

"No, don't do that. Not yet. There's no hurry, is there? There's nothing she can do about it while she's in Vienna, after all."

"But if she retained you, you'd have a little money…" Lizzie trailed off and glanced up at him surreptitiously.

"Which you think might prevent my indulging any further in robbery."

She gave him a half-apologetic smile that melted his heart.

"You needn't worry," he assured her. "You've helped me see the error of my ways."

She sighed, tugging the dog onward when he lingered too long at a particular tree. "Now you're laughing at me again."

"Actually, I'm not," he said ruefully.

Last night, he'd got into Sonia's carriage with her, drunk but far from incapable, and when they'd reached her apartment on the Graben, he'd merely kissed her and walked away. Because at the last moment, he'd realized where all his emotion and lust, all his ill and good humors were directed. It was Lizzie he wanted and some barely understood chivalrous instinct made him back off, even though Sonia wouldn't have understood if he'd explained it to her, and even though Lizzie would never know, nor care. Even for Colonel Vanya.

"I promise you," he said, "I won't steal anything. And even if we never meet again, I'll be a better man."

As Dog gave one of his sudden lunges, he shot out his arm and grabbed the leash to hold him before the animal dragged Lizzie off her feet. His fingers closed over hers, sweet and shocking.

He heard the sudden catch in her breath, felt the delicious warmth of her closeness. Her lips parted and he remembered only too well how they felt under his. But her eyes, gazing steadily up into his, were almost…fearful. Was she remembering, too? Or just frightened that the thief might be about to take advantage and become unforgivably amorous?

"Let me take him," he managed, extracting the lead from her.

"Thank you," she said breathlessly.

※

WHAT WAS THE matter with her? Until she'd come to Vienna, she couldn't ever remember noticing any men in particular. Yet at the Emperor's ball, where her main concern should have been the necklace, she'd let Colonel Vanya, a complete stranger whose face she'd never even seen, kiss her. And even though his behavior had been completely reprehensible and quite disrespectful, she'd caught herself harboring silly romantic dreams about encountering him again. And now, she'd actually felt a dangerous tug of attraction to Johnnie the thief! As if he was becoming confused in her mind with Vanya, just because he was Russian and roughly the same height and build…

At least she actually knew Johnnie, which was more than she could say about Vanya, but still, this just wasn't done. And certainly not by her.

Perhaps the dark and the moonlight had a peculiar effect on her. But she didn't want to think about this; it was too uncomfortable. She *liked* Johnnie, and wished him a good life and happiness. That was all.

Johnnie himself didn't seem to notice. There had been an instant over Dog's lead, when she'd been sure his gaze had flickered to her lips, but that had probably been a trick of the light and her own suddenly depraved imagination, for he behaved with perfect decorum all the way back, talking quite naturally about nothing in particular until she felt quite recovered enough to brush the moment aside.

Supper was even more fun than lunch, since much of the worry over their patient had been lifted. Johnnie was wonderfully entertaining, making the children laugh, and Mrs. Fawcett's dry wit and acerbic manner made her excellent company. After the table was cleared away, they sat by candle light and played some of the word games Lizzie had invented with the children, and the story game that involved a long, rambling tale with everyone taking a turn to add more.

They took it in turns to check periodically on their patient, who still slept like a baby. They all agreed that it wouldn't be necessary for anyone to stay in his chamber all night, but that he should be visited every couple of hours, just in case he woke and was hungry. Lizzie checked on her way to bed with the children, while Johnnie and Mrs. Fawcett, neither of whom seemed to sleep much, promised to take the next two turns, after which he could be left until dawn.

With Dog taking up position across their bedroom door, Lizzie finally fell into bed beside her sisters and was asleep before her head touched the pillow.

⁓⁓

Eleanor Fawcett had retired to her own chamber some time before she was due to check on their patient. She let the maid undress her and prepare her for bed, then wrap her in the voluminous robe in which she was most comfortable. The maid then went to sleep on the truckle bed and Eleanor read her book for an hour—difficult by the poor candle light—before visiting the injured man.

He opened his eyes as she held the candle over him.

"Who *are* you?" he asked in German.

"I'm Eleanor Fawcett. Who are you?"

"No one," he said on the ghost of a laugh.

Eleanor, pleased to see signs of humor, even if she couldn't understand it, smiled back. "Are you hungry?"

He shook his head, his eyes already closing once more. "Tired. So very tired..."

Eleanor left him to it. As she closed the door, a scraping chair on the floor below drew her attention. Curious, because she'd thought everyone had retired, including the staff, she walked down the stairs and through the darkened house to the open taproom. A single lamp burned there, showing her Johnnie in his shirt sleeves, a glass and a bottle in front of him.

He glanced up. "Mrs. Fawcett."

Although the place didn't smell very good, she went over to join him.

He got to his feet, still remembering his manners. "Brandy?"

"Well, maybe just one."

As she sat in the other chair, he went off to find her a clean glass. At least he didn't lurch.

"I'm not drunk," he said, as though he felt her disapproving stare on his back.

"Just getting there," she said dryly. "Is this a nightly habit with you?"

He seemed to consider. "Sometimes."

"Are you unhappy?"

He picked up a glass and walked back towards her. "No."

"Then I think it's time we had a talk."

"What about?" Johnnie asked, sitting down and pouring a generous measure of brandy into each glass.

Eleanor leaned forward and picked hers up, letting the aroma filter up to her nostrils. He'd found the good stuff, of course. Over her glass, she fixed him with the stare which had reduced many men from all walks of life to gibbering jellies.

"About who the devil you are, Johnnie."

# Chapter Twelve

THE MAN WHO still kept trying to think of himself only as Agent Z, closed his eyes once more. The sun shone through the window. The English girl had given him gruel which he'd managed to eat by himself and the combination of food and sunshine made him long to get up and outside. But although he needed very badly to get back to Vienna, he doubted he could get farther than the chamber door unaided.

Maybe after this little nap…

The awareness that had kept him alive through so many difficult situations, prickled his spine an instant before the door silently opened. He even felt under his pillow for a weapon, which, of course, wasn't there.

He tensed, waiting to see who crept in before he decided what to do about it.

A child slid around the door and softly closed it before turning toward the bed. For a long moment, they stared at each other. The girl couldn't have been much more than ten years old.

"Who are you?" he asked at last. Since being shot, his life seemed to have taken a very bizarre turn and he wasn't including the fevered dreams.

"I'm Georgiana Gaunt. Are you the man Lizzie shot?"

"Yes."

The girl came farther into the room. "You don't look very fearsome."

"You must forgive me. I've been ill."

Unexpectedly, the child smiled. "You might be funny," she said, clearly reserving full judgement. "I shouldn't really be in here. I just wanted to say, I thought at first it was an excellent thing that Lizzie shot you, because you'd no right to steal her bag."

"I thought I had. But maybe I was wrong."

"I suppose if you're some kind of policeman you might have had *some* right," Georgiana allowed, grudgingly. "Although I can't help feeling you should have asked. Anyhow, she was so upset that you might die, I had to pray for you to live instead."

"Thank you," Z said faintly. "I think."

"Georgi!" came a shout from farther along the corridor. "Where *are* you? Hurry up, we're about to leave."

"Goodbye," Georgiana said, spinning on her toes and rushing from the room.

"Goodbye," Agent Z murmured to the closed door.

He shut his eyes. He'd gone through all this for absolutely nothing. The girl, Lizzie, the whole family, were innocent. Of this, at least.

On the other hand, the Russian was still hanging around. It might have been amorous intrigue, although the English girl seemed too straight-laced for that. The Russian might well be up to something more sinister. If nothing else, the suspicion provided a good excuse for Z to stay exactly where he was.

---

WHEN LIZZIE RETURNED home to Vienna, she discovered the maids had been busy refurbishing her prettier day dress and one evening gown.

"What is this about?" she asked Minerva, who was sitting by her dressing table while Benson dressed her hair. "Am I to go with you to parties, after all? Aunt Lucy isn't ill, is she?"

Minerva laughed. "Of course she isn't. And no one in their right minds would make you a chaperone. You're hardly on the shelf, you know, Lizzie."

"Well, I'm three and twenty, but – ."

"It's because of your Mrs. Fawcett distinguishing you with such attention," Minerva explained. "You must know that she is considered very fashionable in London. And Papa says she knows all the right people here, too. Mama is expecting cards and invitations from her and you are bound to be included, so…" She waved one hand toward the dresses, one of which hung against the door, the other was having a lace trim sewn onto it, cleverly hiding where Dog's claws had torn the skirt last year and the darn at the shoulder.

"Well, I have to say, you're making a very god job of it," Lizzie told the gratified maids. "Thank you!"

"Did you find Mrs. Fawcett recovered?"

"I think she'll be ready to travel here in a few days," Lizzie said evasively. It was rather alarming how often she lied these days, both directly and indirectly, which provided a very poor example for the children… "I said I'd visit her again tomorrow."

"Well, I look forward to her being here," Minerva said frankly. "From a purely selfish point of view."

"Doesn't it get easier?" Lizzie asked sympathetically.

Minerva wrinkled her nose. "It's like the torture that never ends and it's been going on since London. Oh, I know I'm being so ungrateful for all the money being spent on me, but I truly wish they wouldn't. I don't need a grand match."

"No," Lizzie said thoughtfully. "Maybe you don't."

Benson finished fiddling with Minerva's hair and left, sweeping the Viennese maids with her. Lizzie sat down on the edge of the bed. "But you're eighteen, Minerva. Affections can change."

"Well, that would be true with whoever they married me to and I can't help thinking I'd have more chance with someone I actually liked to start with."

"You have a point." Another was the fact that Minerva clearly wasn't comfortable with this world or her place in it. "But you know, if you become a diplomat's wife, you will have to go to dinners and balls and host your own parties for the great and the good. Not necessarily on this scale, of course. This is quite different."

"And I would have a function. A role to play that didn't involve *selling* myself. As something I'm not."

Lizzie blinked. "Do you really think of it like that? Selling yourself?"

"All the debutantes are. Have been and will be. We're like wares being shown off to buyers, which is bad enough when you're an article people want."

"Oh, Minerva." Lizzie slid down to kneel by her cousin and take her hands. "What's brought on such a depression?"

Minerva smiled and squeezed Lizzie's fingers. "Oh, I'm not actually depressed. To be honest, if anything, I actually feel more comfortable at the balls. I danced with someone at Prince Metternich's, who persuaded me to find my own particular entertainment in it all. It makes me a little less self-conscious, although I would still be glad to have you there to laugh with. Or Gordon."

Lizzie frowned. "It seems to me that you and Gordon need to spend a bit more time together to discover if you really want each other." And Lizzie needed to see them together more to judge. Not that she was a great matchmaker, but over the years, she'd observed many couples—friends, servants and tenants—and thought she recognized pretty well when a relationship worked.

"How?" Minerva asked in despair. "I'm sure Papa has guessed my partiality and keeps him away from me."

"I don't know yet," Lizzie said, releasing her cousin's hands and rising to her feet. "But if you're not prepared to make a stand over him, Minerva, he isn't the one for you."

"What sort of a stand?" Minerva asked dubiously.

"Well, to displease your parents at least to the extent of stating what and who you want. But let's start slowly. Leave it to me. Now, I must go and see your mother and thank her for primping up these old gowns."

ALTHOUGH LIZZIE UNDERSTOOD that the repaired gowns were meant for attending Mrs. Fawcett's future gatherings in Vienna, she hadn't been forbidden to wear them earlier. So, that afternoon, she donned the green day dress, which now looked rather pretty, before Dorothée's carriage arrived for her.

"Goodness, it does look bang-up," Henrietta said admiringly from the window. Michael's vocabulary was clearly invading her own, but Lizzie let it go. "What a pity Aunt Lucy has gone out. You will give Madame Dorothée our regards? And Dog's!"

Lizzie laughed. "Of course I will. Be good while I'm gone and don't let Dog get into any trouble."

Lizzie, who had for some reason, expected a tête-à-tête with her new friend, was surprised to find several other people already present in the faded salons of the Kaunitz Palace. This made it somewhat fast of her to arrive unattended, but Dorothée met her in the hall, greeting her with unaffected delight, and they entered the main salons together.

It struck Lizzie that Dorothée was actually a little lonely. The defeated French, after all, were only just tolerated at the Congress, and no one wished to have much to do with the scheming Prince de Talleyrand, Dorothée's uncle, who, as a former revolutionary and disillusioned Bonapartist, was definitely suspect.

However, the few ladies and gentlemen present, were all very amiable, if mostly French. She was slightly stunned to meet the Duchess of Sagan herself, already one of the most famous hostesses of the Congress, an exotically beautiful woman with dark blonde hair and tragic brown eyes. Tiny and vivacious, the duchess couldn't help but draw all eyes.

Dorothée introduced her as "my sister, Wilhelmine." Which certainly explained her presence. Already married twice and, it was rumored, soon to be divorced for the second time, the duchess was a slightly scandalous figure, but so great an heiress that society forgave her.

"I didn't realize you were sisters," Lizzie said.

"Well, we haven't been much in each other's company," Dorothée said carelessly.

"She's trying to tell you there are ten years between us, without insulting me," the duchess explained. "And then, we were all married off so young that we've been scattered about Europe without much opportunity of meeting. Another reason to love Vienna. Come, tell me your thoughts of our Congress so far."

"You mean it has begun?" Lizzie asked in surprise, an answer that the duchess seemed to find very witty.

The afternoon passed most pleasantly in amusing conversation with very interesting people, though she also found time to talk alone with Dorothée, who, she discovered, was missing her own children. Indeed, she was still mourning a baby daughter who had died.

"I suppose I was so restless with grief that when my uncle suggested coming to Vienna for a change of scene, I jumped at the chance," Dorothée confided. "But now, I could wish the city were closer to Courland so that I could visit them more."

"You've done so much with your life already," Lizzie said wonderingly. "We are the same age and yet you have children, run a palace, and act as hostess for a great statesman. I feel I've been buried."

"Well, England was cut off by the war for so long," Dorothée excused. "But your mind is not buried."

Lizzie laughed. "There are those who wish it were a little more subdued," she admitted. "It rushes off on its own, but I don't have your education, either." Although augmented by her own voracious reading, her formal education was very basic compared with Dorothée, who was fluent in several languages, understood complicated mathematics and was used to discussing literature, economy, and politics with some of the greatest minds in Europe. "I'm beginning to feel I've wasted my life," she said with a rare twinge of something that might have been envy, but felt a little more like longing.

"Oh no," Dorothée said at once. "Never feel that. You have something none of us will ever have, no matter how hard we try."

"What is that?"

"Happiness," Dorothée said.

Lizzie felt her jaw begin to drop, but before she could ask for clarification, Dorothée stood up to say goodbye to her sister who was rushing off to her next engagement, with a young military man as her escort.

At the last moment, the duchess turned back and presented Lizzie with a card. "I hope you'll come," she said with a fleeting smile, and swept on toward the exit.

"Will you?" Dorothée asked eagerly.

"I'll ask my aunt," Lizzie said lightly.

"You could take them all. Wilhelmine won't mind."

Lizzie, well aware of the honor just done her, knew equally well that her aunt's rigid sense of etiquette would never permit her to "tag along" on another's invitation. Or, probably, allow Lizzie to accept one so casually given and certainly not without a proper escort. However, the new arrival of a distinguished, solitary man drew Dorothée's attention and saved Lizzie having to reply.

A few moments later, she ushered the young man over to Lizzie. "I bring you a fellow countryman. Mr. Grassic is claiming previous acquaintance, so I'll leave you to renew it."

As Dorothée flitted away, Lizzie searched the newcomer's face for inspiration as to where they'd met previously. Although she found none, it was a good face—not handsome, but interesting, and his eyes laughed.

"Forgive the exaggeration," Mr. Grassic said gravely. "In fact, we've never met, though I do claim acquaintance with two of your cousins and an aunt. I blame my poor French for the misunderstanding."

"You should speak English to Madame de Talleyrand," Lizzie advised. "Hers is better than my own. So, you know my cousins, James and Minerva?"

"James, certainly, though I don't believe I've had the honor of meeting Miss Minerva. No, the cousin I was thinking of is Cedric Gaunt. We were at school together."

"He's a very distant cousin," Lizzie observed. "I think I only met him once. Or was it twice?"

"Well, we won't speak of him," Mr. Grassic said, so smoothly that Lizzie was sure he shared her low opinion of the absent Cedric who would, had Ivan the Terrible not existed, have inherited Launceton from her father.

"Let's not," she agreed cordially. "What brings you to Vienna? The Congress?"

"Only partially, and only for curiosity. Like everyone else, I'm enjoying my new freedom to travel on the continent. In fact, I'm researching a book on early Christianity with the eventual worldly aim, I confess, of advancement within my profession."

His eyes twinkled so much that Lizzie smiled back. "You are a clergyman, sir?"

"Unlikely, I know, but there it is. I have the honor to be the Vicar of St. Anstell in Gloucestershire."

"I wish you all fortune with your book," Lizzie said cordially.

"Thank you. And you, I know, are here with Mr. And Mrs. Daniels. James told me how things were left with you." The twinkling eyes were serious for a moment. "I'm sorry for your difficulties."

"Thank you. We're lucky to have my aunt and uncle."

"Cedric, for all his faults, would not have treated you so."

"But Cedric, sadly, was not my father's heir."

"Alas," Mr. Grassic agreed. "And have you met the new baron yet?"

"No, nor want to," Lizzie said frankly. "He's in Russia still, I believe."

"Oh? I had heard a rumor he was in Vienna with the rest of the world."

"Oh dear, I hope not, for I have the gravest fear my sister will shoot him!" Especially now that Lizzie had given her the idea.

"Rumors are rarely true," Mr. Grassic observed. "And in London, one Russian is much like another."

This may well have been the case, but over dinner that evening, just to be sure, Lizzie made a point of asking her uncle if he'd seen or heard anything of the new baron.

Uncle Daniels snorted. "I had an insolent letter from his man of business questioning the inventory of Launceton Hall. Our solicitor is dealing with it."

"Then he is still in Russia and nowhere near Vienna?"

"Or in England, I suppose. Why the sudden anxiety?" Mr. Daniels seemed inclined to be amused. "I would certainly have heard if he were here."

"Of course you would," Lizzie agreed and returned to her soup.

In truth, she wasn't quite sure why the question niggled at her, but she really didn't want to meet or even see the man who now owned Launceton, and held so much power over the people she'd grown up among.

However, she was quickly distracted by James' unusually gloomy countenance. He barely contributed at all to the dinner conversation and there were lines of anxiety around his mouth that she couldn't recall ever seeing there before. So, when everyone went to prepare for the evening's outing to the Castlereaghs' soiree, she followed James as far as his bedroom door, calling his name.

"What?" he asked, without much interest.

"I just wondered what was wrong. You seem very low."

His hand slid off the door handle. "I am, but there's nothing anyone can do about it."

"Louise?" she guessed.

"How did you know?"

"I guessed. What happened?"

James heaved a sigh. "I don't know. One evening she's all grace and affection and the next she looks straight through me with no more than a distant smile."

"Well, she *is* married, James. I expect your devotion was making her life difficult."

"Maybe. But Fischer had always seemed pleased when his wife was admired, flattered even. He never objected to my being alone with her."

"Well, you must take your congé like a man," Lizzie said, giving him an encouraging nudge with her elbow, "and not let the world see how cast down you are."

"Of course," he said gloomily. His fingers twisted on the handle, played over the latch, but didn't open it.

"What else?" Lizzie asked.

"I owe him money. Fischer. I lost a lot at cards. And not just Fischer. I don't know how I'm going to pay. I've spun them some yarn about waiting a day or so for my allowance to reach the bank in Vienna, but the truth is, I'll never be able to pay. Even if I tell Papa, he doesn't have that kind of money. He can't even sell the wretched Launceton necklace with your Ivan the Terrible breathing down his neck. I'm ruined, Lizzie."

"Oh no, James, I'm sure that's not true. There's always a way out…" Although right now, she couldn't think what it was. There didn't even seem any point in telling him off, since he was already miserable over it. "The first thing you have to do is stop playing cards altogether," she said firmly.

"I have. I thought I could solve it all by just one decent win, only that never happened. I just got in deeper and deeper."

"Let me think about it," Lizzie advised.

A faint smile lit up the gloom of his face. "You're a great gun, Lizzie. But there's nothing you can do about this one."

"Wait and see," she said and turned back to her own room to help Minerva.

# Chapter Thirteen

"Johnnie," she said, urgently, the next day as she bearded him in the inn stable. In his shirt sleeves, he was brushing down the big, black stallion and seemed to be murmuring softly to it in Russian. Lizzie found that rather touching and wished she hadn't interrupted, but he turned to her at once and came to the open stall door.

"What's wrong?" he asked.

"Are you living here?" she countered.

"No, but the horse likes it."

"Johnnie!"

"I just rode over."

"We didn't see you on the road from Vienna."

"I didn't come from Vienna."

"I'm not prying," she assured him. "I just wanted to ask you…since my aunt still has a necklace and as your man went away to Bohemia, do you think we could steal it and sell it again?"

Johnnie eyed her with bemused fascination. "Because it worked out so well for us the last time?"

Lizzie laughed. "Well, it did. Up until the last moment. We got the money and we didn't get caught."

"Yet. Need I remind you there's a policeman in the house, whom you shot?"

"No, you needn't, and Mrs. Fawcett says he's doing much better. I'm about to go up and visit him."

"To ask him to look the other way when you—we—commit your

next crime?"

"Do you think he would?" Lizzie asked with mock seriousness.

"Never."

"He does seem very…serious about his work."

Johnnie returned to brushing the horse. "Are *you* serious?"

"About stealing the necklace again?" Lizzie reached up and stroked the velvet nose of the stallion. He was a magnificent animal. "Not really. I think I want it removed from my 'possible' list, so that I can come up with something else. Besides, I'm reluctant to involve you in any more thefts when I've been lecturing you about mending your ways."

"The inconsistency wasn't lost on me. What do you want money for this time? Michael's cavalry regiment?"

"Oh no, he and Henrietta have quite decided between them that her rich husband will take care of that. No, my cousin, James, is in a bit of a pickle. So much so that I did wonder if I shouldn't give him *our* money, only I do want it for the children…"

"You should let your cousin find his way out of his own scrapes. That's how you learn not to get into them." He laughed suddenly. "Listen to me, preaching morality."

"Hardly, and you're right of course. Only James' scrapes reflect badly on my uncle and, therefore, on British interests in Vienna. How did you come by such a beautiful horse?"

There was a pause, then: "Don't ask," Johnnie said lightly. He moved around to the stall door and the horse nuzzled his neck. Johnnie slipped him some sugar. "I'll think about James if you leave off hiring another thief for the time being."

"Done," Lizzie agreed. With an effort, she dragged her fascinated gaze away from man and horse and moved back out of the stall. For some reason, she'd been holding her breath and let it out now in a rush.

Johnnie followed her, closing the stall door. "Come then," he said, grabbing his old coat off a peg on the wall. "Let's go and visit our policeman."

However, when they got to their patient's bed chamber, they found he already had visitors. The children had apparently discovered Mrs. Fawcett there, and Georgiana and Michael were interrogating him about his wound, while Dog dragged Henrietta around the room, sniffing at everything.

"Oh dear," Lizzie said. "It's not enough that I shoot you; I bring my entire family to stay with you, too."

Although her victim, who called himself Herr Schmidt without much conviction, was still looking pale, he seemed much better. Mrs. Fawcett said she only managed to keep him in bed with the promise that he could get up for tea this afternoon, provided he allowed her footmen to carry him downstairs.

Herr Schmidt seemed baffled by such attention. Looking directly at Lizzie, he said in English, "I know you didn't mean to shoot me. I know you weren't knowingly involved in any plots against my government. I'm not going to arrest you for my own misjudgements."

Lizzie blinked and then smiled.

"Huzzah!" Michael exclaimed. "Would you care for a game of cards, sir?"

Johnnie laughed. "Did you think leniency would get you off the hook, Herr *Schmidt*?"

The policeman glared at him. "I thought it might, *Herr Johnnie*."

Lizzie, looking around for the cards, brought her gaze flying back to Herr Schmidt's face. Although everyone knew Johnnie was an unlikely name for a Russian, she didn't care for the hint of threat in the policeman's mockery.

"Johnnie did no more wrong than I did," she pointed out anxiously. "You're not going to arrest him either, are you? You'd have died without him."

"I'm aware of it," Herr Schmidt said, his gaze still locked to Johnnie's. "And no, I could hardly arrest him for what you did."

"He just doesn't like Russians," Johnnie mocked. "We're not in favor any more, now that our army has served its purpose and defeated Napoleon."

"Are you trying to rile me?" the policeman asked without noticeable heat. If anything, he appeared to be amused, although it was hard to tell from that expressionless face.

Johnnie laughed.

"We weren't in favor of Russians either," Michael said, "on account of having a vile Russian cousin, but Johnnie's different. He's a great gun. Are we all playing?"

⚜

WITH HERR SCHMIDT recovering his health, Lizzie felt able to turn her mind to other problems, namely those of her cousins. Minerva's budding romance and James' debts both required attention.

Once Mrs. Fawcett took up residence in her Vienna establishment, Minerva could meet unexceptionably with Mr. Corner there. James' difficulties would require rather greater ingenuity.

She began to toy with the idea of visiting the Fischers, wild notions of threatening the husband or begging the intercession of the wife tempted her, though she didn't hold out much hope of success from either ploy. Besides which, gentlemen's gambling debts were hemmed in by such ridiculous rules. *Debts of honor*, she thought disparagingly. What was remotely honorable about a stupid game? Let alone about wagering money you didn't have, or ruining a man's family just to obtain money you didn't need, won at said stupid game? Men really were *childish* at times.

In the meantime, she took advantage of any opportunity to observe Minerva and Mr. Corner together. One such chance arose when Aunt Lucy had claimed the rare attendance of her husband to go shopping on her own account, for once, rather than on Minerva's. Thus, when Mr. Corner arrived with a large sheaf of papers, there was no one else to receive it from him.

While Minerva managed to blush and brighten at the same time, and the children tried to prevent Dog from knocking Mr. Corner over—he took it in good part, which was definitely in his favor—Lizzie received the papers and laid them aside for her uncle. She presented

Mr. Corner with a pen to write a note to go with them.

While he did so, Lizzie said, "You are the solution to our problem, Mr. Corner!"

"I am?" he said, glancing up with raised brow, as if not quite sure whether to be alarmed or gratified.

"Minerva and I were wishing to take a walk around to my friend's house," Lizzie said blatantly. In fact, although it had been Lizzie's wish to go to Dorothée's, she'd mentioned no such thing to her cousin until now.

Minerva's eyes widened.

"Only James is out," Lizzie proceeded, "and we have no escort. Do you, perchance, have an hour to spare us, Mr. Corner?"

Mr. Corner straightened, laying down his pen. His gaze drifted to Minerva and he smiled. "Why yes, it would be my privilege."

"Excellent," Lizzie said, seizing Minerva by the hand. "Then give us two minutes to gather our things..."

Leaving the children to entertain the happy Mr. Corner, Lizzie dragged Minerva upstairs to their bedroom. In fact, Minerva had no need to do more than choose her bonnet and pelisse, though Lizzie had to change from her old, darned dress into the refurbished one.

"What friend?" Minerva demanded, fastening the gown for her. "Did you make her up? Or is Mrs. Fawcett finally in Vienna?"

"No, but I think she might come tomorrow. Or the next day. And I mean my friend Dorothée. I wasn't going to go today, but when Mr. Corner appeared, it struck me we could all go with propriety. You and Mr. Corner may converse without the—ah... distractions of Dog and the curiosity of the children."

"Won't your Dorothée object?"

"Oh no. She and, indeed her sister, told me you are all welcome."

However, as they turned into Josefstrasse, it seemed Dorothée had changed her mind, for a carriage pulled up beside them and Dorothée herself, stuck her head out of the window.

"Lizzie!" she exclaimed. "Are you on your way to visit me?"

"Well I was. We were—"

"I changed my mind. I'm going to my sister's, instead." She pushed open the carriage door and kicked down the step. "Come with me."

Lizzie blinked. "I haven't introduced my cousin, Miss Daniels. And Mr. Corner who's on my uncle's staff…"

Dorothée bestowed a blinding smile on them both impartially. "Of course, you must come, too. My sister will be as enchanted as I and, as you see, there's plenty of room."

"I don't think we should intrude on your sister's party—" Lizzie began, since it was not part of her plan to create a scandal around her cousin.

"Oh, it isn't a party," Dorothée said carelessly. "I doubt there will be anyone else there, but Wilhelmine is always good fun."

Lizzie only hesitated a moment, for although the famous Duchess of Sagan was a rather more public figure than she would have chosen to host her cousin's assignation, it could surely be quite unexceptionable in the afternoon.

Mr. Corner, certainly, appeared to be all in favor, for he handed Minerva into the carriage without protest and they all settled in for the short drive to the Palm Palace. On the way, Dorothée regaled them with amusing anecdotes of her sister's rivalry with her fellow tenant, Princess Bagration, which was when Minerva at least began to realize who Dorothée's sister actually was.

"Lizzie," she hissed, as they dismounted from the carriage. "This will be as bad as the rest." Meaning, presumably, all the other large social gatherings she was dragged to.

"Nonsense," Lizzie replied bracingly. "No one will pay any attention to anyone save the Duchess, unless it's to Dorothée, so you may just relax and enjoy the conversation." Although, following Dorothée up the elegant staircase to the duchess' salons, she hoped devoutly it was true.

Without any formality, Dorothée introduced them as her English friends and the duchess graciously remembered Lizzie. Although even more dazzling in her own territory, there was nothing but civil warmth in her welcome, and since there appeared to be just a few other people present, Minerva relaxed visibly.

"We're having tea and cakes," the duchess said, waving a hand to a table at one end of the room. Lizzie's view was partially blocked by two men in front of it, deep in conversation, with their backs to her. "You must try them all, because each is decorated with the emblem of a Congress country. Even France, because, although they've been defeated, everyone knows they make the best cakes."

Lizzie laughed, noticing as she walked with the duchess that Minerva and Mr. Corner were already at the table with Dorothée, pointing out various iced emblems to each other.

The duchess' gaze swept across the table. "Vanya, what did you do with the Russian cake?"

At the sound of the name, Lizzie's stomach performed an annoying somersault and she tried not to hold her breath as she followed the duchess' gaze towards the window. However, her search never got that far. The two men by the side of the table both turned at the duchess' accusatory question and as Lizzie's gaze passed over them in pursuit of the elusive Colonel Vanya, it caught, instead, on the taller, darker man next to the table.

He wore a gorgeous green and gold uniform somewhat casually and a lock of unruly black hair fell across his handsome face. With laughter just dying in his rather hard eyes and on his sculpted lips, he appeared perfectly comfortable among his aristocratic companions. Nevertheless, he was, undeniably, Johnnie.

# Chapter Fourteen

H IS CARELESSLY TIED cravat would have appalled James; and yet he looked every inch a gentleman.

For an instant, Lizzie's own shock seemed to be mirrored in his eyes, fixed unblinkingly on her face. Confused explanations tumbled through her brain: that their theft had been discovered and this was somehow part of her punishment; that Jonnie was in the midst of some fresh mischief that she needed to save her kind hostess from; that Johnnie wasn't a thief and never had been, whatever she'd seen him do in the theatre that night; that he was something much worse, or much better…

Another faint, almost apologetic smile touched his lips and vanished as he dragged his gaze from her face to the duchess, and spoke in French. "It's my belief Boris pocketed the whole Russian cake to give to the tsar."

"Go to the devil," said another voice close by, presumably Boris'.

Numbly, Lizzie registered that he knew these people, that they knew him, in whatever capacity. And then the duchess was inviting her to try the French cake and inquiring of Minerva what she thought of the Bavarian one. Like an automaton, Lizzie allowed herself to be herded away to a little circle of sofas and chairs around a low table. Before she sat, she couldn't help glancing over her shoulder once more.

He was still watching her, although as soon as she met his gaze, he shifted his own, significantly, to another door at the end of the salon.

Lizzie looked hastily away and sat, murmuring thanks for the tea, and began to eat her cake with the elegant little fork.

"Miss Gaunt, what a pleasant surprise," someone greeted her in English. It spoke volumes for her distraction, that although she knew she'd met him, she couldn't, for a moment, think who he was.

"Mr. Grassic," she remembered at last. "How do you do?" Greetings over, she introduced him to Minerva and Mr. Corner, who seemed to be getting along famously on their own.

"So which patriotic cake has the honor of your plate?" Mr. Grassic asked humorously.

"The French, since we're all allies now. And since I'm assured French cakes are always the best."

"The Viennese might dispute it." Mr. Grassic waved one hand to an abandoned plate on the occasional table, presumably his own.

"Austria is next on my list, although if I try them all, I'll need six stout footmen to carry me home."

Only when Mr. Grassic's eyes lit with surprised laughter did she realize this was hardly a ladylike thing to say. However, she liked the laughter that lightened his rather secretive face. Perhaps that was the reason she didn't give him the set-down she should when he inquired about the identity of Mr. Corner.

"He's on my uncle's staff," she said repressively. "Almost one of the family and *excessively* respectable."

"I'm relieved to hear it," Mr. Grassic assured her. With a quick glance around them—in fact, for the moment, there was no one else close by—he lowered his voice further. "I was hoping your cousins weren't *both* running wild."

Lizzie, who'd used the moment to try to rediscover Johnnie, brought her frowning gaze back to Mr. Grassic. "What do you mean?"

"Just that I hear disturbing stories of the company James has been keeping and the debts he has incurred along the way."

Again, it might have been distraction that prevented the set-down hovering on the tip of her tongue. Or perhaps it was the fact that he was a clergyman and that there was something very likeable about his worldly understanding. At any rate, she swallowed her sharp words, saying instead, "My cousin will find his own way. Don't all young men learn from their mistakes?"

"Preferably before they fall flat on their faces," Mr. Grassic said wryly. "Fischer's is no place for him."

"He knows it," Lizzie said, suddenly uncomfortable discussing the issue which she thought of as private between herself and James. And Johnnie, she realized. "Excuse me," she added as Dorothée caught her eye. Although it was hardly a summons, she used it as an excuse to stand up and move across the room to her friend.

All the time she listened to, and even conversed on, various subjects from the importance or otherwise of having more than the strongest powers represented at the Congress, to the best dressmakers in Vienna, she knew she needed to speak to Johnnie and find out what in the world he was doing here. After the first shock of over-speculation, she couldn't begin to imagine.

Eventually, she excused herself from Dorothée's little group, too, and wandered across the room, pausing to exchange greetings with the few people she already knew, mostly from Dorothée's "at home". Drifting through the door Johnnie had appeared to indicate into the next salon, she found it was empty, but, curious now, she walked through the elegant apartment and out the door at the far end, which led to a hallway. On the other side of the hall, Johnnie himself leaned in a doorway.

Surprise—surely surprise—made her heart thud. He straightened at the sight of her and retreated into the room. With a quick glance around her, she followed him and closed the door.

"Johnnie, what in the world...?" she began urgently, only to break off when he took her hand and swung her unexpectedly into his arms. Furiously, she seized his lapels. "Are you *drunk*?"

"No," he groaned. He swooped and kissed her mouth with stunning thoroughness.

Her hand, already raised to box his ears, stilled at the sheer, hot hunger of his lips which should have frightened her and yet didn't; and then, slowly, she let her wrist and then her palm drop to his braided shoulder. Along with the butterflies in her stomach and the delicious weakness of her limbs, recognition began to dawn. At last. Unforgivably late.

"Vanya," she whispered against his lips, which finally loosened as he smiled.

"There. I told you it would work. And it should explain everything."

She stared at him, trying desperately to gather her wits from the rather delightful daze she'd been sinking into.

"*Explain* everything?" she said indignantly. "It makes everything even *less* comprehensible! Which are you really? Johnnie or Vanya?"

"Both. Johnnie is a sort of a rough translation of Vanya."

"But....but the tsar knew you. You *are* Colonel Vanya! In which case—oh." She broke off as understanding swept over her like a cold bath.

Whatever she'd seen him do in the theatre that first night, he wasn't a thief. He wasn't a one-time sergeant but a current officer of the Russian army. And with the collapse of what had come to be such a large part of her world, came the humiliating understanding of her own idiocy. She'd been blind, unable to see beyond the boundaries of supposed class. And he'd been making a fool of her the whole time.

She slipped out of his arms. He didn't try to stop her.

"Why?" she said, in a small, hard voice.

His hands fell to his sides, but his gaze never released her. "Because you enchant me."

She turned away from him because she wanted too much for that to be true. And she could no longer trust him.

He said, "You needed a thief and when you didn't recognize me with my mask on, I couldn't help trying to make you notice me."

"I should have known," she said, frowning at her shoes. "All the warnings were there that you were neither a thief nor a common soldier. I suppose you were laughing at me."

There was a pause, which she didn't expect to hurt quite so much.

Then he said, "I think I meant to. But I ended up laughing *with* you. All of you."

"I don't believe you," she said desolately. She didn't even know what hurt most. That the encounter with Vanya wasn't the spontaneous moment of romantic attraction that she'd been imagining, or that Johnnie, whom she'd grown so stupidly to trust, had been lying to her the whole time.

Wishing only to be far away from his scrutiny, she moved blindly toward the door. His fingers, rough and warm, closed around her wrist, staying her. The last thing she wanted to do, especially when her skin seemed to glow under his touch, was look at him. But she forced herself, because she'd show him no more weakness.

In truth, she didn't know if she glared or pled, if anger or misery stared out of her face. But after an instant, his hard eyes oddly stricken, his hand fell away.

Without a word, she walked out of the room, unsure even where she was going. Fortunately, she retained enough sense not simply to keep walking until she left the Palm Palace, abandoning her cousin. Instead, she found herself back in the main salon, where she couldn't possibly cry.

Fixing a social smile to her face, she wandered up to the table full of cakes which was at least temporarily bereft of patrons. At least she could pretend to gaze at them as if contemplating her next choice while trying to pull herself back together. It wasn't the end of the world. It wasn't.

"How about a slice of Austrian cake?" said the man suddenly beside her. She couldn't think how she'd failed to recognize that deep, teasing voice, so obvious now as belonging to both Johnnie and Colonel Vanya. He must have followed her across the hall and back into the main reception room, for he stood very still beside her now, overwhelming her, his gaze burning in to her averted face. "In honor of our friend, Herr Schmidt," he suggested.

She gasped, spinning to face him in outrage—or was it laughter? In any case, her suddenness attracted a few curious glances. If she wasn't careful, she'd start scandalous rumors, on top of everything else.

"You really are shameless, aren't you?" she said, struggling to keep her voice light.

"No, I'm thoroughly ashamed," he said quietly. "I should have told you before this."

She realized she was staring at his deft hand, cutting a slice of the iced cake emblazoned with eagles. "Then why didn't you?"

"I suppose I liked that you looked—differently—on Colonel Vanya."

"You should have told me before the ball, when I first met you outside the theatre, that I'd got it hopelessly wrong!"

"I know. But I was drunk and then I didn't want to explain the sordid story of Madame Fischer's necklace. I still don't want you to think about that."

"And besides, I expect it was all very amusing." She couldn't quite keep the indignation from her voice, especially when a soft laugh broke from him.

"Oh, it was," he agreed. "Right up until you shot Herr Schmidt and, even then, if I'm honest. I do have fun with you, Lizzie Gaunt."

She blinked at the slice of cake which appeared in front of her. Her hand took the plate without her conscious volition.

He said, "I imagined we had fun together."

She glanced up at him, the rare urge to hurt warring with her belief that there was no way she *could* hurt him, short of slapping him. Or shooting him.

She didn't expect his eyes to be so serious, so…anxious. Stupidly, it gave her hope, although of what, she couldn't even begin to guess.

He said intensely, "Lizzie, there's more."

"Oh no." Right now, she couldn't take more.

She spun away from him and came face to face with Mr. Grassic.

"Ah, the Austrian, I perceive," the clergyman said blandly. "Come and sit over here and tell me your verdict."

Grateful for any reason to walk away from Vanya—or Johnnie—just then, she went with him.

"Is that man bothering you?" Mr. Grassic asked with rather more seriousness than she had yet heard from him, as he settled her on a quiet sofa and joined her there.

"Colonel Vanya? Of course not," she said hastily. "We had a disagreement over cake."

"Cake," Mr. Grassic repeated. He seemed to be gazing at her very closely, uncomfortably so. "You are aware he has a most unsavory reputation? Brawling, dueling, gambling. And—forgive me—women."

"His reputation is nothing to me," she assured him.

She didn't care about the first three, and the last...well, she'd always known it. It had been there in his eyes the first time she'd met him in the carriage and he'd gazed at her so warmly through the darkness. And in his practiced flirting at the Emperor's ball. She could recognize that now for what it was. She just wished it didn't hurt. Nothing had ever hurt like this. What in the world was the matter with her?

"But of course it is." Mr. Grassic was frowning at her. "It has to be... Good God, you don't know who he is, do you?"

"Oh, I do. Colonel Vanya." A quick glance showed him still alone by the table, still watching her. She didn't know if that made her indignant or furiously happy.

Mr. Grassic leaned forward, blocking her view. "Vanya is not a surname in Russia," he said urgently. "It's a diminutive of the Christian name Ivan."

Something stirred in her brain and in her stomach. Ivan was the Russian form of John. Vanya then would be like Johnnie, just as he'd said. But the clergyman wouldn't stop talking.

"The rumor here is," Mr. Grassic said relentlessly, "that the colonel has recently come into an English inheritance."

Ivan the Terrible. "No," she said aloud. But the blood was singing in her ears. She had to fight down the dizziness. None of this could be true.

"Perhaps," Mr. Grassic said pityingly, "you would allow me to escort you home?"

He stood, holding out his hand to her. Ignoring it, she raised her eyes to Vanya, gazing at her—glowering at her even—from the cake table. *There's more*, he'd said.

She couldn't bear it.

"Thank you," she managed to say to Mr. Grassic, standing and handing him her untouched slice of cake. "My cousin and I have Mr. Corner's escort. And it's time we returned home."

---

IT AMUSED MR. Grassic that in Vienna great business as well as small seemed to be conducted mainly at glittering social events where nothing should have mattered but the cut of a coat or the color of a gown, and nothing more important than the latest scandalous *on-dits* were discussed. Here, his complicated life was made much easier by everyone with whom he needed to do business, great and small, thoughtfully gathering together of an evening under one roof.

On this particular evening, the roof was Lord Castlereagh's, and everyone who was anyone in Europe attended, including the tsar and several of his dashing officers, not least the smirking Major Blonsky and the glowering Colonel Savarin who, everyone said, was spoiling for a fight. The Austrian Emperor Francis was there with the Austrian Empress, and Prince Metternich, of course. Sir Charles Stewart arrived drunk as usual; and, as Grassic had hoped, Mr. Jeremy Daniels and his family.

He looked around in vain for Miss Gaunt, but in the end, had to make do with Miss Daniels, who danced with him under the jealous eye of young Mr. Corner and the approving gaze of her mama. As he'd hoped, word about his prospects and his private wealth had got around and Miss Daniels could yet be useful to him. Not that he had any intention of marrying where there was no money. Not for anyone less than the oddly dazzling Miss Gaunt, at any rate. Which provided, he acknowledged, yet another reason to get rid of the troublesome Colonel Savarin.

However, in the continuing absence of Agent Z, his first business of the evening was with Mr. James Daniels, whom he discovered not at the card tables, for once, but dancing dutiful attendance upon his mother and sister.

"Hello, Daniels," he greeted him in friendly spirit. "Eschewing the cards for tonight?"

"Forever," James said gloomily. "I only ever lose."

"It is a fool's game," Grassic agreed. "You should rejoice at being free of it."

"I would, only…" He cast a glance over at his family, then shuffled a few paces away from them.

Grassic followed. "Only what?"

"Only I'm in rather deep already. I say, old fellow, I hate to ask a friend, but you couldn't lend me a couple of thousand, could you?"

"I couldn't," Grassic said apologetically. "I don't have that kind of money. Contrary to popular rumor. Who knows where such stories start?"

"Sorry I asked." James, clearly mortified, blushed furiously.

"Don't be," Grassic said kindly. "I would help if I could. It's just—" He broke off as if a bright idea had just occurred to him. "Of course. Look, I don't have nearly enough for your needs, but I can put you in the way of earning some."

"A clerk's salary won't really cut it, Grassic, but thanks for the thought."

Grassic moved closer. "I'm not talking about clerking. I'm talking about serious money. It's there to be earned in Vienna right now and better it goes to you than to someone a lot less worthy."

James stared at him. "What do you mean?"

"I mean people pay for information to be laid neatly before them."

James' jaw dropped. "Spying?" he uttered with loathing.

Grassic laughed. "Hardly. We'll leave that to Metternich, shall we? No, the information I mean is freely available, just not all in one place. You'd be breaking no one's trust, no one's laws or your own honor. But you could earn…what? Somewhere between five hundred and a thousand pounds, just by setting down the gist of the secret discussions between the British and the French. With proof, of course. And there's more, much more that a young man in your position could do for the smooth running of the Congress."

✦

VANYA DIDN'T EVEN know what he was doing at the Castlereaghs' ball. He'd known Lizzie wouldn't be there and, yet, part of him had hoped. After all, she shouldn't have been at the Duchess of Sagan's either but there she'd been.

But, of course, she wasn't at the ball. Although he did spot her aunt and cousins, and that smarmy clergyman whose face he wanted to punch almost as much as he wanted to punch Blonsky. Although if they were all here, then Lizzie was at home. Alone. Apart from her brother and sisters and the infamous dog.

Without a word to anyone, he left the ballroom and strode out of the house. Ten minutes later, he knocked on the door of number twenty-five Skodegasse, and asked for Miss Gaunt.

"Miss Gaunt isn't here," said the maid with such surprise, that he knew it was true.

"Then where is she?" he demanded, peering past her. He'd fully expected at least one of the children and the dog to be tumbling downstairs to greet him by now.

"There was a note from the English lady and they all left," the maid said, unable to keep a hint of indignation, or perhaps worry, from her face.

"English lady? Mrs. Fawcett?" Vanya demanded.

He never heard the maid's reply. Her nod was enough to set him running for the nearby stable where he kept his horse.

✦

THERE HAD, INDEED, been a note from Mrs. Fawcett. A somewhat cryptic note merely demanding Lizzie's instant presence. Which she was glad to give. She would have been glad to do anything that didn't involve sitting around the house and thinking. About whether to forgive Johnnie for being Vanya and about whether or not Mr. Grassic was right when he accused them both of being Cousin Ivan the Terrible.

Since she was unsure of Mrs. Fawcett's crisis and whether or not it would be necessary to stay the night at the inn, she rounded up the children and Dog and took them with her in the kindly supplied carriage. A scribbled note to Aunt Lucy explained where she had gone.

"I do hope Mrs. Fawcett hasn't *truly* been taken ill," she said worriedly as the carriage bowled over the cobbles on its way out of the city.

"Perhaps Herr Schmidt is worse," Henrietta suggested.

"Oh dear, I hope not!" Lizzie exclaimed. "I wish she'd just explained and then we wouldn't need to be worrying."

"Perhaps we'd have worried more if we knew," Michael said helpfully.

"Oh *dear*," Lizzie said again, biting her lip.

However, when they reached the inn, hurrying inside in a chaotic, anxious huddle, they discovered Mrs. Fawcett playing cards with Herr Schmidt in the private parlor, quite oblivious to all the drunken noise from the taproom.

Mrs. Fawcett glanced up and smiled, as if they'd just come from upstairs. "Good evening. What are you all doing here?"

"We got your message," Lizzie said, inclined to indignation at the clear health of Mrs. Fawcett and the almost as clear recovery of Herr Schmidt.

Mrs. Fawcett's attention returned to her cards. "What message?" she asked vaguely.

Inexplicable unease began to claw at Lizzie's stomach. "Where is Johnnie?" she asked.

"Isn't he with you?" Mrs. Fawcett asked.

# Chapter Fifteen

THAT EVENING, MISHA, Vanya's servant, had sustained a visit from the one being in the world he feared. His master's mother.

"Where is he?" she demanded, sailing into the attic the instant Misha opened the door. In a gorgeous evening gown of midnight blue silk, with jewels at her throat and ears, and in her elaborately dressed hair, Countess Savarina was clearly on her way to a party, even though she couldn't have been in Vienna for longer than an hour or two. He couldn't believe that any of her servants wouldn't have warned him, or Vanya himself, had it been any longer.

Misha could do no more than blanch and get out of her way. "I couldn't say, Madame."

"Why not, Misha? I've never known you to be anything other than fully cognizant of where my son spends his evenings."

"He had several invitations, Madame. I don't know where he went first."

Countess Savarina gazed around her with distaste, ran one gloved finger along the mantel shelf, checking it for dust. Finding none, she sniffed. "Well? Hazard a guess, Misha."

"Lady Castlereagh's ball," Misha said, hoping his master wouldn't kill him for the betrayal. Surely he would understand…?

The countess was flicking through the cards of invitation propped up against the clock. She sniffed at the Duchess of Sagan's. And at Princess Bagration's. Then she found the note from Mrs. Fawcett, and since it wasn't sealed, she simply read it.

"Who is Mrs. Fawcett? Vanya's latest paramour?"

Misha choked. "God, no! She just sort of...looks after the young lady." As soon as the words left his lips, he'd have given anything to take them back. Not for the first time, he wished he didn't babble in front of the countess. Or at least not when he was trying to hide things from the countess.

"What young lady?" the countess inquired sweetly.

"I couldn't say, Madame."

"Oh, Misha, of course you can. And will. Is she that bad?"

"Oh no, Madame, she's no lightskirt! Never seen him chase a girl, a *lady* like this before..." Too late, he realized he'd said the wrong thing again.

The countess' eyes narrowed, so that they appeared to be spitting through slits. "You mean this female wishes to *marry* my son?"

"Oh no, I'm sure *that* never enters her head," Misha said in relief. After all, Miss Lizzie thought the colonel was a hired thief.

"You are both imbeciles," the countess said with contempt.

"Yes, Madame," Misha said meekly.

"So, my son is with this Mrs. Fawcett right now?"

"No, Madame," Misha replied with some relief that he could tell the truth on that score. "He hasn't read the message yet. It arrived for him after he left for the evening."

"Good." The countess opened her fingers, letting the note flutter to the floor while she walked across the room to the door. "Where will I find Lady Castlereagh's establishment?"

※

"WHY WOULD YOU expect Johnnie to have come with me?" Lizzie asked suddenly.

The question came suddenly into her head more than an hour after their arrival, since Dog had broken into the taproom almost immediately and had to be extracted from the local drinkers who'd found him highly entertaining and hadn't wanted to part from him. After which, there had been refreshments and health questions and

Lizzie had been so relieved to find Mrs. Fawcett in perfect health and Herr Schmidt so far *un*-relapsed as to be downstairs fully dressed, dining and playing cards, that she'd allowed herself to be distracted.

Despite having dined already, the children consumed the leftovers from the meal. Lizzie didn't even try to prevent this now, since she'd long accepted that Mrs. Fawcett insisted on over-ordering in both quantity and variety, and even with a companion, had no hope of ever finishing any meal. She had absolutely no concept of economy, which was fine, since she appeared to have the means to indulge such extravagance.

It was only after the meal had been cleared away and the children were demonstrating to Herr Schmidt how high Dog could jump to catch his ball, that the oddity of Mrs. Fawcett's words came back to Lizzie. "Why would you expect Johnnie to have come with me?"

"I thought you might have met on the road from Vienna," Mrs. Fawcett said vaguely.

Lizzie frowned. Mrs. Fawcett was never vague about arrangements. She'd summoned Lizzie in writing. "No, you didn't," she said frankly. "Or at least not with good reason. Either it wasn't you who wrote to me—and it did look like your handwriting—or Johnnie should have been with us. Why should Johnnie have been with us?"

"Oh drat you, girl, can't an old lady indulge in a little intrigue? It's not as if *you* haven't."

Lizzie's eyes widened. "What on earth do you mean, ma'am?"

"I mean you tried to pull the wool over my eyes. You never eloped with Johnnie or anyone else in your life. It isn't in your character. In fact, it isn't even in his. You let me think he was an officer while you thought he was a thief."

Lizzie had the grace to flush. "Forgive me. It wasn't really my secret to tell. And in any case, we had to account for us being here together and I doubted you'd believe I would elope with a thief who swept up leaves in our back garden."

"Did he?" Briefly distracted, Mrs. Fawcett looked willing to be entertained by the story. Dog, leaping to catch the ball that had bounced off the ceiling, landed on his back amidst a hail of laughter from the children and bounced back up, panting. Mrs. Fawcett shook herself visibly and frowned. "However, I could see at once he was a gentleman." Her sharp gaze lifted to Lizzie's. "Why couldn't you?"

Lizzie looked away. "I don't know. I suppose I saw what I wanted to see and ignored everything that didn't fit. People often do. I just didn't realize I was one of them."

"And yet my revelation doesn't appear to surprise you."

"I met him at the Duchess of Sagan's and saw at once how blind, how idiotic I'd been. I, of all people, should know that clothes don't make the man."

"Well, in mitigation, I'm sure he played to your assumptions."

Lizzie smiled unhappily. "I was going to ask you to employ him, so that he wouldn't have to steal anymore."

Mrs. Fawcett laughed. "What a splendid idea! Although, you know, he wouldn't have made my life at all peaceful. I like my servants peaceful."

"Well, it's hardly relevant since he'll never be one. Or not in that way. So you did write to me? And to him?"

Mrs. Fawcett sighed and nodded. "I confess. I hoped you'd meet on the way, that you'd see him at last as a gentleman and realize…"

"Realize what?" Lizzie demanded.

"That he was a gentleman," Mrs. Fawcett said in a rush, with rare repetition. "But there, you worked it out for yourself without my help, and my plan didn't work anyway, since he isn't here."

"Actually," Lizzie said with a resumption of unease, *"why* isn't he here?"

Mrs. Fawcett shrugged. "I suppose he didn't get my note. He may already have been out for the evening."

Lizzie nodded. It seemed likely and there was no real reason for her unease. She swallowed. "Do you know…" *Do you know who he is?* But she couldn't yet ask that question. She shied away from the answer. "Do you know about Russian names?"

"I know they use patronymics as well as surnames," Mrs. Fawcett said. "But I have very little familiarity with *actual* names. I'll bet Herr Schmidt does, though."

Herr Schmidt, in the act of throwing the ball for Dog, glanced over at the sound of her raised voice. "What do you want to know?"

"Is Vanya a Russian surname?" Lizzie blurted.

"I've never heard it used as such," Herr Schmidt said. "It's a common diminutive of Ivan, the Russian form of John."

Lizzie drew in a painful breath and gazed at Mrs. Fawcett. "Please tell me he isn't Ivan the Terrible."

---

VANYA LAY FLAT on his back, winded and disoriented, gazing up at the stars with rare appreciation. He'd always loved sleeping under the stars...

Only he wasn't asleep. He'd been riding full tilt from Vienna to the inn when, without warning, something had struck him hard in the chest, knocking him backwards off his horse. It was if he'd ridden into a tree branch in the dark, only the force was too great and between them, he and the horse were used to avoiding such obstacles...

He'd been a soldier too long. He'd survived too many battles and ambushes. Even dazed, he listened to his warning instincts and right now they were screaming.

Vanya rolled, leaping to his feet and drawing his sabre in a smooth, practiced action, just as a sword slashed at the ground where his neck would have been. And with new, sickening fear, Vanya remembered that Lizzie and her siblings had passed this way already this evening.

Trying to blink his dizziness away, Vanya saw there were three of them—big, vicious bruisers. He didn't wait for them to attack again. He was in too big a hurry because he needed to know what had happened to Lizzie. Instead, he flew at them with his best Cossack war cry. His horse whinnied in instant response, so he knew the animal hadn't gone far without him.

Taken by surprise by the force of his attack, the enemy fell back before him. Only one of them had a sabre. The others had vicious daggers and clubs. And they were undoubtedly strong. He'd have thought them street brigands, thugs, except for the fact they swore in Russian. It wouldn't save them. Not if they'd touched so much as a hair on Lizzie's head.

Dropping one villain with a vicious sabre swipe to his right arm, he seized the club of the second and wrested it from him by means of a kick in the chest. As the man staggered back, Vanya drove in, smashing the club left handed into the man's head while he fended off the third man with the sabre.

Seeing his fellows both out of action, the third man panicked and dropped his weapon. Vanya kicked his feet from under him and fell on him, holding the sabre across his throat. He imagined his victim doing the same to Lizzie and barely managed to stop himself from cutting the bastard in two before he'd even asked the question. As though seeing it, the villain's face contorted in abject terror. He knew he'd never been closer to his Maker.

"Who else have you attacked on this road?" Fear reduced Vanya's voice to a little more than a whisper, but the hiss must have sounded even more sinister to his attackers, for the one he'd beaten with his own club stopped crawling toward him, while the man with the sabre sobbed out, "No one, Excellency! I swear!"

Could he believe him? He thought he could. The man had been too surprised by the question. But he didn't yet dare to relax. "Who sent you?" he barked.

It was an ambush. On a quiet stretch of road too late for most traffic. Someone had sent them, and since they were Russian, it had probably been for him rather than Lizzie. In which case, he could guess who was behind the attack. He was going to have to do something about Blonsky.

"Mercy, Excellency! Mercy!" the brigand babbled.

"Major Blonsky?" Vanya demanded.

"No, no, not him," the man replied as though relieved to be able to tell the truth to his bloodthirsty tormentor. "The Englishman. He gave us gold, too much to refuse."

Surprise caused Vanya to lift the sabre. His victim clapped a hand to his throat but otherwise didn't move. Vanya rose and stood back. Blood dripped down the side of his face and trickled under his sleeve and over his hand. He didn't think it was serious.

"Englishman?" he repeated. "What Englishman?"

"Don't know his name," the soldier wailed.

"But you're Blonsky's men, aren't you?" Vanya said shrewdly. "That's why you didn't mind having a poke at me. You think I'm your major's enemy."

"Aren't you?" the one with the slashed arm said bitterly from a few feet away, as he cradled his badly bleeding limb.

Vanya said, "I was under the illusion we'd all just fought in the same army against a common enemy. We're all Russians."

"Didn't stop you trying to kill the major!" came the indignant response.

"Swordplay," Vanya said with a dismissive wave of one hand. "No one had any intention of killing anyone else." At least Vanya hadn't. He hadn't minded the fight, though. He hadn't minded at all showing the boy who'd once bulled him and humiliated him so often exactly who was now the stronger, better man. But this was different. This was malice. Murder, initiated surely by a total stranger, not the drunken brawl he was used to among Russians.

Vanya tore off his cravat and cleaned his sabre with it before returning it to its scabbard. His horse snorted down his neck and he reached up absently to stroke its nose.

"Well," he told his attackers who still sat on the ground staring at him with their mouths open. "You'd better get back to your English master and tell him I'm coming for him next. And if I see your ugly faces again, I'll have you hanged. In fact, I might anyway unless you do *my* bidding. If I call you at any time, you jump to it, Major Blonsky notwithstanding."

Without waiting for a response, he threw himself onto his horse's back and galloped off toward the inn. Lizzie. He had to know that Lizzie and the children were safe.

Mrs. Fawcett's face gave nothing away except incomprehensible frustration. "Elizabeth—"

"It's Johnnie!" Michael reported from the window and Lizzie, conscious still of that nagging fear for him, leapt to her feet, hurrying toward the door before it flew open and Johnnie—Vanya—strode in, wild-eyed and bloody.

A strange animal-like sound escaped her lips as his gaze swept around the room.

"Good God!" Mrs. Fawcett exclaimed. "What on earth happened to you?"

His gaze found the children, seemed to count them, moved on to Lizzie, where it blazed like some strange, flaring firework. Then he closed his eyes and simply sat down on the floor.

Lizzie threw herself to her knees in front of him. "Johnnie!" Seizing his face between her hands, she turned it up to hers. Someone—Mrs. Fawcett—thrust a damp napkin at her and she wiped the blood from his face. "Where are you hurt? What—"

She broke off as his hand closed on hers, holding it still against his face.

"I'm fine."

"Goodness," Henrietta said from the window. "Mrs. Fawcett, you are quite cast in the shade. The most dazzling creature imaginable has just stepped from her carriage into the inn."

"I passed someone almost at the gate," Johnnie said, his voice so blessedly strong and normal that relief swept over Lizzie, drowning even the commotion of, presumably, the fine lady's entry to the inn.

"Georgiana," Mrs. Fawcett said calmly, "run up to my chamber and fetch Cartwright and my medicine box so that we can tend Johnnie's hurts. What happened to you?"

"Ambush," Johnnie said succinctly. "Don't worry, this is only a scratch. It's just…I was sure Lizzie and the others weren't far in front of me and I didn't know…"

The door burst open again before Georgiana even reached it and a positively dazzling lady in silk and jewels sailed inside with the innkeeper and his wife both bowing and protesting like importunate dogs at her heels.

"Oh the *devil*," Johnnie uttered.

# Chapter Sixteen

THE FINE LADY, who seemed to take in every occupant in the room with one withering, haughty glance, said tartly, "I'll thank you to mind your language." Without even turning her head, she snapped "Be gone, sirrah," to the landlord. "And take your good woman with you."

The landlady, her mouth opening and closing without making any sound, gazed at Mrs. Fawcett as though asking somewhat apologetically for permission to escape from a situation she no longer understood. Mrs. Fawcett waved one impatient hand and waited until the door closed.

But even then, the fine lady was before her. Fixing Lizzie with a glare of loathing, she demanded, "What have you done to my son?"

Lizzie blinked. "If this is your son, I wiped blood off his face."

The lady, holding herself rigid, advanced on Johnnie. Her face looked rather white. Johnnie, in spite of Lizzie's instinctive movement to prevent it, rose to his feet. He seemed perfectly steady, even bent to take Lizzie's hand and raise her, too. "Thank you," he murmured. Then, dropping Lizzie's hand he turned to the fine lady. "Forgive my dirt and blood. Consider yourself embraced with due filial duty and affection."

Only by the unfurling of her tightly fisted fingers did the lady give away any relief. "Well, since your hurts are clearly not serious, you had best present these people to me."

As though resigned now to the inevitable, whatever that was,

Vanya said, "Of course. Allow me to introduce Mrs. Fawcett, from England. And the Misses Gaunt and – "

"Gaunt?" the lady uttered with apparently fresh loathing. *"Gaunt?"*

"Gaunt," Vanya said firmly, fixing her with an expression Lizzie could only describe as ferocious. Even more surprising, the lady subsided, while Vanya also introduced Michael, who was hanging valiantly on to the dog with Henrietta's aid, and Herr Schmidt. "My mother," he finished with what appeared to be reluctance. "Countess Savarina."

"Savarin?" Georgiana repeated with quite as much hatred as the countess had uttered "Gaunt. Your mother is a Savarin? Johnnie, what does this mean?"

"It means English children have no manners," Countess Savarina said tartly.

"Of course they do," Lizzie countered. "But even the best of manners tend to lapse in the face of bejeweled strangers who turfed them out of their family home the same day they buried their father. *Manners* doesn't really cover that one. Children, come, it's time we left."

The countess, whose jaw had actually dropped during Lizzie's speech, narrowed her eyes. "Past time," she said grimly.

Which is when Michael let go of the dog.

Lizzie didn't move. She knew Vanya would catch Dog before he knocked the countess over. And he did, almost distractedly. But that didn't stop her petty pleasure in the countess' suddenly alarmed backsteps.

Lizzie walked to the door, ignoring Vanya's burning gaze on her face. "Don't take my words personally, Countess Savarina. I was referring to your son. Good night, Mrs. Fawcett. Thank you, as always, Herr Schmidt."

"Lizzie," Vanya said quietly. There might have been a plea in his voice, but it was far too late for that. Dignity, belatedly, was all she had left. And for once, the children, and even Dog, following submissively on her heels, allowed her to have it.

"*JOHNNIE? JOHNNIE IS Ivan the Terrible?*" Michael's stunned voice drifted through the closed door, dripping with loathing as he spoke the hated name.

Into the silence in the parlor, Mrs. Fawcett said distantly, "Excuse me. I must instruct my coachman."

The countess barely waited until she was out of the room before she exploded. "Ivan the Terrible? Do they think that is funny?"

"No," Vanya said, irritably, throwing himself into a chair by the table. "They think it's apt since you evicted them before their father was cold."

"This is the first time I've left Russia," she objected, clearly affronted.

"You sent your orders, Mother. They were carried out. Let's not demean ourselves further by pretending otherwise."

The countess sniffed. "Well. They'd kept your poor dear father's inheritance from him for too long."

Vanya blinked. "A week?"

"All his life!" his mother corrected waving one encompassing arm with indignation. "And then to be treated like—"

"You know there was nothing to inherit before the old man died," Vanya interrupted. "My grandfather and my father both made good lives for themselves in Russia. None of us were ever left destitute. Which is what you did to the Gaunts. And then you swan in here dripping with diamonds and contempt. What kind of reception did you expect, exactly?"

"I didn't know she was a Gaunt," the countess muttered. "What I expected was a little affection from my only son."

Vanya regarded her with the powerful mixture of frustration and affection she induced in him so easily. "Mother, what in God's name are you doing here?"

"I got it out of Misha that you came here with the so-called young lady. I thought she was inveigling you into marriage, so when I went to the Castlereaghs'—isn't her ladyship a quite eccentric dresser?—and discovered you'd already left, I assumed you'd come here and made Misha show us the way."

"No, I mean what brought you to Vienna in the first place?"

His mother shrugged elegantly. "You, of course. You never write to me, so I thought I'd come in person. And then I thought we could go on to England when this Congress is over and see this Launceton of yours..." Her eyes swept over him and narrowed. "Why are you bleeding, Vanya?"

"When I find out, I'll let you know."

"Does that man speak French?" the countess inquired, fixing her erratic gaze on Herr Schmidt who was gazing pensively out of the dark window.

"I imagine so. And I imagine he speaks perfect Russian, too, so there's no point in changing now."

"What is he doing here?"

"Recovering. We shot him." Vanya stood up. "I'll order you a cup of tea while the horses are refreshed. Then we're going back to Vienna."

---

"IT WAS THE mother who threw us out," Henrietta said quietly as the carriage bowled through the darkness. "Johnnie didn't know. When he heard the truth from us, he helped you steal the necklace to make up for what she'd done. He was trying to do the right thing."

"That's a very charitable interpretation," Lizzie said. "Only I don't think he did steal it. There's no replica. Aunt Lucy's still wearing it because he never took it in the first place, just induced her to take it off for that evening under some pretext. She said something about a broken clasp that turned out not to be broken. No wonder he wasn't bothered about his buyer discovering paste instead of diamonds..."

Michael, who'd seemed quite devastated by "Johnnie's" betrayal, brightened. "You mean he just *gave* us three thousand pounds? Out of his own pocket?"

"I think he might have," Lizzie said dully. "Which is really…annoying of him, because now I feel obliged to give it back."

"Oh no, Lizzie," Georgiana said earnestly. "Don't do that. It's really the least he could have done."

"But it makes us beholden to him!"

"How?" Michael demanded. "Did he attach any strings to it?"

"No, not yet, but—"

"It seems to me," Henrietta said, "that he went out of his way *not* to attach strings, so that we—you—would have no qualms about accepting it."

Lizzie rested her head on her hand and closed her eyes. She had no idea what to think anymore.

---

THEY GOT BACK to the house in the Skodegasse just after the rest of the family. Lizzie sent the younger ones off to bed and joined her aunt and Minerva in the drawing room to inquire after the ball. For once, it seemed, Minerva had enjoyed herself hugely and the reason soon became clear. She had danced twice with Mr. Corner, and since one of those had been the supper dance, she's spent a good part of the evening in his company.

"You're wasting this opportunity!" Aunt Lucy scolded.

"It didn't feel wasted," Minerva muttered. "I like being with Mr. Corner. I feel comfortable."

"Comfortable," Aunt Lucy repeated as if she'd no idea of the word's meaning. "You might as well spend the evening with your brother."

"James is not at all like Mr. Corner," Minerva said with dignity. And at last, her tone seemed to pierce Aunt Lucy's fantasy of a great match and untold family wealth.

"Oh no," she said. "Minerva, no. It will not do. He has nothing."

"I know," Minerva said miserably.

Lizzie, ignored by both of them up till now, chose to take a seat by Minerva, facing her aunt. "I believe my uncle had nothing," she remarked, "when you married him. And now he is to be made an

Ambassador and given a knighthood."

"That is not to be talked of just yet," her aunt said with dignity. "And even so, it has taken us twenty years of struggle. I don't want that for you, Minerva."

"Why not?" Lizzie asked. "Your house was always the most pleasant I knew. Not huge like Launceton Hall, but there was rarely any bad-tempered shouting or tension, either. It always seemed to me you and my uncle ran a happy home. I *would* want that for Minerva."

Aunt Lucy stared at her as if stricken. Then it turned into a glare. "You don't know what you're talking about, Lizzie. If you've nothing helpful to contribute to the discussion, you may go to bed."

"As you wish," Lizzie said, standing up. In fact, a little oblivion seemed very attractive.

"I'll go, too," Minerva said, following her.

Inevitably, Minerva poured out her heart on the way upstairs. Lizzie listened patiently and made sympathetic noises. She rather thought things would work out for Minerva in the end, if she just held out. It was her own happiness that seemed suddenly impossible.

As she undressed and lay down beside Georgiana, she tried desperately to get back her contentedness with the future she'd already worked out: a pleasant cottage in the country with the children, a successful London season for Henrietta, followed by a brilliant match, and at least a few years of governessing for Lizzie. Michael would get a commission in the army, Georgiana would be provided for and she, Lizzie, might even find a place with one of them, helping out.

*Poor relation*, a voice whispered unkindly in her head.

*And besides, what if Henrietta falls in love with a poor man? Are you going to be like Aunt Lucy and push her into a marriage she doesn't want just so you can stop worrying?*

In any case, it was all moot now. She was going to have to give the money back to Johnnie. Vanya. Cousin Ivan…

"Be still, Lizzie," Georgiana muttered.

But she couldn't settle. To avoid disturbing the others, she rose, wrapped a shawl around her nightgown in the dark, and left the bedroom. The rest of the house was in darkness, too. Everyone must have retired. Lizzie lit the candle left in the hall and walked silently downstairs. If she had a plan at all, it was merely to pace around the drawing room until all this churning within her was quiet and she could sleep.

But as she quietly pushed open the drawing room door, she saw there was a light already there, another person with another candle. James stood by the bookcase, his candle beside him, thumbing through the heap of papers Mr. Corner had left for Mr. Daniels.

"Are you thinking of going into diplomatic service, too?" Lizzie asked.

James jumped visibly, almost leapt in the air, muffling a cry. "Good God, Lizzie, don't creep up on a man!"

"Sorry. What are you doing?"

"Oh, nothing. I couldn't sleep. Just looking for something to do."

Since she herself was wandering about for no better reason, perhaps she shouldn't have doubted him. But she knew him very well. And even if she hadn't, she had enough younger siblings to spot shiftiness when she saw it. Even in the poor light, he made no effort to meet her gaze. She could have sworn he was blushing and he certainly held himself with unusual stiffness.

Lizzie walked further into the room. James made what looked like an involuntary shooing motion with his hands, then seemed to force himself to stillness.

"If you're in more trouble," she said carefully, "it might help you to tell me?"

"Of course I'm not. Why should you imagine I'm in trouble just because I can't sleep?"

"Oh, I don't know. It might have something to do with the fact that you owe several thousand pounds you can't pay to some not very pleasant people."

"Oh, thanks for bringing that up," James said petulantly. "No wonder a fellow can't sleep!" And he stormed past her without a word of good night.

JAMES HURRIED ALONG the Skodegasse in the direction of the Graben. He thought, after his initial shock of finding Lizzie there watching him, that he'd handled himself rather well. He was almost home and dry. And out of the woods. Although it was late, the Graben was by no means deserted. James walked up one side and down the other, then walked breadth-wise back and forth across it. But he could see no sign of Grassic who, however, had made it clear he might not attend their meeting in person.

He gave James to understand he was a very busy man with a great deal of importance that most people never realized. All James saw were some rough looking characters he doubted had any lawful business in any land. One of them detached himself from a tree on James's third horizontal foray and ambled toward him.

James braced himself. Almost over. And then someone seized his arm from behind and marched him back the way he'd come.

After the first shock, James dug his heels in. "What do you think you're doing?" he panted, trying to detach the viselike fingers from his arm.

"Getting you out of even more trouble," said the tall man beside him. Although James was no weakling, he seemed to have no ability to resist his abductor.

"Who are you? What do you want?" James demanded.

"I'm your big cousin Ivan and I want to teach you a lesson."

IN THE MORNING, although Lizzie still tried very hard to re-conjure her optimism of the last couple of weeks, she couldn't help feeling that all she had were a lot of problems with no likely solutions. But there were a few things she knew she had to do and so, as soon as she discovered that her aunt was awake, she knocked on her door and sat on the end of her bed, watching her drink coffee in an unusually morose manner.

"Is something wrong, Aunt Lucy?" Lizzie asked.

Aunt Lucy sighed. "No, nothing that cannot be mended. Did you wish to talk to me about something in particular?"

"Actually, yes." She took a deep breath, reluctant to upset her good-natured aunt any further. "Did you know that Countess Savarina is in Vienna? Cousin Ivan's mother?"

Aunt Lucy wrinkled her nose and set down her coffee cup. "Yes. Dreadful creature, dripping quite vulgarly in diamonds. She was at Lady Castlereagh's. Her ladyship was kind enough to point her out to me."

"Were you wearing the necklace?" Lizzie asked.

An almost mischievous smile flitted across her aunt's face. "Well, I was, but funnily enough the clasp was loose again, so I took it off."

"Probably best," Lizzie said gravely.

"I thought so."

"Maybe you should send it back to England with the next dispatches?"

"Or I could call on her and return it in person. But, oh Lizzie, apparently the son is here, too. You know, Ivan the Terrible? Only you really must stop using that name now, just in case we're obliged to meet him."

"I'll try," Lizzie said breathlessly.

Benson came in, bearing a silver plate with a card on it. "If you please, ma'am," she said grimly, presenting the plate.

Aunt Lucy picked up the card. Her jaw dropped and she all but threw the card at Lizzie. "Countess Savarina! Now what do I do? Benson, have them tell her I'm not at home. No, wait, of course I am, it's eleven o'clock in the morning… Drat it, Lizzie, do I want to offend the woman or not? Do I receive her?"

"With icy composure, if at all," Lizzie advised.

"Benson, has Mr. Daniels left yet?"

"Yes, ma'am, an hour ago."

Aunt Lucy gnawed her lip, gazing at Lizzie, then, abruptly, she threw back the covers. "I'll be down directly," she announced with decision. "Give the wretched woman refreshment. Lizzie, you must come with me."

"Oh no, Aunt, that wouldn't be a good idea."

"Why ever not? You are my strength and besides, I want to show her exactly who she displaced."

"Yes, but I...I met her last night when I was with Mrs. Fawcett at the inn and I'm afraid I wasn't terribly...conciliatory. We didn't...get along."

Aunt Lucy's smile was uncharacteristically ferocious. "What a shame," she uttered.

"Shall I change into the better dress?" Lizzie asked, bowing to the inevitable.

"On no account," Aunt Lucy ordered.

If Aunt Lucy expected to make the countess feel guilty for her treatment of the late baron's family, Lizzie thought she was barking up the wrong tree. Countess Savarina did not strike her as the kind of woman who even noticed other people's misfortunes, let alone accepted responsibility for them. On the other hand, Lizzie caught herself up for accepting Henrietta's explanation of Johnnie's—Cousin Ivan's—conduct and blaming everything on his mother. She wanted to believe it too much.

Ten minutes later, she entered the drawing room in Aunt Lucy's wake and discovered the countess seated stiffly on the chair by the fireplace. She rose as they came in and movement by the window caught Lizzie's attention. Another figure turned to face them, in full military uniform. Lizzie's heart seemed to dive straight into her stomach, churning up everything that was meant to be there. She couldn't look at him, though she was fairly sure he bowed in their direction.

"Countess Savarina," Aunt Lucy said coldly, dropping a stiff curtsey which Lizzie echoed. "I'm so sorry to keep you waiting."

"I assure you it's of no moment." The countess swallowed. "I apologize for calling upon you so early, but I felt I had to come immediately when my son explained to me how matters had been handled at Launceton."

"Indeed?" Aunt Lucy was still impressively frosty. Lizzie hadn't known she had it in her.

"I have come to beg your pardon," the countess said with a clarity that sounded odd to Lizzie's ears, as if she were enunciating very carefully in order to make the words easier to say. "And more particularly, the pardon of Miss Gaunt and her sisters. I never dreamed those imbeciles would evict you as they did. It was quite unforgivable and so I have written to them. They are, of course, dismissed. I can't have my instructions so misconstrued."

Not for a moment did Lizzie believe they had been misconstrued. On the other hand, she'd no intention of letting the countess take all the blame for this.

"We were told," she said, "that the instructions came from the new Lord Launceton."

The countess opened her mouth to reply, but before she could speak, the colonel said, "In my name, certainly, and for that I take full responsibility. I was entirely at fault and beg your forgiveness."

The humble speech sounded so unlike him that she made the mistake of actually looking at him. His intense gaze captured hers at once, but she could find neither mockery nor insincerity of any kind there.

"Really?" she asked seriously.

At that, sudden laughter did spring into his eyes. Just as if they had truly been friends. "Really."

"Lizzie," Aunt Lucy hissed with a kind of strangled mortification.

"Forgive me," Lizzie said without contrition, "are my manners at fault again? Lord Launceton, my aunt, Mrs. Daniels."

As the colonel bowed again, Aunt Lucy frowned, peering at him more closely. "Colonel…Surely, Colonel Vanya?"

His smile twisted. "Only at masquerades. Colonel Savarin everywhere else. My father took my mother's family name when they married; it works better in Russian than Gaunt."

"Then you won't use your title?" Aunt Lucy said. "Your English title."

"Of course he will," the countess answered for him, taking his arm.

"Once this silly Congress is cleared up."

"Thank you for seeing us," the colonel said stiffly. "We'll take up no more of your time."

"No, please sit down," Aunt Lucy said without cordiality. "I have in my possession a necklace that is part of the Launceton estate. My late brother lent it to me, but it undoubtedly belongs to you." She blushed, no doubt recalling whatever had passed between her and the unknown Colonel Vanya concerning the necklace at the Emperor's ball. That something had occurred, Lizzie didn't doubt.

"Thank you," the countess said, as though surprised by such honesty.

"I have no need of necklaces," the colonel said, ignoring his mother's stare. "Why don't we continue the loan? We are, after all, cousins."

Aunt Lucy's eyes widened. Lizzie knew how she felt. The pain in her stomach seemed worse when she couldn't keep hating him.

"But you will want to give it to your wife," Aunt Lucy said faintly.

Just for an instant, Lizzie couldn't breathe. She'd never even considered a wife. And yet such a being could make no possible difference to Lizzie's fate.

Another twisted smile flickered across the colonel's lips and vanished. "I'm not married. And if I were, I understand there are other jewels." He reached out, firmly drawing his mother's gloved hand through his arm. "Good day, Mrs. Daniels. Miss Gaunt."

---

"AM I FORGIVEN now?" his mother demanded as he handed her into her carriage.

Vanya sighed. "Yes, Mother, you are forgiven. Provided you interfere no further."

"Well, the aunt is very British but perhaps not so bad. The girl, on the other hand, has far too much to say. Her spirit is too independent. Unbecomingly so."

"For one totally dependent, you mean?" he said wryly.

"Why do you defend her, Vanya? What is she to you?"

"A friend," Vanya said firmly. *Or at least she might have been if you hadn't turned me into Ivan the Terrible.* He kept the words to himself, though, and even as he strode off down the street alone, acknowledged that they weren't actually fair, either. He hadn't been interested in the English estate. Like his father, he'd believed the British branch of the family had turned their backs and he'd been in no hurry to build bridges when the old man had written.

His mother had sent on the news of the baron's demise, but even then, he'd done nothing about it. Admittedly, he'd been wounded at the time, but he'd still been capable of stopping his mother in her tracks if he'd cared enough to do so. He could have guessed what she would do and why. For him.

Well, he'd tried to make it right now, as best he could. It didn't and couldn't change how she regarded him. Ivan the Terrible was only the beginning. He'd lied and pretended and made everything worse. The trouble was, he hadn't expected to care. In the beginning, he'd only sought a little amusement while he righted a wrong perpetrated in his name, after which he'd doubted he would ever see her again. Only then, at the Emperor's ball, he'd flirted with her and kissed her and something had changed.

And now he was found out and it was all over, and the darkness was closing in on him, urging him to the devil, to drink himself to oblivion and lose himself in whatever debauchery he could find. It had always worked before. He generally came out of his benders a better man with a sore head. Or at least, so he'd always believed. But in truth, he'd never taken much responsibility for whatever he did in such conditions. For years, it had just become his release from the horror of battle and the aftermath of grief. There was no need of grief here. No one had died, not even Herr Schmidt.

Herr Schmidt. Now there was a man he really needed to talk to. Russian soldiers—Blonsky's soldiers—had been paid by an Englishman to kill him. Almost with relief, he seized on the mystery. He couldn't let the darkness take him yet, because the would-be assassins had known about the inn. Whoever had sent them, had known where he went and it was quite possible they knew Lizzie went there, too.

On impulse, he swerved towards a coffee house where he'd once noticed Blonsky, surely at around this time of the day. There were a few Russians at the tables outside, so he went in, nodding acknowledgement to the few greetings sent his way. But, discovering no sign of Blonsky or any of the men he knew to be friends of his, he left again, and strode on to the next coffee house.

There were a lot of those in Vienna and he had no intention of wasting the entire day on searching them. There were other places he was more certain to meet Blonsky. However, in the third coffee shop, he spotted the major at an outside table by the door. His uniform coat was loosened, but he looked, otherwise, the perfect officer of the royal guard, relaxing off duty with his friends.

Without taking his eyes off Blonsky, Vanya strolled among the tables. The other soldiers nearby stopped talking, watching Vanya advance with varying shades of unease or excitement according to their character. The quiet spread quickly to Blonsky's table, too, where the men tensed. Someone said the major's name with quiet urgency and Blonsky, the last to notice him, finally glanced over, his coffee cup halfway to his lips.

The cup slipped, as if his fingers had suddenly gone slack, and coffee spilled onto the table. Between the fine whiskers, his lips parted. His eyes dilated. And Vanya knew.

Blonsky hadn't expected him to be alive still. He might not have given the order, but he was in on it. Tempting as it was to make the man sweat by sitting next to him for the next half hour, Vanya didn't really have the time to waste.

"Do you know," he said to no one in particular, "I think I'll drink my coffee somewhere more pleasant."

# Chapter Seventeen

IN HER FIRST day in Vienna, Mrs. Fawcett caused a major social stir by having an "at-home" afternoon with not only children but a large and unruly dog present. It was a risky strategy, but since Dog was enough under control to not actually jump on women's elegant gowns and since the Duchess of Sagan, Dorothée de Talleyrand and Lady Castlereagh all chose to be amused, the afternoon was pronounced a success. Mrs. Fawcett was given the instant if undeserved reputation of hosting the most original entertainments.

The entire Daniels-Gaunt household was present, including Mr. Daniels himself and Mr. Corner. Lizzie, slightly alarmed that Vanya would turn up at any moment, dragged Mrs. Fawcett aside, into her bed chamber, and asked her outright if there was any chance of it.

"Oh, I think he's busy until this evening," Mrs. Fawcett said carelessly, "when he's promised to escort me to Princess Bagration's. Why, did you want to speak to him?"

"No," Lizzie said flatly. Then, remembering the money for the "stolen" necklace, she offered, "That is, I don't want to, but I need to."

"Ah," Mrs. Fawcett said, thoughtfully. "Are you condemning him for being Ivan the Terrible or the rakehell everyone in Vienna tells you he is?"

"Neither," Lizzie said. "For lying to me." *And kissing me and making me think…whatever it is I was thinking.*

"Did he really lie? Does it not strike you, Elizabeth, that he did everything you asked of him and more?"

Lizzie gazed blindly out of the window at the uniformly gray sky. Perhaps autumn was finally here.

"You always seemed such good friends," Mrs. Fawcett pursued relentlessly, "that I could see right away why you'd eloped together—in the days I still believed you *had* eloped together."

Lizzie raised one eyebrow. "How many of those were there? One day? Two?"

"Something like that."

"I'm sorry about the stories. I didn't know at first if we could trust you. If *I* could trust you," she corrected.

Mrs. Fawcett smiled faintly and drifted toward the bedroom door. "And now you've forgotten to trust each other. What a waste."

※

WHEN SHE RETURNED to the drawing room, Lizzie was slightly alarmed to see a group of young men all gazing at Henrietta as if not merely dazzled but stunned. Admittedly, Henrietta had that effect on most people. If she noticed it at all, she thought they were rude for staring.

"You have an extraordinarily beautiful family," Mr. Grassic observed, standing beside Lizzie.

"You mean Henrietta," Lizzie said candidly. "She is fifteen years old. By the time she's seventeen, I suspect she'll need a bodyguard."

Mr. Grassic smiled. "She's a most charming, unaffected child. They all are."

"Thank you," Lizzie said, smiling with genuine pleasure. "In England, society would find them far too…*much* for civilized company, but here in Vienna, things seem rather more relaxed. Mrs. Fawcett is very brave to have us all."

※

VANYA, HAVING LEARNED from Mrs. Fawcett that Herr Schmidt had simply disappeared from the inn during the night—"At any rate, he was nowhere to be found this morning," the redoubtable lady had informed him while supervising the disposal of furniture to accommodate her afternoon at home—gave up looking for him in the streets around the police building and went home.

He could have gone in and inquired or even sought an interview with Baron Hager, the police minister, but he suspected Schmidt didn't want that kind of attention drawn to himself. Vanya certainly didn't want to get the man into any more trouble. At least, not unless he gave Vanya any.

"You are coming this afternoon?" Mrs. Fawcett had called after him as he'd left him.

"Sorry, I can't," he'd replied hastily and not entirely truthfully.

"The Gaunts will all be there."

He was almost tempted. The desire to see Lizzie again, even if only to feel her cold glare of contempt on his face, was undeniably strong and when put with the prospect of whatever chaos the children and dog would produce, the pull was almost irresistible.

"Then I'll do them a kindness and stay away. Au revoir, Madame!"

Her voice drifted after him as he grabbed his hat from the hall table. "Well, I insist you come to my masquerade ball on Monday."

"You're very kind!" he called back noncommittedly and bolted.

He decided to go home and write notes to a few friends and, later, to visit Princess Bagration and find out what the rumors were among the Russians and their relations with members of the British delegation. People were usually happy to gossip to him about Blonsky, hoping for some wild or entertaining reaction to take back to the rumor mill.

Misha had left two letters for him, propped up in front of the invitation cards on the mantelpiece. One scented epistle was clearly from Sonia. He threw it on the table and with a groan, tore open the other bearing the tsar's seal.

His Cossacks weren't good at escort duty. They enjoyed showing off and gathering a crowd, and if anyone was ever foolish enough to attack the tsar, they'd slaughter him—or her—on the spot without a qualm. But they weren't stupid. They knew taking the tsar to balls and performing tricks for his friends were trivial, pointless and beneath them as seasoned, skilled warriors. As a result, they were even harder than normal to keep in line on such occasions.

But this wasn't an escort order. It was a personal summons to the tsar's presence. Vanya threw it down with irritation, before realizing that, in fact, a visit to the tsar and his minions at the Hofburg might be extremely useful. Giving his uniform a halfhearted brush down with his hands, Vanya left his rooms again and walked round to the Hofburg.

His first indication that something was wrong came, inevitably, from the courtiers and hangers-on who swarmed around the tsar's ornate public reception room. Those nearest the door all stopped talking as Vanya entered. No one greeted him but, instead, drew back out of his way. Blonsky's friends, perhaps, he thought with a curl of his lip, though as he looked around him there was no sign of his old enemy.

He did glimpse the tsar, seated at his desk while some heavily braided officers and secretaries hovered nearby. One, whose name Vanya didn't even know, caught sight of him, murmured to the tsar and walked forward. The tsar didn't raise his head.

"Colonel Savarin, this way, if you please," the braided functionary requested with cold civility. Vanya followed him across the room, puzzled that he was not being conducted to the tsar but to a chamber beyond, which turned out to be a bare apartment containing one large, empty desk with one chair on either side of it.

"Wait here." The braided stranger left again, closing the door firmly behind him.

Vanya frowned at the discourtesy and paced around the room. Up until now, he'd been used to seeing only the affable side of Tsar Alexander. He'd found the "old soldiers together" camaraderie a bit irritating, certainly, but he'd got used to taking the Imperial favor for granted. It seemed he'd finally done something to annoy His Majesty, though he couldn't imagine what. Even when he and Blonsky had fought their infamous duel, the tsar hadn't shut either of them in a room and deliberately left them to kick their heels ignored for more than a quarter of an hour.

Well, since no one had told him he was a prisoner…

Vanya swerved away from the small window and strode to the door. He was about to wrench it open and go in search of His Majesty, when it opened from the outside and he had to jump back to avoid a collision.

The Polish Prince Czartoryski, whom Vanya had always regarded as a friend, stuck his head in the door, looking harassed.

"Colonel, watch your back and do nothing foolish," he said urgently. "We'll get to the bottom of this."

"Bottom of what?" Vanya demanded, scowling.

But Prince Czartoryski straightened and stepped back, and finally the tsar himself entered the room, closely followed by the braided secretary and Blonsky. Two soldiers waited outside the door.

At sight of his old enemy, Vanya knew this was serious. Almost worse, although Vanya bowed, the tsar offered no greeting, merely looked coldly down his nose.

"Where were you yesterday evening?"

Vanya blinked. "Lady Castlereagh's. I met Your Majesty there."

"You left early," Blonsky uttered. "Before His Majesty."

"Yes, I did," Vanya agreed, staring at him.

"Where did you go?" the tsar demanded.

"I rode outside the city, to an inn where friends of mine were staying."

"British friends?" the tsar inquired.

Vanya raised his brows. "Yes, as it happens. For the most part."

"You see?" Blonsky said triumphantly.

"Then you don't deny it?" the braided man blustered.

"Why the devil should I?" Vanya demanded "Are the British no longer our allies? Did we declare war at Lady Castlereagh's and no one thought to tell me?"

The tsar smacked his palm on the back of the chair in front of him. "Damn it, there is no place for levity here and you would do well to recognize the fact!"

"I beg Your Majesty's pardon," Vanya said mechanically. "Perhaps if you tell me what the problem is—"

"What happened to your face?" the tsar interrupted.

"I got in a fight," Vanya said with a dismissive wave of one hand. "Or at least," he added, gazing directly at Blonsky, "I was attacked. On the road to the inn."

As soon as he spoke, he knew he'd made a mistake. He just didn't know what it was. For instead of looking shifty as he'd done in the coffee shop, Blonsky smiled and lifted his gaze to the tsar's.

"You see, Sire?"

The tsar's fingers gripping the side of the chair showed white. "How long have you been betraying me, Savarin?"

Vanya's lips fell open. "I have never betrayed you." He was too surprised for there to be more than simple sincerity in his words and tone. Perhaps it was this that made the tsar finally look at him.

"And yet the paper is now in the hands of the British," Blonsky observed.

The tsar's fair lashes swept down over his blue eyes and he swung away from Vanya as if the sight of him hurt.

"What paper?" Vanya demanded.

"Do you take us for fools?" the braided man demanded.

"Right now, yes!" Vanya said unwisely. "What is it I'm supposed to have done?"

"You were supposed to stop when the Imperial Guard requested it," the tsar spat. "You were supposed to submit yourself to a search, not half-kill them and go on your merry way."

Vanya closed his mouth, gazing at Blonsky with something like awe as he began to understand. "That's really quite clever," he allowed.

Blonsky had got himself out of any potential charge by getting in a far greater one against Vanya first. Pretending his men had been on the road to stop him passing some paper or other to British allies in the inn.

"You're under arrest, Savarin," the tsar said bitterly. "For treason."

"Am I to have no defense?" Vanya demanded as Blonsky opened the door to admit the soldiers.

"Yes, you will have your say," the tsar said tiredly. "But not now. I can't look at you right now. Escort the colonel back to his barracks where he will remain under arrest until we send for him."

"Your Majesty, his Cossacks will just free him," Blonsky said. "Might I suggest my own regimental barracks, instead?"

Vanya laughed. "I certainly won't escape there."

The tsar nodded and swung away.

"Sire," Vanya said urgently. "It isn't me you want. It's the Englishman."

The tsar paused without turning back to face him. "What Englishman?"

"I don't know yet, but he has to be—"

Blonsky laughed, drowning out anything else, and the tsar didn't stay to listen. "Your sword, Colonel Savarin."

As the soldiers waited, Vanya slowly drew his sword, but he was damned if he'd surrender it to Blonsky. The man's tongue was practically hanging out for it. Instead, he stepped back and turned, presenting it to Czartoryski.

"I mean it," he said. "There's an English paymaster at the bottom of this."

Czartoryski took the sword with a distracted click of his heels. "We'll investigate," he promised.

But, of course, it wasn't down to Czartoryski's investigations or anyone else's. It was down to the capricious will of the tsar, and right now Blonsky was whispering poison in his ear.

Czartoryski nodded, turned on his heels and followed the tsar.

"Take him to the barracks, lock him up," Blonsky commanded. "I must say, Vanya, it will be a pleasure to have you with us again. Almost like old times."

It was a threat as well as a reminder. It crossed Vanya's mind, as he strolled to the door with his escort, that he'd never survive this imprisonment. Blonsky couldn't afford to let him live in case the truth made more sense than Blonsky's lies. Besides which, childish enmity had been turned into something much deeper and more dangerous by the duel they'd fought two years ago. Blonsky wanted Vanya dead.

As Vanya crossed the main reception, the occupants stood back as before and watched him in utter silence. No one, even supposed friends, would speak to the traitor for fear of contamination.

Except Boris, who burst into the room just as they were leaving. For once, his normally calm friend's eyes were wild, boiling with fury and helpless frustration. "My God, it's true! But who the hell gave you to Blonsky?"

"His Majesty," Blonsky snapped. "Stand aside!"

Boris, breathing deeply, stared at Vanya, who smiled and shrugged, more to comfort his friend who was clearly thinking much as he had about Blonsky's custody. Only Boris couldn't know that Vanya had no intention of staying in anyone's custody right now.

"I know you didn't do this, Vanya," Boris said intensely.

"You're obsessed with a legend that was never real," Blonsky sneered and pushed Vanya onward with a contemptuous shove between the shoulder blades.

Vanya added it to his list for payback; it was the only way not to thump Blonsky now and find himself in chains. He walked on with an insouciant wink at Boris.

Outside, the courtyard, usually bustling with the Austrian Emperor's soldiers and servants, was almost empty. Only a courier stood by his horse on the other side of the yard, idly talking with a groom while he waited, presumably, for whatever he was to carry.

"So how am I travelling the ninety miles to your barracks?" Vanya inquired. "Tied across a saddle? Discreetly chained to a coach shared with your watchful self and a loaded pistol? Walking?"

The rumble of wheels and a vaguely sad clopping of hooves drawing closer gave him a clue. Through the open outer gates, a sorry looking horse pulled a battered vehicle behind it.

Blonsky's lip curled. "In the supply wagon. With the rest of the meat."

Vanya laughed, watching the wagon's approach. "That does make your day, doesn't it, Sasha?" Which, in the end, was Vanya's prime motivation, too: he refused to give Blonsky his day.

Without warning, he seized each soldier by the belt and swung them into each other with a crash that would have made his own eyes water had he not been already sprinting across the courtyard, not for the wagon, or even the gates, but for the courier and his horse.

"Shoot him!" Blonsky screamed over the chaotic scuffling and shouting.

"In the Emperor of Austria's palace?" said one of the soldiers, fortunately keeping his head better than his major.

"Just stop him!" Blonsky raged.

The courier, who'd just received his bag from some palace functionary, was staring with his mouth open as Vanya charged directly at him.

"What the…?" uttered the groom, backing smartly out of the way. He still held onto the reins, from some instinct trying to shield the horse from the approaching madman, turning the stirrups away from him.

Vanya didn't need stirrups. He'd learned from the Cossacks. He simply leapt, hurling himself from the ground onto the animal's back. The horse, terrified by the suddenness of the rude arrival in its saddle, reared, neighing with fright, dragging the reins free of the groom's helpless hold. Vanya clung on with his knees, swept up the reins, and urged the horse forward before its front hooves had hit the ground. Since his desires coincided with the horse's instincts to bolt, bolt they did, and with hands and knees and heels, Vanya made sure it was toward the open gate.

Blonsky and one of the soldiers were trying to close it. More soldiers were pouring out of the building, the Russians falling over Austrian guards who'd run out to see what was going on, while the wagon horse and its driver watched proceedings open-mouthed. Up at the open first floor window of the tsar's apartments, heads were sticking out and hands gesticulating. Vanya was sure someone laughed, so in grateful spirit, Vanya lifted one hand from the reins and waved, even while charging full tilt for the half-open gate.

Blonsky, seeing he was never going to close it in time, threw himself into the horse's path instead. Vanya laughed and rode straight at him. He could see the whites of Blonsky's eyes, the rapid dilation of his pupils as the major realized Vanya really would ride him down.

And then Blonsky leapt aside with absolutely no time to spare.

Viciously disappointed, Vanya galloped through the gate and out into the city.

# Chapter Eighteen

JAMES, WHO WAS escorting his mother and sister to the theatre before they were to join Mr. Daniels at some ball or other—Lizzie had become totally lost as to whose party happened when—had a spring in his step as he overtook her on the stairs.

"You're looking more like yourself," Lizzie said, pleased.

James grinned. "Solved a few problems. You can stop worrying about me, now."

"Oh, God," Lizzie said warmly, although, as she followed him more sedately, she did wonder how so huge a problem could have been fixed so quickly. A rich and amiable friend, probably, in which case the problem was merely postponed, not solved.

"Aren't you coming to the theatre this time?" James called over his shoulder.

"No, I'm a little tired," Lizzie excused herself. "Besides, you're all going on to the ball afterwards, aren't you? I'll have a quiet evening with the children."

James grinned. "Contradiction in terms, coz!"

Lizzie smiled, glad to see him so much more his old self. In fact, she should have felt much happier about everything. Minerva, spending more time with Mr. Corner, was reaching an understanding that gave her a rather charming inner glow and Lizzie, having pointed out to her aunt that Mr. Daniels had been in no better a position than Mr. Corner when she had married him, had hopes that parental opposition would disintegrate in time. She usually rejoiced in her wishes and schemes reaching fruition, or at least the hope of fruition, but today she couldn't shake off glumness. Restless and unhappy without reason, she could settle to nothing since returning from Mrs. Fawcett's.

As she played a game of Jack Straws in the drawing room with the children, memories kept floating inconveniently in front of her eyes. Not least of them was Cousin Ivan, when she'd last had any hope that he was merely Johnnie, throwing himself into the inn parlor, covered in blood, yet desperate only to see that she and the children were unharmed. That wasn't the behavior of a monster, but of a protective man, a friend.

In any case, who was she to place such value on honesty? Hadn't she paid him to steal something just because she wanted the money for the children's and her own comfort? It had belonged to her father, but it certainly wasn't hers, and she'd had no right to it. Or to the money still burning a hole in the carpet bag under her bed.

Just for a moment, she thought of Johnnie, Vanya, and Cousin Ivan as one man, and of the fun and excitement and sheer emotion she'd known around him in whatever guise. Her heart skipped a beat, because she had no reason not to trust him, every reason to remain his friend. She'd behaved badly through sheer pride, a vice she hadn't known she possessed until now.

She drew in her breath, distractedly taking her turn in the game, pulling free the straw and watching without interest as the whole edifice crumbled, to cries of outrage from the children.

"Sorry!" Lizzie exclaimed, just as the door opened and the maid announced Mrs. Fawcett—or at least she tried to, but that lady barged straight past her before the maid had got beyond, "Frau—"

Dog and the children launched themselves across the room to greet her, although the children were pulled up short by the sight of a tall, finely dressed stranger and a military gentleman with fine whiskers who looked vaguely familiar. Mrs. Fawcett was dressed for a ball in fine sapphire blue silk with sapphires and diamonds sparkling around her throat and wrists and in her ears and hair.

"Goodness," Georgiana said awed. "You look...gorgeous."

"Don't I?" Mrs. Fawcett said complacently. "But do you know, I believe, for once, I'd rather Dog didn't get to me. Do you think you could take him somewhere else, just to give me a few moments to talk to Elizabeth? You can bring him to my house tomorrow morning and let him jump all over me there, instead."

Laughing, the children obligingly hauled Dog off, leaving Lizzie looking uncomprehendingly from Mrs. Fawcett to the soldier whom she finally placed as Johnnie's cohort, Misha, to the other gentleman who seemed familiar, too. He'd been at the Duchess of Sagan's.

"Elizabeth, this is Count Boris Kyrilovitch Lebedev. He's a friend of...your Cousin Ivan's. Misha, of course, you already know."

Both men bowed, though Misha appeared horribly embarrassed. Until Lizzie looked at him more closely and realized he'd been crying.

Foreboding galloped through her. Her fingers crept up the front of her gown to her throat, nestling there for comfort.

"What's happened?" she asked.

Mrs. Fawcett flapped one arm at Count Lebedev, who said flatly, "Vanya was arrested this afternoon for treason. They're saying he stole a sensitive document and gave it to the British."

Astonishment widened her eyes. She frowned at Count Lebedev. "Why?"

"Why?" he repeated.

"Why would they think such a thing? Why would he *do* such a thing? He wouldn't. It makes no sense. Quite aside from his character, he'd have no reason."

Mrs. Fawcett allowed, "He doesn't need money; he has no grudge against the tsar and no need to curry favor with the British. He's wealthy twice over in two different countries. On the other hand..." She took a deep breath and fixed Lizzie with her piercing gaze. "If a lady asked him, dared him—"

He had a history. He'd stolen the necklace because she asked. Or at least...

"He didn't. And he doesn't. And if you imagine I've been inveigling him to betray his country as some kind of favor to my uncle, or whatever your—"

"I imagine no such thing," Mrs. Fawcett interrupted calmly. "But it may well be what the Russians are imagining. Because of the somewhat...bizarre nature of your meetings."

In the carriage behind the theatre; secretly in the garden, masked at the Emperor's ball, at an unfashionable inn off the beaten track...

Lizzie sank down on the nearest sofa. "But that's silly! Herr Schmidt knew all of that and even he acknowledged we were harmless!"

"To Austria," Mrs. Fawcett pointed out. "Besides which, Herr Schmidt had the felicity of spending time in your company. None of the Russians, save Misha here, ever did."

Lizzie lifted her gaze to Count Lebedev who stood frowning down at her. "If you're his friend, you know he didn't do this."

A smile flickered across the count's face and vanished. "Of course I know. My problem is proving it."

"Speak to him," Lizzie advised, jumping to her feet once more. "Where is he?"

Misha and the count exchanged glances.

"We don't know," Count Lebedev admitted. "He escaped minutes after his arrest, which frankly, has done his cause no good."

Misha exploded in a torrent of Russian, which Count Lebedev translated. "Misha says it's done his survival chances a *lot* of good. You see, it was an old enemy of his who arrested him and probably persuaded the tsar he was guilty in the first place. Blonsky has motives coming out of his ears to set Vanya up for this and everyone knows it. If we can talk the tsar back to rationality, His Majesty will know it, too." He sighed. "For now, he's too angry. Misha thinks Vanya knew he'd be dead before we talked the tsar back round and that's why he bolted."

Lizzie searched Lebedev's serious dark eyes. "Is that what you think?"

"No," the count said. "I think he bolted because he could and he wouldn't give Blonsky the satisfaction. He didn't wait for the better chances he'd inevitably have had on the road. He took the earliest one, in front of the tsar and everyone else watching out of the windows, the one that would cover Blonsky with the maximum embarrassment possible."

She opened her mouth to ask what was between Blonsky and Vanya, but Mrs. Fawcett forestalled her.

"Count Lebedev wants to know if either of us can shed any light on this business. Apparently Vanya blames an Englishman for the undoubted disappearance."

"What Englishman?" Lizzie asked in surprise. "How would it benefit Britain to cause trouble between the allies?" She could tell at once that her question was naive.

"Oh, everyone's jostling for position," Mrs. Fawcett said. "And for allies within the allies, if you see what I mean. Preventing too close an understanding between Russia and Prussia would be seen as an advantage to both Britain and Austria. And probably to France as well, if anyone were talking to the French."

"And this document was related to some agreement between Russia and Prussia?" Lizzie asked, frowning.

Count Lebedev shifted uncomfortably from foot to foot. "I'm afraid I can't say," he said stiffly. "But it's something the British accused the Russians of first thing this morning. Talks are breaking down before they've properly begun and the tsar is not being well regarded. He feels betrayed."

"And Vanya believes an Englishman, not a Russian or even a Prussian, is responsible?" Lizzie said thoughtfully.

Mrs Fawcett swept further into the room and sat opposite Lizzie. "The accusation is that Vanya was bringing the documents to us in the inn when the tsar's guardsmen tried to wrest them from him on the road."

Lizzie's lips parted. "Oh no, that's not right. *We* know we're involved in nothing like that. Yet someone definitely attacked Vanya, whether they believed it to be true or for some other reason entirely.

Oh dear," she added, suddenly stricken. "Perhaps the Russians know that Herr Schmidt was already investigating Vanya and me!"

"Who is Herr Schmidt?" Count Lebedev asked, bewildered.

"One of Baron Hager's policemen."

Count Lebedev paled. "Why?"

"It was a misunderstanding and all my fault." Lizzie dismissed the explanation with the wave of one hand. "Herr Schmidt knows that. So…how do we go about finding who this Englishman is?"

"It must surely be someone who is at least close to diplomatic circles," Count Lebedev said thoughtfully, "though he could be in some menial position, even a servant… but he's probably someone who has a little more money to spend than usual."

Lizzie's stomach gave an unpleasant little twist.

"That doesn't really help," Mrs. Fawcett observed. "There must be hundreds of such Englishmen in Vienna just now…Elizabeth? Have you thought of someone?"

"No, no," Lizzie said quickly. "Just trying to think… If we find the culprit, Count, what would we do? Give the proof to the tsar? Would Vanya then be able to come back? Or would he still be in trouble for escaping?"

"That would rather be up to the tsar. One thing is certain, though, if we don't find the culprit, Vanya will never be able to go home."

"He could come to England, take up the reins at Launceton," Mrs. Fawcett observed. "But it's true his name would be tarnished by such a scandal."

Count Lebedev nodded. Spying, selling the secrets of any country to any other, even one's own, was hardly gentlemanly conduct.

"Well, let's think about it very hard," Lizzie said, "and talk about it tomorrow—at your house, Mrs. Fawcett?"

"Come before two," said the redoubtable Mrs. Fawcett, rising to her feet, "so that we might be private. Count Lebedev, might I have your escort to the ball?"

"Of course," the count said gallantly.

At the door, Mrs. Fawcett turned back. "Aren't you worried about him?" she asked, low. "Don't you wonder how he's coping alone with no roof over his head?"

Lizzie laughed. If it was a laugh with a tiny catch in it, she hoped Mrs. Fawcett wouldn't notice. "Of course not," she said determinedly. "He fought Napoleon's army all through the Russian winter, living off his wits and scraps from the land in between. I really don't think there's much harm an unseasonably warm Austrian autumn can do him."

---

A MAN, VANYA thought, could learn a lot from Herr Schmidt. The policeman had an extraordinary talent for blending into his background, so much so that Vanya, who'd fought with him, been more or less responsible for shooting him, dug a bullet out of his flesh and watched over him during several days and nights of fever, almost walked right past him without noticing him. Which was even worse when he considered he was actually looking for Herr Schmidt at the time.

Under cover of darkness, he'd got into conversation with the coachmen behind the theatre and discovered where several of them passed on their information. It seemed all foreigners' domestic staffs were riddled with spies. And so Vanya walked round to the coffee house and was about to simply walk out again, when a voice at his elbow murmured, "They're looking for you, you know."

Brown hair, gray coat, a pleasant face expressing neither interest nor disinterest, pleasure nor dislike.

Vanya dropped into the chair on the other side of his table. "You're a hard man to find."

"Apparently not."

"How are you?" Vanya asked.

Herr Schmidt blinked, as if surprised by the question. "I'm well. Why are you looking for me?"

"To find out what you know. You've heard of what I stand accused. It's mainly spite against me, but I think a document really was stolen and passed on, and I need to find out who did it."

Herr Schmidt picked up his coffee cup and drank. "I don't know."

Vanya sat back, dug his hands into his pockets. He wasn't yet disappointed since he didn't know whether or not Herr Schmidt was telling the truth. "The men who attacked me last night are under the command of my enemy who accused me. But they claimed to be working for an Englishman. Why would an Englishman want to kill me? So that I couldn't deny it when I was accused?"

Herr Schmidt shrugged. "That sounds more like your enemy's plan."

"Then did Blonsky himself take the document?"

"Probably. I don't know."

Vanya curled his lip. "And yet they say no one sneezes in Vienna without your people being aware of it."

Herr Schmidt set down his cup and regarded Vanya with alarmingly steady eyes. For the first time, he had a glimpse of just how badly this might affect Schmidt's suspects. In his own highly understated way, Herr Schmidt was a dangerous man. He fought dirty, too, as Vanya recalled.

"And you think I owe you help in this matter because you saved my life?" Herr Schmidt inquired.

Vanya raised his eyebrows. "No. It's my belief you're made of old shoe leather and would survive any number of such wounds until you're a slightly tattered old man. I asked from simple friendship, but I see I have assumed." He rose to his feet. "Forgive the intrusion."

Unexpectedly, Schmidt stood, too. "Austria is not the only nation buying secrets," he said quietly and rapidly while he took a handful of small coins from his pocket and counted them out on the table, presumably to pay for his coffee. "Information is being traded like water in a desert, fanning suspicions that were always going to be there and which are now spiraling out of control. I thought at first someone was trying to sabotage the Congress, but now I believe the failure would be just a secondary repercussion. Representatives of all the governments are paying handsomely – far more handsomely than we – for this information. It's become like an exchange and someone is making a lot of money out of it. Especially if he's selling and reselling the same information to lots of different people."

Schmidt, without so much as a goodbye, began to move on.

"Who?" Vanya demanded moving with him. "Who's doing this?"

"An Englishman," Herr Schmidt murmured. "Stay, enjoy your coffee. He has some connection to you and to the Daniels' household. Beyond that, I don't yet know."

Herr Schmidt moved away in front of a waiter, accidentally—perhaps—preventing Vanya from leaving with him. A distracted smile flickered across Vanya's face as he sat back down at the table and asked the waiter for a cup of coffee. But most of his mind was already wrestling with Schmidt's parting words. The connection could be no more than James. But the real, gnawing question was what danger it presented to Lizzie.

"May I take this chair?" The Russian voice was just part of the increased noise that Vanya became aware of. It was time to leave.

"Of course," Vanya said, without thinking.

Perhaps it was his answering in Russian that caused the sharp intake of breath. It would have been smarter not to find out, simply to slink out of the coffee house, meeting no one's gaze. But Vanya had never been good at discretion. He couldn't resist glancing up into the wide-eyed face of an officer he knew. An inn on the road to Paris, a rowdy party with women and too much brandy and a duel with his old childhood bully, Blonsky. And a very young, untried officer bringing him the news of Lord Launceton's death. He couldn't even remember the boy's name, but he was damned sure the boy knew his.

You couldn't wear a sabre with civilian clothes. His only weapon was the dagger in his pocket and that really wouldn't be much use against the swords of…how many? Six officers, not all of whom were yet drunk. He'd make a fight of it, but he didn't care for the odds.

There was no doubt of the young officer's recognition. And he clearly knew Vanya's fugitive position. For an instant, neither of them moved. Vanya didn't really want to hurt him. He'd rather liked him for his disapproval which was probably why he'd taken the time to win him over. A hundred contradictory expressions crossed the boy's face now, revealing his struggle with duty and honor and, probably, belief. Behind him, his friends were arguing over the relative beauty of the Duchess of Sagan and Princess Bagration.

The young man dropped his gaze, lifted the chair, and turned back toward his friends. "No, the Duchess of Sagan is the more beautiful," he said. "Just in a subtler way."

Vanya exhaled slowly and stood. He walked out of the coffee house, well aware what he owed the young officer whose name he couldn't even remember.

―❦―

HAVING SLEPT BADLY, Lizzie rose and dressed early. Her first ambition of the day was to speak to James. If Vanya was suffering for something James had done, then they had to put it right somehow, preferably without James going to prison or disgracing his father. As she walked past James and Michael's room, she paused, closing her fingers around the handle. It would certainly be the quickest, quietest place to talk, although she wasn't sure it was something Michael should overhear. And in any case, James made no sense when he hadn't had enough sleep. There was no point in even trying to talk to him this early.

A scratching and wheefling at the door told her that Dog already knew she was up and about, so she opened the door just enough to release him and quietly closed it again. Dog gave her the usual long-lost-friend welcome and then galloped down the stairs, skidding around the corner into the hall, piling rugs into a heap as he went.

Lizzie followed more sedately, straightening everything as she went. Since she could never be sure which servants were in the garden doing what and if the back gate was closed, she picked up the leash from its hook by the back door and slipped it on Dog before opening the back door and allowing herself to be dragged outside into the pale, early morning sunshine.

There was a definite chill in the air, as if the late summery weather was finally being forced away. Or perhaps it was just her own feeling, colored by recent ominous events. Dog, having stood still for almost ten seconds with his twitching nose lifted into the breeze, made a sudden lunge at the clothes pole and lifted his leg, during which procedure he continued to sniff the air. As soon as he'd finished, he set off down the garden at a brisk trot, nose to the ground, making excited little whining noises as he went.

Lizzie let him pull her on—it was too early for her to have anything better to do than watch Dog and think—until they reached the potting shed close to the gate. Whatever he was after seemed to be in there for he pawed at the door in a most peremptory fashion.

"What do you imagine's in there?" Lizzie murmured. "A cat? You won't like it, you know. Or at least," she amended, "it won't like you." Since the dog had actually managed to paw the door open by this time, she hung on tight to the lead, prepared to be spun in circles as he tried to play with whatever creature was inside.

A shadow filled the doorway and Lizzie dropped the lead anyway, for Dog was hurling himself with joy upon Johnnie. Vanya. Cousin Ivan. Colonel Savarin. And what she called him really didn't matter as much as the fact that he was here. A little rumpled and definitely unshaven, he caught the dog with one hand while holding a letter in the other.

"Are you insane to be here?" Lizzie demanded, fear lending a scolding tone to her voice. "Don't you know they watch this house?"

"The Austrians watch it. The Austrians watch everyone. It's the Russians I have to worry about."

"You don't *look* very worried," Lizzie observed, although she anxiously picked out lines around his eyes and mouth that she'd never seen before. For some reason, they hurt her. Her gaze fell on the letter in his free hand. It was addressed simply to Michael. Frowning, she lifted her uncomprehending gaze to Vanya's. "Why are you here? Why are you writing to Michael?"

"I'm not. I just thought he'd be the first to pass this way in the morning with Dog."

"Have you slept in there?" Lizzie demanded.

"Sort of." He held out the letter. "It's really for you. And James."

"James!" she exclaimed with foreboding. "What is going on, Va—" She broke off.

An unhappy half-smile flickered across his face and died. "Go on. You can say the name without fear of reprisals."

"I don't need to. I need an answer."

"The answer is, I don't know but I need to find out. I think we all do. Someone's playing havoc with all our suspicions and making a lot of money at it. If we want to save peace in Europe, I think we have to stop him."

"Will it save *you*?" she blurted, taking the letter and hiding it in the folds of her shawl.

"I don't know." His gaze drifted up and down the garden and then he stepped out of the shed.

"Where are you going?" Lizzie asked in alarm.

Vanya bent and retrieved the leash, handing it to her before he released Dog with a last pull of his ears. For an instant, the blaze in his eyes melted her bones and her stomach. He smiled. "To the devil, Miss Gaunt. Ask anyone."

Her breath caught as he moved closer and she had the insane desire to touch the stubble on his jaw. She wondered wildly how it would feel against her face if he kissed her… And then he did, a sudden lunge, capturing her lips, hard, and then releasing her almost in the same moment, as if he feared her retribution—or her embrace. The suddenness left her staggering, as he brushed past her to the gate and vanished. His last muttered word drifted back on the breeze, barely audible.

"Sorry."

"For what?" she whispered to the empty garden. Only by the movement of her lips did she realize she was touching them, as if to hold his kiss in place.

She dropped her arm and drew in a shaky breath. Then, giving herself a brisk shake, she dragged Dog back into the house, desperate now to read whatever it was Vanya had written to her and James. Hurrying back upstairs, she saw Michael emerging, yawning from his bed chamber.

"Michael, is James awake?" she hissed.

Michael, about to close the door threw it open once more. "James! Lizzie wants you!" And leaving the door wide, he walked past Lizzie, grabbing Dog by the collar as he went. "Come on, Dog, let's play ball," he encouraged, rushing downstairs with Dog barking at his heels.

Lizzie walked into the bedroom. "James, are you awake?"

James sat bolt upright in bed. "Lizzie!" he expostulated. "What the devil—"

Lizzie closed the door behind her. "Hush, for goodness sake."

"You can't be in here," he protested. "At least not while I am."

"Don't be so silly. We practically grew up together. Who cares? Pull the covers up to your chin if it makes you feel better. I've got a letter for you and I need to talk to you."

"Well, leave the letter and go away!"

"I can't until I've spoken to you." And if she got the wrong answers, she wouldn't give him the letter.

She sat down on the edge of Michael's bed and held his bewildered gaze. "When I saw you in the living room the other night, did you take one of your father's documents?"

A hunted look came into his eyes and her heart sank. Worse, she was sure he meant to deny it or at least evade the question with bluster. Then his shoulders slumped.

"Yes, I did. I was desperate. It was something that didn't matter to *us*, something to do with the Russians and the Prussians."

"Oh, James." How could he imagine that was unimportant to Britain or to the Congress in general? "What did you do with it?"

"I went to meet this bloke who'd promised to buy it from me."

Her heart beating hard, Lizzie said, "Who did you meet, James?"

James' lips twisted. "Ivan the Terrible."

## Chapter Nineteen

Lizzie felt the blood drain from her face so fast she had to grasp the bedclothes to scare off the dizziness. "You met Cousin Ivan?" she whispered. "You sold *him* the document?"

"Not exactly…you know, despite evicting you all from Launceton so indecently fast, he's not such a bad chap. In fact, he's a great gun."

Lizzie pressed both hands into her temples. "But this doesn't make sense. He wouldn't! Even if he would, why should he? Surely my uncle had already seen it?"

"If you ask me, it's you who's not making any sense. He didn't *buy* the document from me. He made me take it back and he lent me five thousand to pay off all my debts in one. I'm going to work for him to pay it back."

Lizzie, feeling like a fish gasping in the air, said, "As what?" in a strangled voice.

"We haven't decided yet. Perhaps helping to manage one of the estates. Who knows? If he goes back to Russia, I might be able to sneak you all home to Launceton Hall."

"Oh James, you idiot," Lizzie said, going to him and throwing her arms around his neck in a brief, hard hug of sheer relief. After a second of stunned surprise, just as she released him, his arms came around her, just as the door opened and Aunt Lucy stuck her head in.

"James, I need you to—" She broke off, her mouth falling open in astonishment. "James?" she floundered. "Lizzie?" In horror, she leapt into the room and closed the door, leaning against it with both palms flat against the wood.

James' arms, fortunately, had fallen away as soon as his mother had opened the door, but neither could pretend she hadn't seen and grossly misunderstood.

"It's not what you think, Mama," James announced. "Lizzie and I are going to be married."

"No you're not!" Aunt Lucy exclaimed.

"No we're not!" Lizzie uttered at the same time.

"You can't," Aunt Lucy declared. "You're first cousins and neither of you has a bean!"

"We don't care," James insisted. "We're engaged."

"We are *not* engaged," Lizzie said irritably. "Stop being so silly, James. You're practically my brother and we are not compromised!"

"But Lizzie, I'm surprised at you," Aunt Lucy raged. "What in the world are you doing in here cuddling James?"

"I wasn't cuddling him!" Lizzie protested. "Exactly. It was just…we'd managed to solve a problem together and it was a great relief."

"Well, there you are, you can't marry a man because you're relieved!"

"Of course you can't," Lizzie agreed and Aunt Lucy, although still a trifle bewildered, began to look mollified.

Until James said determinedly, "But the reason isn't relief; it's love. I love Lizzie and I wish to marry her."

"Since when?" Aunt Lucy demanded.

"Since never!" Lizzie exclaimed. "James, you do *not* love me or want to marry me! Only last week you were in love with that awful Fischer woman!"

But if she'd hoped to fire him into defense of his first love with the insult, she was doomed to disappointment. James merely waved the beautiful Louise Fischer to one side as an unimportant fancy of his youth.

"Perhaps he's still drunk," Lizzie said to Aunt Lucy and left them to it. She had more important things to think about, such as what

Vanya's letter said.

It wasn't much of a letter, more of a military instruction, asking for a list of all the British people she knew in Vienna, especially those who had visited the house or who were at all intimate with either James or his father. Clearly, Vanya, too, was trying to track down the mysterious Englishman who traded in state secrets and, knowing James' moment of weakness with the purloined document, assumed her cousin knew him.

Two hours later, as she sat alone in the drawing room window, mending a pile of stockings, James stuck his head around the door and she beckoned him inside.

"I never had the chance to give you the letter from Cousin Ivan," she said, low.

"I'm a bit worried about Cousin Ivan," James confessed. "Papa's just told me the Russians tried to arrest him and he escaped. They think he stole their document about the secret meeting with the Prussians. Apparently, he fought ten men to a standstill and then leapt bareback onto a horse and jumped it over a meat wagon to get away. Some people say he *killed* ten men, in which case I don't see the tsar ever forgiving him."

"Oh dear," Lizzie said, pressing her hands to her cheeks, then lowering them decisively. "But then, it's probably not true."

Hastily, she repeated the gist of his letter. James sat down there and then to begin writing his list. He made two columns, one for Lizzie's acquaintances and one for his own, so that he could write Lizzie's down while she carried on sewing.

"Oh, you know Grassic, do you?" James said thoughtfully when she came to that name. "What do you think of him?"

"He's good company, amusing and knowledgeable. Beyond that, I don't know. Why?"

James wrinkled his nose. "He's a friend of Cousin Cedric's."

"That certainly stands against him, but I don't believe they're close. Why do you ask? What do you think of him?"

"Well..." James shifted in the chair and took a deep breath. "It was

Grassic told me about the money to be made from selling particular documents."

Lizzie stared at him, letting her work fall into her lap. "*Mr. Grassic* put you up to it?"

"Well, he put me in the way of it, told me where to go and when to deliver it and get paid. But dash it, Lizzie, he's a man of the cloth! I don't think he's the villain Cousin Ivan's looking for!"

"Why not?" she asked baldly. "Just because he's a clergyman?"

"No, dash it, because he's a gentleman. He was just helping me out of a hole, not running some international spying organization."

Lizzie gazed at him in frustration. "James. What sort of a gentleman suggests to a diplomat's son that he steal an important document and sell it to strangers in the dead of night? If you have no concept of what your discovery would have done to your father, you may safely wager that Mr. Grassic does."

James stared into space, digesting that, then brought his eyes back into focus on Lizzie's face. "You think I'm a bit of a fool, don't you?"

"I think your good nature combined with your lack of experience makes you too trusting," Lizzie replied kindly, returning to her needlework. "I suspect it wouldn't matter so much anywhere but here at this particular time. A better question is really what we do about Mr. Grassic?"

After a few moments of thought, she became aware of James' gaze, still riveted to her face, as though he were seeing someone quite other than his familiar and slightly odd cousin, Lizzie.

She frowned. "You *have* stopped all this marriage nonsense, haven't you?"

"Oh no. I think it would be a capital idea to be married, don't you?"

"No! James, there is absolutely no need for this. My reputation is not in need of saving."

"Oh, I know that. And I'll not deny the words first tumbled out in a fit of chivalry, but do you know, I liked them as soon as I spoke them. The idea grows on me all the time. I'd very much like to marry you, Lizzie."

"No, you wouldn't," she said flatly. "I'd drive you insane in an hour. And besides, I'm too old for you and I regard you in something of the same light as I regard Michael, so marriage would *not* be comfortable!"

"I won't give up," James announced, rising to his feet as the sounds of his mother and sister returning from some expedition drifted in through the door.

"James, how can I be clearer? I won't marry you and I won't change my mind!"

He only smiled in the annoying way of men who believe a mere woman can't know her own mind. How could he have learned that and failed to grasp the basics of right and wrong as personified in Mr. Grassic?

James strolled out. Lizzie heard a brief exchange in the hall and then Minerva came in to show her the new trim for her best ball gown which she had already worn several times.

"It's very pretty and will look most charmingly on that gown," Lizzie approved, glad to see her taking an interest at last. It would please Aunt Lucy, although the reason might not. Minerva now wished to look her best for Mr. Corner.

"I want to be an asset to him in every way," Minerva confided. "I quite understand that impressions such as appearance can be important, especially at the beginning of a diplomatic relationship."

Lizzie smiled. "And a romantic one. Are you winning my aunt and uncle around?"

"Not exactly. Mama won't listen to anything about it and I'm fairly sure she hasn't even mentioned it to Papa. But I'm quite fixed upon it."

"And Mr. Corner?"

Minerva blushed. "He wishes to marry me, but he believes we should wait until Papa receives his promotion after the Congress. Mr. Corner will surely rise with him and this will be an excellent time to ask Papa for my hand."

Besides which, it gave the young people time to know each other better. Lizzie's opinion of Mr. Corner's good sense and his care of Minerva rose another notch.

"But what about you, Lizzie? You're really going to marry James?"

"Of course I'm not!" Lizzie said irritably. "James said it in a foolish bout of misplaced chivalry. There is no engagement."

"Oh." Minerva began wrapping her trimmings back up. "Pity. It would have been nice to have you as my sister."

Lizzie didn't point out that she came with two sisters of her own, plus an illegitimate brother. And her own preferred independence in a cottage somewhere was less likely than ever now that she felt obliged to give Vanya the money back.

"Oh, and Mama thinks you will have to start coming out with us," Minerva said brightly. "At least to some events."

"Oh no. That was never in our agreement. None of us would enjoy my being the obvious poor relation and none of us can afford anything different."

"Well, Mama has found a dressmaker who's just starting out on her own so her prices are excellent. She thinks we could afford you a new ball gown. We can share trims to change the appearance."

"You're all so kind, but no, it wouldn't be right." Lizzie put away her work and stood, gathering up the mended stockings.

"But you are going to Mrs. Fawcett's, so what's the difference?"

Lizzie laughed. "Mrs. Fawcett is a force of nature."

"And you go to the Duchess of Sagan's."

"I went once in the afternoon. Because Dorothée took us there. And talking of afternoon visits, I promised to go to Mrs. Fawcett early today…"

The drawing room door flew open to admit an angry maid. "Miss, the dog eats my washing!" she raged.

∞

AT MRS. FAWCETT'S, Count Lebedev began to pass on what he'd learned from Vanya.

"Then you've seen him?" Mrs. Fawcett said eagerly.

"He accosted me in my rooms in the middle of the night," Lebedev said wryly. "He'd been speaking to an Austrian policeman, who told him information is circulating like a plague. The same stolen documents are being bought and sold several times and everyone's paying huge amounts of money in the belief that they're buying something vital that no one else knows about. By now, they must have guessed the information isn't always unique, but still they pay. And one man seems to be reaping the benefits. An Englishman."

"Mr. Grassic," Lizzie said. "He's an English clergyman—or says he is. I've written to the Bishop of Gloucester, who was a friend of my father's, to find out if he really has a living clergyman in his diocese, but it will be some time before we have an answer."

Count Lebedev blinked at her in clear surprise. "So that's it," he said, incomprehensibly.

"I beg your pardon?"

"Nothing. So, we know who…but to save Vanya, we need to know who took the Russian document to sell to Grassic."

"We could ask Grassic," Mrs. Fawcett said grimly. "I have two *very* stout footmen."

Count Lebedev, appearing to see nothing amiss with this plan, nodded thoughtfully. "I know a few Cossacks who'd be willing to hold him down, too."

"I suspect if you beat a man enough he'll tell you what you want to hear rather than the truth," Lizzie said sternly. "Isn't our best chance to – ah – persuade him is to have him do it again and catch him?"

Lebedev eyed her with fascination. "How would we do that? Without opening the tsar's government to further risk?"

"Well," Lizzie said modestly. "I have a plan."

※

Mrs. Fawcett insisted that Lizzie's plan would work much better if she went out more in society and, so, rather doubtfully, Lizzie allowed her friend to buy her two new evening gowns, one of which she wore to Prince Metternich's masquerade ball.

Minerva, delighted to have her cousin's company, was effusive in her admiration. Lizzie suspected she would have enjoyed the clothes and the ball a lot more a week ago. The glittering occasion, the sumptuous surroundings and dazzling guests, to say nothing of their supremely sophisticated host, now left her just a little flat. If it hadn't been for her goal of discovering the English secret-trader, she would have been dull company, indeed.

Instead, she strove to sparkle, to dance and make witty conversation, in which she was helped by Dorothée, who introduced her to a wide new circle of international acquaintances. It would all, Lizzie hoped, add to her attraction as a woman with knowledge for sale. And it seemed to be working. By the time Mr. Grassic approached her for a dance, she only had one place left on her card—deliberately so.

Of course, her success was not universal. As she strolled between dances with Dorothée, they stopped to converse with a group of people who included Countess Savarina and another beautiful Russian woman Lizzie was sure she'd seen at the Duchess of Sagan's. As introductions flowed, Lizzie made a point of smiling at the countess and remarking in friendly fashion that they were already acquaintances, being almost cousins.

The countess, her eyes like flint, gave the smallest, coldest inclination of her head and deliberately excused herself. A week ago, Lizzie might have felt hurt or humiliated. Now, she knew only a childish desire to stick her tongue out at the countess' back.

"Don't worry about her," the younger Russian lady murmured beside her, as conversation endeavored to cover the countess' rudeness. "On principal, she dislikes all women associated with her son."

"One can't help one's birth," Lizzie said lightly.

The lady lifted exquisite, not quite amused eyebrows. "It's hardly your birth that's the problem."

Lizzie lifted her chin. "What do you mean?" she asked directly.

"I mean everyone knows it was you he galloped off to meet every day."

Heat seeped into Lizzie's skin. "I don't know what you mean. I visited an old family friend, mostly in company with my horde of siblings and animals. There is no scandal for the countess to fear."

"Of course not," the lady soothed, quite blatantly disingenuous.

Lizzie gazed at her, uncomfortably suspicious. "I'm sorry, there were so many introductions, I stupidly missed who you are."

The Russian lady smiled. "Let's just say Countess Savarina didn't speak to me, either. Until you came along. Thank you. You are really an excellent distraction. Or were, before his fall from grace."

She'd known, of course; she'd always known about his women. And this one was very beautiful. It was her flippant tone that rankled.

"His fall doesn't concern you?" Lizzie asked.

"Vanya always has a way of landing on his feet, so no, it doesn't." She smiled and tapped Lizzie's cheek gently with her closed fan. "Accept the advice of one who has played the game for a long time and knows him very well. Enjoy the fun and invest nothing of yourself or he'll break your heart. I never cling and he always comes back to me."

"How nice for you," Lizzie murmured inanely. "Excuse me. I'm promised for this next dance."

FOR VANYA, REVEALING the corrupt trade in secrets had become not merely a means of proving his innocence but an end in itself. Anger at his accusers, from the tsar downwards, churned his blood. He was aware that even if he managed to turn this back on Blonsky, that bitterness at his supposed friends' lack of trust, the ease with which Blonsky had turned everyone against him, would always be with him.

But he wouldn't leave it alone. He'd rub his innocence in their faces, kill Blonsky if he could, and then walk away, resign. Go to England and…no, he couldn't bear that, either. Maybe he'd just go to the devil as everyone expected and not care about anything or anyone. It was easiest if he just didn't think beyond the immediate task.

Which was shadowing Blonsky about the city, seeing where he went and with whom he spent time. Tracking down a single enemy in a city wasn't quite the same as finding and laying ambushes for French units in the vast, freezing landscape of Russia, but his earlier experience did seem to stand him in good stead. He moved silently, used whatever cover he could find, and listened. And he talked to people, found out who lived in the houses Blonsky visited. Sometimes Vanya followed him into taverns or public events from troop reviews to masked balls, just to observe who his friends were, especially among the British.

Although he was glad to accept the help of Misha and Boris, he wasn't selfish enough to go near them after that first night. He knew the tsar's agents were looking for him in his own barracks, at his mother's house, even at Sonia's. He suspected they'd been out to the Emperor Inn, too. But, fortunately, they had to be careful in another sovereign's capital. They couldn't tear Vienna apart to find him and he made the most of that.

Misha had smuggled him out some necessities such as civilian clothes and he'd found a grotty room in a run-down part of the city. He only slept a few hours there, washed, shaved, and changed his clothes, so its insalubrious character never bothered him.

What did bother him was when he followed Blonsky into a masquerade ball at Prince Metternich's summer palace and he saw Lizzie waltzing with the Austrian Captain von Reinharz.

In that instant, he lost sight of Blonsky, just in gazing at Lizzie. She amazed him all over again. Her mask had slipped, which was how he'd spotted her so quickly, and she was trying to retie it while continuing to dance. Both she and her partner obviously found this most entertaining. She was so beautiful, laughing, vital, graceful…and in the arms of that *rake*. Vanya actually found himself halfway across the dance floor to snatch her from the man and knock him down, before he remembered he had neither the right nor the luxury. Besides which, she would hardly thank him for such a scene. He should be glad that her family had let her out to have a little fun, and part of him was. But the other, darker, stronger part was eaten up with the sort of fury that could only come from jealousy. And the total impossibility of his feelings.

Swerving off the dance floor, he tore his gaze away from her and went in search of Blonsky, instead. Vanya found him paying court to Sonia, who was far too experienced a flirt to treat him with more than amused indifference, only bestowing the odd glance, enough to give him hope. Once, Vanya had looked upon that as a challenge, one he'd risen to and won. Too easily, perhaps. It struck him that, although they were both aware of the rules of the liaisons game, he hadn't treated Sonia terribly well. He'd led her back into their old affair and then abandoned her because he'd discovered he didn't even want to touch a woman who wasn't Lizzie.

He'd thought at first he just needed to wait for the obsession to go away, for he knew when she found out he was the reviled cousin, Ivan the Terrible, there would be no chance for him. And so it had proved, although just for a moment, the look in her face when he collapsed at her feet in the inn with relief at her safety had given him hope. If she could forgive him for the Vanya-Johnnie mix-up, maybe she would look afresh at Cousin Ivan…

But, of course, she didn't. Her hurt tore him up, not just because of her suffering but because it proved some measure of care for him, for Vanya or Johnnie. If it hadn't been for Ivan the Terrible, he might even have stood a chance.

But he didn't. There was no chance. And now, to cap it all, he stood accused of treason and had bolted rather than answer the charge, which probably made him a deserter, too. And his obsession only grew worse, making him yearn to hit old friends who had the temerity to dance with her.

An almost-distraction from his own pain occurred when, from his brooding position behind a pillar, he saw Blonsky move away from Sonia and into the path of the man just passing Vanya's pillar.

"Grassic," someone murmured, by way of greeting, and the man passing Vanya made a polite response.

Grassic. Tall, dark, elegant… The name had been passed on to Vanya by Misha in a bare note passed in a crowded market square. Vanya took it for what it was, the name of the Englishman at the root of the problem, the likeliest mutual acquaintance of James Daniels and Blonsky.

Vanya kept his gaze on Grassic and on Blonsky's approach. They did, indeed, exchange greetings, but they moved on without stopping or even bowing. Still, Vanya resolved to observe them both and elected to follow Grassic for the rest of the evening.

He shouldn't have been surprised when the Englishman danced with Lizzie. He certainly wasn't prepared when the pair slipped through a garden door to take some fresh air in the rather more licentious atmosphere outdoors. Now fear for her overcame the fresh surge of jealousy. It hadn't struck him before that Lizzie might actually be in danger from Grassic. Surely she was too smart to fall for his nonsense, especially now she knew about James and…and how much did she know?

From the shadows of the building, Vanya watched over her. Anger and anxiety bubbled up, seething, for she seemed to be *flirting* with him. Certainly they talked a lot, though Vanya couldn't make out the words through the distant music and conversation from the building. At least, when Grassic took her hand, she slid it free at once and began to walk back to the ballroom.

And suddenly, Vanya just wanted it all over and done.

# Chapter Twenty

Mr. Grassic reached his room at the top of a tall, narrow Viennese house, by an outside staircase for which his landlady frequently apologized, thinking it unseemly, apparently, for a man of the cloth to have to climb so far out of doors. Grassic always assured her with great patience and good humor that the exercise was good for him and brought him closer to God. In fact, he preferred the freedom to come and go unobserved, and had quickly learned how to do so without making the rather rickety stairs screech.

Mr. Grassic was in an excellent mood. He'd had a good day's trading and was well up in his takings. What was more, and just a little exiting, he was sure he had Daniels' niece just about in his pocket, which would more than make up for the loss of James. Miss Gaunt was pretty, charming, clever – and Cedric's cousin. He couldn't make up his mind whether he should marry her or just ruin her. On the whole, he inclined to marriage, since she was such a refined catch. A man could go far with a noble wife, even if she was poor. *Especially* if she was poor, since it made her hungrier…

Mr. Grassic smiled as he climbed the stairs, counting to avoid the noisy steps and weaving to avoid the areas that creaked. His door and the lock were well oiled, too, so his key slid in silently and he was able to enter his attic and even close the door without a sound.

Only then did everything begin to unravel. Without warning, lamplight blinded him, as if someone had suddenly thrown off a heavy cover. Instinctively, Grassic lifted his hand to block the light, while still trying to peer through it to the still figure who sat by his desk, bathed in the white glow.

Although not a physically brave man, Mr. Grassic was not used to fear. He relied on his wit and intelligence to keep himself safe. That and the protection of the cloth. None of those things had kept a stranger out of his room.

He swallowed. But before he could even begin his poor man speech, a deep, soft voice said, "Don't make a sound. Don't move a muscle. Or I'll shoot you were you stand."

Only then did Grassic see the pistol pointing steadily through the light. Fear paralyzed his brain as well as his body.

"We understand each other?" the stranger inquired.

Grassic nodded desperately and, at last, his brain began to work. "Of course," he said hoarsely and cleared his throat. "I think you are a troubled man. I'd like to help you."

"Oh, I am," the stranger agreed. "And you will. You paid Blonsky's soldiers to assassinate me."

So that was it... Colonel Savarin. Probably the worst of all the possibilities Grassic had been imagining. Plus, he'd found his way here. There was no point in denying it.

"My hand was forced," Grassic croaked. "All I could do was persuade them not to try too hard and that obviously worked."

"You're good," Colonel Savarin allowed. He sounded amused. Grassic wasn't sure yet whether that was a good thing or a bad.

Cautiously, now that his eyes were more used to the light, he studied his opponent. Savarin wore civilian dress and looked a little rough, like a working man wearing a rich man's cast-offs.

"I presume," Savarin said, as if he didn't much care, "that my doting cousin, Cedric, paid you to—ah...get me out of the way, so that he can be the next Baron of Launceton. When that didn't work, you and Blonsky made the best of the tsar's discovery of stolen documents and implicated me, instead. My death was bound to follow one way or another."

"I know nothing about that," Grassic said anxiously.

"About stolen documents?" Savarin said in stark disbelief. "My dear sir, they are your whole raison d'être! And the amount of money you were prepared to pay James Daniels, you must sell the same information over and over to everyone."

"I keep it circulating," Grassic admitted. "Although I confess I exaggerated the pay to Daniels so he'd make the first theft. After that, with the hold, I could force him to many more for no more money."

"You really are a nasty little worm, aren't you?" Savarin observed.

For some reason, Grassic felt his whole body flush at the other man's contempt. That was rare and he didn't like it. "If you say so. You have the gun."

Savarin spared it a glance. "So I do. On the other hand, unless I kill you here in cold blood, which I am, of course, prepared to do—might as well be hung for a sheep as for a lamb—I won't always be the man with the gun. And if I shoot you, there is still Blonsky, who, by the way, is preparing to sell you down the river. So…I have a proposition for you, Mr. Grassic. As a man of business."

Grassic shifted position, frowning. "Sell me down the river? How? What do you mean?"

Savarin shrugged. "Once you've got rid of me, he won't need you. He'll tell the tsar I sold the documents to you. The tsar will tell the Austrians and the British and the Prussians, even the French, and your lucrative little business will be over. Worse, someone, probably the British, will throw you in prison and lose the key."

Grassic narrowed his eyes. "You can't know that."

"Actually, I can. I've been watching and listening to both of you very closely over the last few days. As if my life depended on it."

Grassic moved closer to his enemy and sat down in the other chair. Savarin didn't object. "So what do you propose?"

"An alliance," Savarin said. "You and I against Blonsky."

Grassic eyed him with something like fascination. "And how, exactly, would that work?"

Savarin shrugged. "I've got documents that everyone will want. Direct orders from the tsar to me in the last months of the war that prove his future ambitions. Plus…a letter from the tsar, supposedly to the Prince de Talleyrand but quite clearly to Bonaparte himself. Trust me, the Allies will bite your hand off for that one."

Grassic felt his blood stir with excitement. This was exactly what he needed. Too good to be true? Probably. "And you would give me these," he said slowly, "in return for how much gold?"

"I don't need gold. I need Blonsky behind bars. I want proof of his treachery to the tsar. In return for that, I'll give you the documents I have. And when my position is restored, we can come to a fresh arrangement."

Grassic raised his eyebrows. "Colonel, you're unexpectedly naive. I don't keep documents that could incriminate me or my associates."

"Of course you do," Savarin said wryly. "If you didn't, how could you control them? But," he added, getting to his feet, "if it turns out you're not quite so clever as I'd imagined, I'll have to find some other way to reverse my position."

"Don't rush off," Grassic said hastily, then laughed because it was quite bizarre to be suddenly trying to keep the dangerous man with the gun here. "Supposing…just supposing I had such a document incriminating Major Blonsky. You would accept that as sole payment for the documents you mentioned?"

"I would. Providing it incriminates Blonsky."

The blood flowed faster through Grassic's veins. He could clean up with such documents, acquired with no outlay whatsoever. He might even be able to retire before the end of the Congress. "There's a coffee house by the Theatre an der Wien—" he began.

"No," Savarin interrupted.

"Very well. The corner of the Graben, where you found young Daniels—"

"No," Savarin said again. "At the risk of hurting your feelings, Mr. Grassic, the exchange will not happen in one of your haunts or some dark back alley where I can be murdered quietly by, say, Blonsky's thugs. Or anyone else's that you might have a loan of. It will happen at Mrs. Fawcett's masquerade ball, where even you would dare do nothing outrageous."

Although Grassic rather liked being considered so dangerous, even by proxy, Savarin's idea seemed even more risky.

"Mrs. Fawcett's?" Grassic frowned. "Won't the tsar himself be there? Even if he isn't, several of his minions will be. You'll be arrested before you set foot in the place."

"I'll wear the same mask I wore to Metternich's ball tonight."

Grassic forced his eyebrows back up. "You do like to live dangerously, don't you, Colonel Savarin?"

"No, I'm fed up with it, which is why I need you on my side and Blonsky out of the way."

"And poor Cedric?" Grassic inquired.

Savarin shrugged. "Tell him I'm dead or in prison and about to die, that he'll be Baron Launceton any day. I don't care. With what I'm about to give you, you won't need Cedric's blood money anyhow, though I'm sure you'll still find a way to get it."

Savarin brought up the pistol, gazing at it as if in surprise. In spite of his returned confidence, Grassic held his breath. Then Savarin pocketed the weapon and inclined his head. "Until Mrs. Fawcett's," he drawled and sauntered out of the room. He didn't even trouble to walk quietly down the stairs. Everyone in the house would know Grassic had had a late night visitor.

***

GRASSIC WAS GLAD he didn't need to go looking for Blonsky. They met quite by accident at the morning hunt in the Vienna Woods.

"He'll be at Mrs. Fawcett's ball," Grassic murmured as they both waited for the animals to be released.

"Who will?" Blonsky demanded, his none-too-great mind clearly on the prospect of more immediate slaughter.

"Who do you think?" Grassic said beneath his breath. "Just make sure your soldiers are there."

After all, his little game here was nearly over. Savarin's future services were of no real interest to him, not after he'd acquired the explosive Bonaparte letter which would be Grassic's swan song, as it were. Once that was in his hands, Blonsky could do what he liked with the bastard. What Savarin had failed to take into account was that Grassic simply couldn't have people breaking into his home, wherever that might be. It was bad for business.

---

"Don't be so sad," Henrietta said anxiously. "You look beautiful."

Realizing her sisters had come in, Lizzie pulled herself together and gave a bright smile. "Oh, I'm not sad, just thinking," she assured them. "I don't want to get too used to this life!"

"What, three parties in one week?" Georgiana said disparagingly. "Minerva has been to dozens."

"But people will look for Lizzie more because she's seen less," Henrietta said.

Lizzie didn't know if it was shrewd or not. Her new socializing, largely at Mrs. Fawcett's expense, had one motive: to exonerate Vanya. After that, her life was a flat, blank canvas, bleak and dull, so she concentrated quite hard on her immediate aims. Which should come to fruition tonight, all being well.

Lizzie wore a new white silk gown draped in gold gauze. Its high waist fitted perfectly and the skirts fell around her with particular elegance. The bodice was cut a little lower than she liked, but she was pleased with that, too, since she needed to use all her wiles on Grassic.

Minerva had dressed her hair in a vaguely Grecian style that her sisters were admiring with silent awe. But she wore no jewelry, despite the efforts of Minerva, Aunt Lucy, and Mrs. Fawcett to lend her some. She wished to continue the image of a penniless young woman, driven to desperate measures. It wasn't so far from the truth, although she cringed when she remembered what those desperate measures had been, in reality, only a couple of weeks before.

"Aunt Lucy's calling for you," Henrietta said. "You'd better go. Michael has Dog shut up, so he won't get to you!"

Lizzie walked over to the bed and picked up her reticule, which was a little fatter than normal because it contained a well-folded document headed with Lord Castlereagh's name and position.

"Wish me luck." Lizzie flung the words over her shoulder as she hurried downstairs to join the others.

As they entered Mrs. Fawcett's rather charming house in the old, inner city, Aunt Lucy murmured, "Don't you see a big change in Minerva? She seemed, finally, to be enjoying herself. It must be your company that gives her confidence, my dear."

"I shouldn't think so," answered Lizzie, who was fairly sure it had more to do with her cousin's happiness in her understanding with Mr. Corner.

Mrs. Fawcett, unmistakable since she was welcoming her guests, stood resplendent in black and silver and glittering diamonds, her mask and domino cloak matching her gown.

"A bold choice," Lizzie approved. "You make the rest of us seem bland and underdressed."

Mrs. Fawcett leaned closer. "Between you and me, some *are* underdressed. Wait until you see Princess Bagration. But you, my dear, are tasteful and delightful and anything but bland! He's here, already," she added under her breath. "Scarlet domino."

Lizzie saw him almost as soon as she entered the ballroom—a tall, rather elegant figure of a man. She marveled yet again at his skill in appearing the perfect gentleman, the academic and yet ambitious churchman. Of course, he might really have been all of those things as well as a treacherous weasel.

"Let me have two dances." James's voice interrupted her.

She was about to nod with vague, uninterested agreement, when the meaning of his words penetrated her distraction. "None," she laughed. "Go and dance with girls your own age!"

The relaxing of her aunt's shoulders just in front of her, showed James' mother was listening in with some relief.

"But I've learned that I don't really like girls my own age," James confided. His eyes developed an alarming burning. "I prefer older women."

Lizzie didn't know whether to laugh or slap him. Instead, she raised one eyebrow. "Then it's as well for both of us that I'm developing a strong dislike of very young, very gauche men."

"Go and fetch us lemonade, James," Aunt Lucy commanded and James, very red-faced, bolted to do her bidding. "I'd ask you to nip this very odd affection in the bud, Lizzie, but James seems to be doing an excellent job of it himself."

"I imagine it's a passing phase," Lizzie said ruefully and turned to answer the greeting of Captain von Reinharz, easily recognized beneath the mask by his blond whiskers, who'd come to ask her to dance.

She spent the next hour flitting around the ballroom, avoiding Grassic until after the tsar arrived. If Alexander didn't make an appearance, the whole play would be lost and all to do again, but eventually Lizzie saw his familiar, tall, blond figure being welcomed by Mrs. Fawcett with a low curtsey.

Deserting Minerva, she made her gradual way around the ballroom, hoping Grassic would notice her. The orchestra struck up a waltz and without warning, an arm snaked around her, whirling her around.

For an instant, a tiny instant, her heart leapt with furious excitement, for the height of her masterful partner, his dark hair and mask and his bright red domino, all combined to make her think it was Vanya.

But, of course, it wasn't. She knew as soon as she looked at his mouth, before he even opened it to say, "Forgive my urgency. Our waltz, I think."

"I don't have you on my card," Lizzie said lightly, fighting her unreasonable disappointment. After all, Vanya couldn't possibly come here. He was in hiding. She didn't even know if he was still in Austria, let alone within the city. "But I believe I will allow it this time, since I have no other partner."

"I thought all your dances would be taken by now."

"No, I've been doing my best to keep them free, at least until our business is conducted."

"You've brought such business here?"

"I have."

"Then I have the recompense. Where would you like to conduct such business? There are two alcoves on the other side."

"Anyone might come in. We'll meet on the terrace, after the next dance." She named the terrace more from some instinct to avoid any place chosen by him rather than from some innate preference. Grassic looked pleased.

Lizzie wanted very much for tonight to be over. And yet, with Vanya restored to innocence and, presumably Imperial favor, she couldn't help wondering forlornly what she'd do then.

---

WHEN VANYA STROLLED into Mrs. Fawcett's ballroom and bowed to his hostess, she clearly knew him at once.

"Welcome, M. Rouge!" she greeted him gaily, following it up with, under her breath, "What the devil are you doing here, you young idiot? You'll get yourself arrested!"

"I don't plan on it. How are you, Mrs. F.?"

"I *was* very well. I hope you're not going to spoil everything..."

Vanya smiled grimly, "What makes you imagine I would dream of doing such a thing? I'll finish it, one way or another."

"For God's sake be careful, Vanya," she pleaded, sotto voce. "Major Blonsky is here with the tsar, *and* Grassic..."

"I'll endeavor to avoid the spilling of blood in your house," he said, though it didn't seem to comfort her noticeably. "Dance with me, Mrs. F, and tell me all."

"I can't dance. I'm the hostess!"

"Well, no one else will come now, will they?" And then he saw Lizzie. Just the sight of her made him smile, softened his mood and gave him...not quite hope, but a moment of happiness. Before the jealousy surged in, for she was dancing in another man's arms.

"Is that Reinharz with Lizzie?" he demanded.

Mrs. Fawcett peered over his shoulder. "Yes, I believe it is. He's quite taken with her. Lots of men are. She's become quite a success since she stepped into society. She could make a brilliant match."

He should rejoice for her. He should.

Mrs. Fawcett pinched the back of his hand. "Johnnie. Has it not occurred to you that you could be the most brilliant of all? You could give her back her old home, provide security to that gaggle of children and dogs."

"And remind them constantly who took it from them? Ivan the Terrible!" He took a deep breath, tried to smile. "You know I'd do it if she cared for me. If I could clear my name. But she doesn't. I'll be glad if she marries a good man who makes her happy. And if he doesn't, I'll kill him."

Mrs. Fawcett gave a croak that sounded very much like laughter. "Why don't you just find out? After...oh Johnnie, there's another late arrival, you'd better conduct me off the dance floor—and then stay away from anyone who might recognize you!"

Although it struck Vanya that Mrs. Fawcett was up to something, he thrust it to the back of his mind and scowled behind his mask as he went in search of Grassic and Blonsky.

He needed to know the position of the latter before he approached the former. Having already reconnoitered the grounds, he knew five of Blonsky's men were stationed there, though he doubted there were any more in the house. The tsar, like the other crowned heads who'd thronged to Vienna, had grown very relaxed about personal security and was quite used to attending parties, and even just wandering about the city streets more or less unattended.

Blonsky was playing cards, with his mask rakishly up at one eye. He looked restless, his attention not on the game, which was a sure sign to Vanya that he was up to something. Vanya walked on past the card room door without going in.

He had a nasty moment when he almost walked into Boris, who, through sheer surprise, could easily have given him away. Boris lifted his idle gaze, running it over Vanya, and moving on before returning in haste, much widened. But at least he said nothing.

Vanya winked and walked on, for he'd just spotted Grassic at the refreshment table. Amusingly enough, he wore a domino of the same scarlet color as Vanya's.

Vanya strolled up to him and reached over him for a glass of champagne. "Mr. Grassic," he drawled. "Saved any souls recently? Or do you hold, primarily, with predestination? Careful," he added, reaching out in time to catch the glass which slipped from the Englishman's fingers. "You need a seat in a quiet room." Setting down both glasses, Vanya took Grassic's arm with a mock solicitude and steered him across to the nearest alcove, letting the curtain fall back behind them.

"I unsettle you," Vanya observed. "So let us be rid of each other's presence as soon as possible. Are we conducting business this evening?"

"I have business to conduct," Grassic allowed, sitting on one of the two chairs set by an occasional table in the middle of the alcove. "Let me see yours."

"You first," Vanya mocked, strolling nearer.

Grassic took something from inside his coat, where he must have had a secret pocket sewn, and held a folded paper up beside his ear, waiting. Vanya took his documents from the waist of his dark pantaloons and gravely offered them to the Englishman. They swapped.

Vanya unfolded Grassic's paper and discovered it to be a letter from Blonsky, speaking of the enclosed documents and the price. Although it didn't mention Grassic by name, addressing him merely as "My dear sir", it was certainly enough to show that Blonsky had provided documents of some kind for money. No wonder Grassic had kept it. Vanya refolded it.

Grassic was still reading his, laboring, presumably, through the French, and comparing the hand of the military orders with that of the letter to Napoleon on Elba. At last he returned, frowning, to the letter. "Some of it's in Russian," he complained.

Vanya winked. "That's the really interesting bit. It's as good as an unbreakable code to most prying eyes. I trust this concludes our business."

"So do I," Grassic said.

He didn't rise when Vanya strolled away.

As Vanya emerged from the alcove, Blonsky came out of the card room on the other side of the ballroom. Ignoring him, Vanya walked straight up to the tsar who was flirting outrageously with an Italian beauty Vanya had once danced with, but whose name he could no longer remember.

Vanya bowed. "Forgive the intrusion, Sire." He presented the folded paper. "I believe this will reveal your spy."

The tsar's eyes widened in suspicion, if not recognition, as his fingers closed mechanically around the paper. Vanya gave him no time, merely bowed again, turned on his heel and walked purposefully towards Blonsky.

At first, Blonsky seemed to confuse the scarlet cloaks and assume he was Grassic, for he came blithely enough to meet him. Then the major's military boots faltered. But there was no real surprise on Blonsky's face. He'd known Vanya was coming.

Vanya smiled and changed direction to walk openly out onto the terrace. After all, he'd promised Mrs. Fawcett not to spill any blood in her house.

※

LIZZIE, HER HEART drumming with impatience while she listened to Captain von Reinharz tell some apparently amusing campaign story, caught a flash of Grassic's red domino on its way out onto the terrace.

"Excuse me, Captain," she interrupted. "I see my aunt…" To make him feel better, she even set off in her aunt's direction. That matron, gossiping happily with Mrs Fawcett and another middle aged lady, paid her no attention. Though Mrs. Fawcett caught her eye for a moment of silent communication.

When Lizzie was still several yards away, she swerved, and made her way, instead, to the terrace door. There, she paused and looked again toward her aunt, although it was, in fact, Mrs. Fawcett she needed.

Mrs. Fawcett was already watching her. She inclined her head and rose, murmuring something to her companions.

Satisfied, Lizzie slipped outside.

The welcome breeze cooled her face, but at least the colder weather meant no amorous couples seeking solitude in the open air. The terrace was well lit, too—a further discouragement, perhaps.

From the corner of her eye, Lizzie caught again the flash of scarlet and waited, taking a deep breath for courage. The scarlet figure remained very still, so Lizzie turned slowly toward it. Suddenly, it moved with almost frightening speed, seizing her against a hard chest with arms powerful enough to break her. Before she could even cry out, her mouth was crushed under another, hot and reckless.

Outraged, Lizzie flung out one arm, ready to deal a sound buffet to the side of Grassic's head.

But Grassic could never kiss like this. So bold and passionate and tender. So knowing. So...impossible.

"Vanya," she whispered into his mouth, for he was right. She knew, she would always know him by his kiss. The hand she'd meant to hit him with closed in his hair. "Vanya..."

Throwing her other arm around him, she gave herself up to his kiss, returned it with aching fervor because it was what she'd wanted for so long.

"Lizzie," he whispered. "I love you more than my life. You *are* my life, my love..."

And then his mouth claimed hers again and again, and when he raised his head at last with a shuddering breath, she reached up and took back his lips. Everything else had flown out of her mind. There was only the joy of his arms around her, beneath her cloak, his closeness, the hot, melting pleasure of his mouth....

From nowhere, it struck her that the hard, cold metal digging into her hip was a sword. Unexpected laughter trembled in her throat, on her lips. Only Vanya would come to a ball in civilian dress wearing his sword because, of course, he could still be captured or killed by his own people.

"Vanya, you have to get away from here," she said urgently against his lips.

"Come with me," he got out. "I know I shouldn't even ask you—I wasn't going to let myself speak to you tonight, never mind touch you, but I have to ask. If I can clear myself tonight, come with me."

Before she could even speak, his mouth took hers again, and she gave back the kiss gladly. Just as a world of noise suddenly erupted around them.

Mrs, Fawcett said in despair, "Oh drat! Back everyone, I was mistaken!"

But it was too late. A voice drawled in amusement, "Who the devil is that?"

And the unmistakable tones of the tsar himself uttered, "That, if I'm not much mistaken, is our Colonel Savarin."

"Stay behind me," Vanya breathed and released her, turning to face the crowd who'd poured out of the terrace door with Mrs. Fawcett.

She'd only been meant to bring the tsar and Boris Lebedev, though Lizzie had even forgotten about that in her astonished delight at discovering Vanya. Her Vanya. And, apparently, a shipload of embarrassment. Aunt Lucy would never forgive her for this.

"It's a masquerade," Vanya said. "Allow a lady the privilege of her anonymity."

And then came a sneering laugh as Major Blonsky, Vanya's old enemy, pushed through the crowd. "What, did none of you know that the Gaunt girl is his doxy?"

Vanya wrenched his sword from its scabbard. His eyes clashed with Blonsky's. "There are no doxies here, you foul-mouthed, traitorous weasel," he said softly.

And then, unexpectedly, someone got between them. James.

James?

Staring at Vanya, he said with dignity. "I'll deal with his foul mouth in a moment. For the moment, sir, you'll answer to me for manhandling my cousin, my fiancée."

Lizzie cast her eyes to heaven and pushed out from behind Vanya to give them all a piece of her mind—only the words died in her throat, for running across the grass to the terrace were several soldiers. Metal screeched on metal as they drew their weapons.

"Vanya, run," she whispered.

"Not a chance," Vanya said and knocking James to one side, he flew at Blonsky with an emotion that looked very like joy.

Lizzie clutched both hands to her head. "Stop it," she raged.

But no one heard her, not least because the tsar had, somewhat surprisingly, commanded the soldiers to stand by. Someone was ushering the women back into the safety of the house.

"Don't worry," Captain von Reinharz said in her ear. "Savarin can eat two of that dog before breakfast. But in the meantime, if you need someone to marry to get you out of this fix, I'm your man."

It may have been hysteria, but Lizzie wanted to laugh.

"Take her inside," Reinharz said quietly and someone placed her hand on a male arm, drawing her away from the fight, which was now raging across the lawn.

With indignation, Lizzie saw that Vanya was actually enjoying himself, but even so, she couldn't look away. With every clash of steel on steel, Vanya drove Blonsky back, every slash and cut and thrust so vicious that Lizzie was sure he meant murder.

"He mustn't kill him," Lizzie said in horror. Her gaze sought and found the pitilessly observing face of the tsar. "Your Majesty, Vanya mustn't kill him! Please!"

The tsar glanced at her. A tiny smile flickered across his lips and then he returned to watching the fight.

Lizzie could no longer see it. She'd been drawn too far away, beyond the terrace door, in fact, to shadows at the side of the house, where a little gate led around toward the front.

Frowning, Lizzie tried to tug free and, for the first time, looked at her companion, Mr. Grassic.

# Chapter Twenty-One

From surprise and sheer instinct, Lizzie jerked away from him, but found her arm held with calm, inexorable strength. Which at least made her brain start thinking again of more than male stupidity and the pointlessness of Vanya dying, either by Blonsky's sword or the tsar's justice. What was the point of being exonerated from treason if you then committed murder in public?

But then, what was the point of her beautiful plan to have the tsar witness Grassic buying documents from her and forcing him to confess his accomplices, if all the tsar witnessed was her indiscretion with Vanya, and she then conducted the business without anyone at all seeing? At least Grassic would still have the document on him.

So, she took a deep breath and forced herself to relax. "You're right, of course. I don't wish to see. Shall we conclude our business, Mr. Grassic?"

He paused, his free hand on the gate latch, now that she'd stopped struggling, and gazed at her through the darkness. Although she couldn't make out his expression in the gloom, she had the impression it was surprised, even admiring.

"Let us just move—"

"I'll be more comfortable when it's done," Lizzie said firmly. "No one is paying us attention whatsoever."

"Then give me the document."

Lizzie drew her hand free of his arm and opened her reticule. Extracting the thickly folded paper, she held it out to him. While he pocketed it, she said, "My recompense?"

Gravely, he handed over a small purse, which couldn't have contained anything like the kind of money James had been promised. As she tucked it away in her reticule, she extracted the spare hairpin before closing the little bag.

"Let's go inside," she said lightly, turning back toward the light.

His fingers closed around her upper arm, sudden, intrusive, controlling. "I don't think that would be a good idea. Come with me."

"Why?" she demanded.

"I have a new plan now. This game is ending, yours and mine."

"What do you mean?"

"I mean we need to leave. Both of us. My business is coming under far too great scrutiny to last beyond the sale of what I have. Many people will be after my blood. While you need to escape social ruin. Let us do so together, go to a new city. Together, we would be unstoppable."

Lizzie blinked. "Social ruin?"

"You were discovered by half of Europe's elite rulers and their wives, in the arms of a Russian traitor. There is nothing for you left in respectable society, unless you accept the offer of the poor and ridiculous cousin. Or the libertine Austrian captain." His free hand insolently pushed up her chin. "What, were you hoping for an offer from your other cousin, the Russian traitor? It was notable by its absence, was it not?"

*Come with me*, he'd said. Not *Marry me*. It shouldn't have hurt; it didn't matter. And she wouldn't let it.

"Mr. Grassic. You are, without doubt, the most unprincipled and repellent creature I have encountered in my life, and I have no intention of going beyond this gate with you."

❦

"STOP," THE TSAR commanded.

Vanya had Blonsky on the ground, straddled him, one hand to his throat, the other raising the sabre high for the kill. In the lust of battle,

Vanya had almost forgotten who he was fighting, where and why. He could have been in the icy wastes of Russia, fighting the French. It was as if his body took over from memory without troubling his brain for orders. The tsar's command barely penetrated, until it was repeated, and a voice he knew and trusted said urgently, "Vanya!"

The red mists began to clear; his sword arm held still. Staring down at Blonsky's dazed yet terrified face, it was as if the last twelve years had never been. Was he really still fighting this same, childish battle? Right down to the audience of avid, blood-thirsty males, old enough now, surely, to know better. He couldn't blame it all on Blonsky. It wasn't even about Katia any more, if it ever had been.

Irritated, he leapt to his feet and lowered the sword.

"Take the traitor," the tsar instructed. As the soldiers closed obediently on Vanya, the tsar added, "Not him! Blonsky. Arrest Major Blonsky for treason."

Vanya turned to face the tsar. "You read it?"

"It was a surprise to me," the tsar admitted. "Of course, I never truly believed in your guilt."

"Clearly," Vanya said sardonically.

"And this makes a lot more sense. Even without the proof. We old soldiers should trust each other."

"Proof?" Blonsky blustered, springing to life again suddenly in the hold of his guards—his own slightly baffled men. "What proof? You can't possibly have proof of treachery I never committed!"

The tsar waved a document in the air. "This!" he thundered. "This agreement between you and Grassic, our trader in information!"

Blonsky scowled and then his eyes began to widen with recognition. "But…but where did you get that?"

Of course, there was only one place it could have come from and the knowledge was written on Blonsky's stained, white face.

"I got it from Grassic," Vanya spelled it out for him. "He swapped it."

Blonsky turned eagerly to the tsar. "There! You see? Savarin gave Grassic something for this! Savarin is guilty! Ask him what he gave

Grassic for this supposed proof of my guilt."

"I'll show you," Vanya said, looking around him. "Where is Grassic?"

"He took Miss Gaunt into the house," Reinharz volunteered.

More than unease, a spurt of positive alarm had Vanya charging into the house. A female squeal at the sight of his bloodstained sabre, reminded him to put it away. Mechanically, he cleaned it on his handkerchief first, while scouring the ballroom with his urgent gaze. But this was no time for discretion.

He raised his voice. "Where is Miss Gaunt?" he demanded. "And the Englishman, Grassic?"

The excited hubbub died away. People exchanged glances and shrugs but no one spoke up. Striding forward, he eventually found Mrs. Daniels and Minerva. "She isn't with you? Did she come in?"

A blood curdling scream suddenly rent the air. It came from outside. In a wild mixture of intense fear and fury that he'd never known before, Vanya barged back across the ballroom to the terrace door, just as Lizzie walked in leading Grassic by the hand. Blood streaked across her fingers.

With a roar, Vanya seized the Englishman's collar, wrenching him away from her, pulling back his fist. "What have you done to her?"

"Nothing!" Grassic said bitterly. "The little bitch stabbed me in the hand!"

Vanya hit him anyway for that. Over the fallen body, and the shocked gasps and cries of the guests backing away from the scene, his gaze met Lizzie's. A smile flickered across her rather anxious eyes. "With a hairpin," she admitted. "I didn't expect it to cause so much bleeding. You didn't kill Blonsky."

He began to smile, just because she was there. "I will if you like."

Her gaze flashed around the room at Mrs. Fawcett's most interested guests and color rose to her cheeks. "I don't like," she muttered.

Minerva brushed past him, put her arm around her cousin in comfort and support.

The tsar and Boris entered behind Lizzie and Mrs. Fawcett bustled over to meet them.

"Such goings-on," their hostess said comfortably. "So what have we learned? That Mr. Grassic here buys and sells information to everyone, promoting distrust and endangering the whole Congress? That Colonel Savarin is innocent—"

"Not necessarily," one of the tsar's older aides pointed out. "Blonsky says Savarin gave Grassic something. Best see what it is."

Grassic, who'd staggered to his feet once more, fended Vanya off with both hands. "Keep that madman away from me!"

"Then be so good as to empty your pockets, sir," the tsar said with dignity.

Grassic lifted his chin. "While I have every respect for Your Majesty both as a sovereign and as a man, I believe I owe you no obedience, certainly none that impugns my honor."

"Nevertheless," said quite another, very English voice haughtily as its owner eased his elegant way through the crowd. It was Lord Castlereagh, the British Foreign Minister. "Nevertheless, I believe you must do it. If you don't, I will most certainly have you arrested on suspicion of treason while the whole matter is thoroughly investigated."

Grassic curled his lip. "On your own heads be it. The documents in my possession incriminate the very people who accuse me." He removed a few folded papers from inside his coat and all but threw them at the British minister.

"What are these?" Castlereagh murmured, unfolding the first.

"That," said Grassic smugly, "is what Miss Gaunt stole from her uncle and sold to me for a few schillings."

"My niece stole nothing from me," Mr. Daniels said with dignity. "Though I confess I thought I was doing the right thing by buying information from Mr. Grassic in the past."

"Then what is this?" Lord Castlereagh asked without emphasis, still holding the document in front of his eyes. "What direct meeting did *you* have with M. de Talleyrand?"

"None," Lizzie said unexpectedly. "If you pass a candle over the top, you'll see I've written something on it. In lemon juice. It's a trick my brother learned somewhere."

With a glance of reluctant amusement, Castlereagh accepted the candlestick someone passed him and waved the paper above the flames for a few moments.

"Ah, there it is," he observed, and read out, "This is a forgery designed to trap Mr. Grassic. It was entirely invented by me, Elizabeth Gaunt, the 25$^{th}$ day of October, 1814."

Vanya began to laugh. "Nicely done, Lizzie! Apparently great minds think alike."

"You forget, I also have what *you* sold me!" Grassic snarled. There was a wildness in his eyes now that Vanya hadn't seen before, as if he'd never imagined being in the situation where other people were flim-flamming *him*. He took out a handkerchief and mopped the sweat and blood from his face.

Castlereagh bowed to the tsar and passed the remaining documents to him.

"The supposed orders from Your Majesty to me," Vanya said. "Except, as you'll be aware, you never gave me any such orders, and neither of us were in the places stated in the orders—ever, I suspect."

"And the letter to Bonaparte?" Castlereagh asked, as if fascinated.

"The part in Russian explains it."

The tsar's scowl vanished. "Let me read it to you. *This letter is a lot of nonsense composed by Ivan Petrovitch Savarin purely to confound the Englishman, Grassic.*"

Into the general laughter, Lizzie cried, "Minerva!"

And Vanya saw that he'd been unforgivably careless. Grassic's physical cowardice had fooled him. There must have been a penknife wrapped in the handkerchief he'd used to wipe his face, for he now held the weapon to Minerva Daniels' throat.

Dragging her in front of him as he moved across the ballroom, Grassic said, "No one should come near me if they want the girl to live."

Vanya began to calculate distances and times, to go over in his head the likely places he could intervene between here and the street... And then everything changed again as, quite unexpectedly, a pleasant looking young man who seemed too stunned even to move, suddenly acted, punching Grassic ruthlessly in the side of the jaw and snatching Minerva in his arms. The knife clattered to the floor as Grassic staggered into a pillar. Vanya grabbed him before he fell and, this time, didn't let go. Boris searched his pockets, while Vanya twisted his arm up behind his back until he yelped.

Meanwhile, Mr. Daniels said warmly, "That was excellently well-done, Corner! Perfectly placed! I can't thank you enough."

And when Vanya glanced again at Minerva he saw her gaze locked with her cousin Lizzie's. Lizzie closed one eye and Vanya wanted to laugh. So this was the unsuitable young man Minerva had chosen.

"Well, at least you've done someone a favor," Vanya murmured to Grassic.

"So *now* Vanya is vindicated," Mrs. Fawcett pursued.

"Colonel Savarin is a true Russian hero without a stain on his record or his character," the tsar pronounced. Miraculously, a glass had appeared in his hand. "A toast! I give you... Vanya!"

"Vanya!" echoed all the gentlemen, especially the Russians, while the ladies clapped their hands with apparent delight.

Lizzie stood alone, faintly smiling, but the frown tugging at her brow troubled Vanya, until a crash of glass made her jump. The tsar had thrown his crystal glass into the fireplace, though fortunately for Mrs. Fawcett, the other Russians forbore to emulate him for once. Instead, they all looked expectantly at Vanya, who felt laughter rise.

Snatching a glass from the proffered tray, he raised it high. "To Mr. Corner!" he shouted and drank.

"Mr. Corner!" responded Mr. Daniels and the other Englishmen with enthusiasm, while the young man himself blushed endearingly.

"Mr. Corner," the tsar said graciously and drank, though this time he didn't feel compelled to throw his glass in the fireplace.

PRESUMABLY IN RECOMPENSE for his week on the run, the tsar insisted on providing his own carriage to convey Vanya back to his attic. Vanya didn't much care. The Daniels' had gone, taking Lizzie with them, and he hadn't had a moment's opportunity to speak to her again first. Everyone seemed to conspire to keep them apart, perhaps because of the scene far too many people had witnessed on the terrace, although thankfully the much more exciting subsequent events seemed to have driven the indiscretion much lower in the gossip chains.

Vanya, who'd barely slept for a week and had drunk too much with the tsar on an empty stomach, was dog-tired as he bade his hostess farewell and thanked her for all her help in changing his fortunes. She gave him a brief, uncharacteristic hug, but fortunately, didn't bring up the subject of Lizzie. He was in no condition to bear that.

As he left the ballroom, a masked man by the door said, "Well done, Colonel Savarin."

Vanya barely spared him a glance and a mechanical smile. He even walked on another step before recognition dawned and he stopped.

"Herr Schmidt. You really are alarmingly good at invisibility."

"The mask helps."

"I'll take your word for it. What did I do well?"

"Discovered your spies and exonerated yourself. It makes my life simpler and gives the Congress a chance. Thank you."

Vanya blinked. "Well, if we're thanking each other, it was your information that put me on the right track." He held out his hand. "You're a strange fellow, Herr Schmidt, but I'm very glad to know you."

Herr Schmidt stared at the hand as if he didn't know what to do with it. Vanya wouldn't have been surprised if the policeman had simply walked away. But after a distinct pause, the man grasped his hand briefly and returned his gaze to the ballroom, eternally watchful. Vanya wondered if Mrs. Fawcett had actually invited him, or if he'd barged, much as Vanya himself had.

Vanya tramped down the path to the street where the tsar's own carriage awaited—not one of the Imperial Austrian green coaches on loan to visitors—muttered his address to the coachman and climbed in.

Only as he threw himself moodily back in the seat and the vehicle began to move forward, did he become aware that he wasn't alone. The outside lights on the carriage shone in the windows on the girl seated opposite.

Tiredness, drunkenness all fell away like a heavy, wet towel cast aside. "Lizzie," he uttered, launching himself across to the other seat and taking both her hands. "What the devil are you doing here?"

He heard the catch in her breath, the unsteadiness in her voice. "You said to come with you. Here I am."

He stared at her, then slowly lifted her hands to his lips, one after the other. "You are wonderful."

"Not really," she said. "I'm afraid, wherever we're going, we need to stop off first at my aunt's and collect the children. And Dog."

His lips twitched. "Of course we do," he said gravely. "But I think I might have a better plan. I'll take you back to the Skodegasse and restore you to your aunt for the night. In the morning, I'll call again and…and I don't really know how one does this. There's no one I can ask formally for your hand, is there?"

Only by the faint upward twitch of her lip did she betray that she hadn't even been sure of that.

"Oh Lizzie, what do you take me for?" And yet, even thinking that, even in all her uncertainty, still she'd come. "God knows I don't deserve you. I can't even find the words to ask you because I don't want to say what everyone else has said before."

"I didn't need words to know you," she said. And taking it for the invitation it was, he took her in his arms and kissed her with aching tenderness. Her response was sweet and immediate, and when he ended it, she put her hand up to his cheek and kissed him again.

"Was that my proposal of marriage accepted?" he asked huskily.

"Yes, please. Only…"

"Only what? Are you concerned that we're cousins? It's a very distant relationship—"

She waved one dismissive hand and clutched his lapel. "No, no, that doesn't matter."

He searched her eyes, frowning. "I promise I'll care for the children, and Launceton—"

"Oh, I never doubted that. It's just… I know you're not a monogamous man," she finished in a rush.

He drew back to look into her face. "Who told you that?"

"Countess Gelitzina." She caught his hand to her face while he struggled with shame and words. "I don't mind about her," she assured him. "Or about any of them. But I don't want to know. And I don't want the children to know."

"Lizzie. I wish Sonia hadn't…but there, she had every right to say, to think, what she did. I didn't treat her well. I haven't treated a lot of women very well. But now there is you, there is only you. Not just from duty but from desire, from reality. Only you."

For several moments after this, neither of them could speak. At last, Vanya realized the carriage had stopped. They were outside his building. Releasing Lizzie, he stuck his head out of the window and instructed the coachman to drive to the Skodegasse.

The carriage rumbled back into motion.

"And your mother doesn't like me," Lizzie confessed.

Vanya gave a shout of laughter. "My mother will like you, once she realizes you like me and no longer call me Ivan the Terrible. You won't, will you?"

"Not unless you become tyrannical," Lizzie replied, smiling as she laid her head on his shoulders. "I like being with you, Vanya."

"I certainly like this much better than our first meeting in a carriage."

"Did you despise me very badly?"

"Lord no, you intrigued me beyond belief. I wanted to kiss you then. And a lot more besides."

Even in the shadows, with her face averted, he saw her flush. He kissed her hair. "We'll get to that, too," he promised. "Very soon. Very, very soon. If you have no objection to the Orthodox rite, we can be married before the end of the week. Sooner. Tomorrow."

She gave an unsteady, breathless little laugh. "You really don't care about gossip, do you?"

"No." He caught her chin in his fingers, caressing as he turned her face up to his. "But I would like to waltz with you again on our wedding day."

She smiled, dragging his hand to her lips and kissing it. "I'd like that, too. In fact, I might insist upon it."

# Epilogue

TEN DAYS LATER, Lizzie waltzed publicly in the arms of Colonel Ivan Petrovitch Savarin, also known as John Gaunt, fifth Baron of Launceton. That was unlikely enough. What really took her breath away was the fact that he'd just become her husband.

Despite the protests of Aunt Lucy and Lady Castlereagh, they'd been married by a Russian Orthodox priest in a beautiful church near the meat market. The tsar and tsarina had both been there, as were the Duchess of Sagan, Dorothée de Talleyrand, and her uncle.

To the accompaniment of exquisite singing, crowns had been held over her head and Vanya's. The words giving her to a man she'd known less than two months, whom she'd hardly had a moment to lay eyes on in the last ten days, had been spoken in a language she didn't even understand. And when it was done, when he kissed her, the heat of his mouth almost stopped her breath.

The magnificent wedding breakfast was hosted by her proud aunt and uncle at Mrs. Fawcett's house since it was much larger. The children, though gleefully excited, were unprecedentedly well behaved. James, while privately maintaining his heart was broken, ate with cheerful gusto. Minerva, Lizzie's chief attendant, despite sitting beside Mr. Corner, kept watching her with puzzlement, as if wondering how Lizzie could have wished to marry someone as alarming as Cousin Ivan.

Laughter bubbled up inside Lizzie. She felt animated, almost sparkling as she drank champagne and flitted from guest to guest. And yet, only when the orchestra struck up and Vanya led her onto the floor and into his arms, did she feel she'd come home.

And this time, she remembered not to look at her feet, but into his devouring eyes. The warmth there both thrilled and frightened her.

"Do you want to dance all night or shall we make our escape?" he murmured. His deep, low voice vibrated through her, making her shiver.

*Already?*

A friend of Vanya's had given them his summer place outside the city for a week. After the whirl of excitement and frenzied activity leading up to the wedding, she longed to be alone there with him, even though her stomach twisted almost painfully with anticipation. And with the inevitable virginal fear she was determined to hide from him.

"Maybe after this dance," she managed.

He smiled, holding her closer. Just a little *too* close. Vanya would never care for propriety. Instead, he steered her through the couples who'd joined them on the floor, dancing circuitously but inexorably towards the ballroom doors, and out into the hall—where they literally bumped into Herr Schmidt.

Vanya laughed and held out his hand to the policeman. "I didn't think you'd come."

"Neither did I," Herr Schmidt said. Although he shook Vanya's hand and bowed in Lizzie's direction, his attention was all on the ballroom beyond the open doors. "Congratulations on your marriage," he added, "but I'm afraid I'm here in a professional capacity."

"I didn't do it," Vanya said flippantly, while Lizzie followed the policeman's gaze across the ballroom—surprisingly enough to a young woman in a pale blue gown, sitting with an elderly gentleman.

Since Mrs. Fawcett liked this lady, Lizzie had met her a few times at social gatherings over the last week and found her both funny and peculiarly tense. Although perhaps not conventionally beautiful, she was attractive, clever, and just eccentric enough to appeal to Lizzie, as well as to many gentlemen of her acquaintance. In fact, she was engaged to marry the Crown Prince of Kriegenstein.

"Miss Esther Lisle," Lizzie said aloud, wondering at Herr Schmidt's interest. "She's going to be a princess."

"No, I'm afraid she isn't." Herr Schmidt sat down on one of the upright chairs to the left of the doorway.

"Oh dear," Lizzie said, frowning at him. "What—"

"It isn't your problem, Lady Launceton. I haven't come to— ah…cause you trouble. I imagine you'll have enough of that from your husband. Good evening."

"Good evening," Vanya said wryly. and taking Lizzie back into his arms, he danced her across the hallway to the front door.

Half-protesting, half-laughing, she gave in, letting Miss Lisle's unknown troubles dissolve in her own personal excitement. She would always feel this around Vanya…

Miraculously, a carriage awaited them in the street. Vanya handed her in, closed the door and sat very close to her. As the horses set off, he wrapped a warm cloak around her. Lizzie's heart beat and beat, and when he began to kiss her, she gasped and held on to him as if to her only salvation.

As soon as they entered the sumptuous summer palace, he dismissed the waiting, wooden-faced servants with a handful of coins, before simply leading her upstairs and into a huge bed chamber.

Lizzie trembled as he stilled at last. Tipping up her chin with one finger, he gazed into her eyes, reading, it seemed, what she tried to hide, for his kiss was soft on her lips, gentler than before.

"We're still waltzing," he said unsteadily and swung her back into the familiar steps. Only now, he held her thrillingly close, so close that their bodies held very few secrets from each other. "It's just another waltz…"

And then, with care and fun and, ultimately, with breathless, blinding passion, he taught her the joy of the dance.

## The End

## Author Bio

Mary Lancaster's first love was historical fiction. Since then she has also grown to love coffee, chocolate, red wine and black and white films – simultaneously where possible. She hates housework.

As a direct consequence of the first love, she studied history at St. Andrews University. Several jobs later, she now writes full time at her seaside home in Scotland, which she shares with her husband and three children.

Mary's books include several historical novels with strong romantic elements and a new series of light, fun Regency romances set at the Congress of Vienna.

Connect with Mary on-line:

Amazon Author Page:
amazon.com/Mary-Lancaster/e/B00DJ5IACI

Newsletter sign-up:
http://eepurl.com/b4Xoif

Website:
www.MaryLancaster.com

Facebook Author Page:
facebook.com/MaryLancasterNovelist

Facebook Timeline:
facebook.com/mary.lancaster.1656

Email Mary:
Mary@MaryLancaster.com

Printed in Dunstable, United Kingdom